rode

rode

Thomas Fox Averill

UNIVERSITY OF NEW MEXICO PRESS

Albuquerque

16 15 14 13 12 11   1 2 3 4 5 6

Library of Congress Cataloging-in-Publication Data

Averill, Thomas Fox, 1949–
rode / Thomas Fox Averill.
     p. cm.
ISBN 978-0-8263-5029-9 (cloth : alk. paper)
1. Self-realization—Fiction.
2. Horses—Fiction.
I. Title.

PS3551.V375R63 2011
813'.54—dc22

                    2011000118

This book is for my children,
Eleanor and Alexander Goudie-Averill,
who listened,
and who keep me listening.

Preface

first heard Doc and Merle Watson sing Jimmy Driftwood's "Tennessee Stud" at the Walnut Valley Bluegrass Festival in Winfield, Kansas. Doc's voice was perfect for the song—from the once-upon-a-time of "along about eighteen and twenty-five," to descriptions of "the Arkansas mud," to the confrontational "he fell with a thud" when Doc drummed on his guitar, to the urgent "loped right back across Arkansas."

I soon learned the song, and when I joined a folk/blues/bluegrass band, the short-lived Rock Island Line, I did the vocals and played my homemade slide guitar, thudding for guns and tapping for horses' hooves.

"Tennessee Stud" was written in 1953, but made its recording debut, sung by Jimmy Driftwood, on *Wilderness Road*, an album released in 1959. Soon, it was covered by Eddie Arnold, whose performance won Driftwood a Grammy Award nomination. Since then, "Tennessee Stud" has been recorded by dozens of artists, including Johnny Cash, Doc Watson, Tennessee Ernie Ford, Bill Barwick, Ramblin' Jack Elliott, Hank Williams Jr., and Arlo Guthrie. Groups as diverse as The Little Willies, The Nitty Gritty Dirt Band, and The Chieftains have added it to their repertoires. "Tennessee Stud" has been absorbed into American popular culture, and the lyrics can be found on numerous Internet sites. Fans can even download the song on iTunes and convert it into a ringtone. I hear it before I answer my own cell phone.

The song became part of my family culture, too. When my daughter was born in 1982, I thought of songs I might sing to her as lullabies. Long and narrative seemed best, and "Tennessee Stud" worked well.

She grew up with the song, as did my son, who was born fourteen years after his sister.

Singing the song countless times, I became curious about the story behind the lyrics. A short phrase like "I had me some trouble with my sweetheart's pa" made me wonder who the sweetheart's pa was, what form the trouble took, what convinced the narrator of the song to take flight rather than fight. Same with "Me and a gambler, we couldn't agree. We got in a fight over Tennessee." Complicated details lurk behind such terse lines. I began to imagine complex scenes, first in the dark as I rocked my children and sang, then as I began to research the time period of the song. I visited the Jimmy Driftwood Collection at the University of Central Arkansas in Conway. There, with the help of Jimmy Bryant, director of archives, I found the basis of the song, a family story, not much more fleshed out than the song itself:

> Uncle Jess Goodman, my wife's grandfather and a veteran of the Civil War, used to tell me how his grandfather, Uncle John Merriman, owned the greatest horse that ever lived, The Tennessee Stud. The great exploits of this horse were legion. Seems that John got into trouble with his sweetheart's folks and rode off to the Arkansas Territory rather than fight his loved one's people. However, after having ridden this wonderful horse all over the Great Southwest and into Mexico, and after having made a sack full of money from racing and filing a notch or two on his gun, Young Johnny came back to Tennessee, thrashed his potential in-laws, and carried the girl away to Arkansas. The Merriman story must have had its impact on Uncle Jess Goodman, for after coming out of the Civil War at 16, he came to Arkansas, became one of our greatest bear hunters, a silver-tongued Baptist minister, and a keeper and racer of fine horses. He went back to his home state for his stallions, and always kept one that he called The Tennessee Stud.

I traveled the same route the song chronicles, from Tennessee into Arkansas, through Texas and into Mexico. I visited racetracks, Spanish missions, historical museums, a living history farm, and national parks where the landscape might still be what it might have been "along about eighteen and twenty-five." I also read books from that time period for vocabulary and attitude. The use of some words in reference to African Americans and Native Americans is customary to that time and not a reflection of my own attitudes. I apologize in advance for any pause such words give contemporary readers.

After the research, inspired simply by the narrative arc of the song, I invented my own characters. I have not been slave to the story, but faithful to the spirit of this quintessentially American tale of a man who flees violence only to become what he flees, a man who holds love in his heart even while adventure rules his time, a man who finally learns something about himself, his love and his promise, and who fights for and wins what he values before heading off to make a new home in the territories. I offer my imagined version not as a substitute for anyone else's imagination, especially Jimmy Driftwood's, but as a tribute to the power of his family story in my life. Ultimately, this is a love story, ending with the births of foal and baby. I'm writing to that same baby, now full grown. ∎

Sections of *rode* have appeared in the following publications:

"First Verse." *descant* 46 (2007): 19–30.
"Red River Valley." *New Letters* 74, no. 1 (2007–2008): 89–105.
"Memphis 1825: The Nerve and the Blood." *North American Review* 292, no. 1 (January–February 2007): 17–24.
"Fugitive Interlude." *Blue Earth Review* 7, no. 2 (Spring 2009): 18–21.
"Preacher." *North American Review* 294, no. 6 (November–December 2009): 25–28.

There are no dreams of now that were not then.

—Joseph Stanley Pennell,
The History of Rome Hanks and Kindred Matters

eighteen and twenty-five

Robert Johnson sneaked into his father's barn loft just past twilight. His father had milked the cow, bedded the horses, and was no doubt eating cold beans in his near-dark house. *He prays in the dark, just as he should*, Johnson thought. He stumbled over the warped boards, feeling the dark walls of the loft, hands grasping for his granddaddy's saddle, time-worn, cracked, gnawed in spots by mice. Robert wanted it for the saddle horn, the leather long ago given way to expose the metal shank beneath.

Ever since Robert Johnson had started building his cabin—felling trees, stripping bark, cutting notches, laying foundation from smooth river rock, winching logs as the walls grew, setting timbers for roof, cutting shakes, sawing holes for windows, chinking cracks, smoothing boards for a door—he imagined the final touch, a door handle fashioned of the very saddle horn his hand suddenly gripped, the metal cool.

He recalled his granddaddy leaning forward in the saddle, one hand on the horn, the other reaching down to pull Robert, three years old, into his lap. They galloped away so far along the river that Robert wondered if his granddaddy could ever find his way home. With an equal measure of fright and excitement, Robert held onto that horn so tight he felt the impression of it the next morning as he lifted his fork of fried corn mush to his mouth.

Robert hefted the old saddle from the peg in the loft wall, climbed down the ladder, and hurried away into the now-black night toward his cabin. Johnson's granddaddy never could stay in one place, was a man who had cursed his home and left, a man never happy, never meant to build a cabin and live in it sunrise to sunset, year after year until his final season. Granddaddy was a rambling man, a drinker sunk to the bottom of an ocean of whiskey. No wonder Robert's father stood against his father. As Robert stood against his father.

Though newly built, Robert's cabin already seemed occupied by ghosts. Dead granddaddy. Dead brother. Dead mother, the consumption taking her just as Robert reached his majority, her last request the promise that Robert's father give him the forty acres along the creek, disputed in ownership though it was, where he could raise horses in peace. His father seemed a ghost, too, living, as he said, "closer to God every day, while you seem hell-bent, living closer to the world."

The old man pored over the Bible in the tiny circle of tallowed light he allowed himself each night. Daylight drove this man to work, and when he finished, he walked his fence line, measuring each rail to the precision of the one before it, mended harness and clothing with the same wide stitches, put up wood until the pile was high as his cabin. And Sundays meant the ten-mile ride to Holy Brethren to be baptized, purified, sanctified in the blood and the word all over again.

Robert drilled holes in his door to the same pattern as in the saddle tree, then laced the saddle horn to the door just as it had been laced into the saddle. Each time Robert Johnson entered or left his cabin, he would touch the saddle horn, talisman and touchstone. What, he wondered, would he find beyond his world of ghosts?

Jo Benson—she of the golden hair and freckled skin, as determined as Robert to move herself beyond her birth—found him. Like Robert's, her mother was gone. Robert's went to reward, Jo's to punishment, if the village whisperers were to be believed. Jo lived in a dungeon of dangerous men. Her father? Trouble. Her brothers? People called them *outlaw*, and conjecture was not often far from truth in Tennessee. The Bensons cared well for their horseflesh, less so their humankind.

Early spring, just as the days warmed, he glimpsed Jo Benson in the trees along the path to the creek. Having yet to dig a well, he fetched water from the creek that ran between his property and her father's. One morning, the bucket on his porch was full. The next morning, he rose early. She carried the heavy bucket with both hands clutching the rope handle, her face a grimace of effort. She heaved the bucket onto the porch with a thud, water sloshing, then rocking back and forth, trying to find its level. By the time he put on his pants, she was running away, feet bare, dress flouncing.

Some days she watched him at work cutting timber for what would be a large barn. Some days he crossed the creek to approach her house close as he could, to catch a glimpse of her life. She dug in the garden, readying the soil for seed. She fed chickens, collected eggs, dragged clothes across a washboard with furious effort. She hung up the clothes, especially her dresses, with great care. Just as she did, he always made sure she knew he was there. He picked the earliest wildflowers to leave on his porch. The bucket was full, the flowers gone the next morning. When she left a handkerchief on the line, he took it home and placed it in his window.

One morning he waited behind the cabin. When the bucket thumped on the porch, he showed himself. "Can we talk?" he asked.

She shook her head.

"You can speak, can't you?" he asked.

She blushed in the early light. "Pa says I musn't. Manny and Randolph, too. They don't like you." She backed away.

"Do *you* like me?" Robert sat on the porch.

She stopped. "They don't like me to think for myself."

"My momma always liked *you*," said Robert. "She wished she could look out for you, back when we'd see you in town."

"I was just a girl," said Jo. "Now I'm a woman. Sixteen."

"You still look like a girl to me," said Robert.

She put her hands on her hips, held her head back. "I can carry water. I can sew. I churn cream to butter. I can do what any woman can do."

Robert blushed, then, his thoughts racing to what he might do with a woman. "We've been trading favors," he remarked. She crossed her arms over her chest. "Water, flowers, and so on. I've been watching you."

"I've watched you," she said, her arms relaxing. "You aren't like some men. You care for things. Your cabin. Your horses. Your land. I like a man who cares for things."

"I could care for you," Robert said. He stepped toward her.

"Pa will wonder where I am," Jo said, and ran away.

Next morning, when he went for water, a soft singing rose from the creek. He silenced his boots in the brush. Jo was in the creek, at a deep place where sometimes he noodled for fish on the shady side of the bank.

She was neck-deep in the water. He stood behind a tree. She paddled to the bank, and rose up, her back to him. She *was* a woman, her buttocks strongly muscled, yet with a softness that moved his heart toward his throat. He was moved elsewhere, as well, though he suppressed carnal thoughts. Just as she stepped from the creek, she hesitated. She turned slightly and backed into the water. "You might enjoy a good bathing yourself," she said.

Robert shrank, as though he were the one naked. She swam to the middle of the bend in the creek and looked up to the ash he hid behind. "If you're like my menfolk, you haven't bathed all winter."

Robert scrambled down the bank to the edge of the water. He'd never been naked in front of a woman. He turned his back to her, stripped off his clothes, and jumped in. He swam toward her, then found the bottom of the creek and stood, his shoulders above the waterline. "You're sure enough a woman, Jo Benson," he said.

"I told you that." She swam away.

He swatted a spray of water after her.

She splashed back. "Do you want to love me?" she asked.

"I do," he said.

She swam quickly to the bank where he'd left his clothes. She climbed out and gathered them up. She jumped in with them and swam to her side of the bank.

"My clothes are even dirtier than I am," he warned her.

She climbed onto the bank, picked up her clothes, and bundled them with his. "Hope you have more than one change," she said, then ran up the path.

"Jo Benson," he called after her. She did not return. He walked home naked but for his boots.

Next day he went back. His clean clothes smelled better than they had in a long time. But his bandana had gone missing. He spent part of the day waiting for Jo, but she didn't return. The next day, she was in the creek and he ran down from his hiding place. He stripped and swam to her. He thanked her for washing his clothes. She asked for a kiss as reward, and then reward turned to prize.

For the next several weeks they met. Warm and sunny days they took off their clothes. Gray or raining days they sat under the canopy of a tarp and talked of the future they'd have once they solved the problem of her father, her brothers. "They say I'm not to marry soon, and not until they find the suitable man. As though they could judge a man like they would a horse. And decide which one I might want."

"I could talk to them," Robert said.

"We could run away," Jo said.

"I want to raise horses on this good land." Robert stood to stretch.

"You think you do," said Jo. "But why would you want to live near your father? Why would I want to live near mine? Or my brothers?" She stood under the tarp and picked up a rock. She flung it into the creek, breaking a surface already pocked with gentle rain. "Sometimes a tangled rope needs to be cut, the knots are so tight."

"You're mighty young to feel so trapped," said Robert.

"Aren't you mighty young to feel so settled?" she asked.

"If I was settled with you," Robert said. He moved closer to her. "What would anyone do if you just came to my cabin? We could marry on the sly in Pleasant View. Old Charlie Rhodes makes a good justice of the peace when you hand him enough money."

Jo stepped away. "You're older than me in years," she said, "but I believe I've been reckoning my future longer than you have."

"Make my cabin yours," Robert said. "I can take care of you."

"You can't take care of my brothers and pa." She ran from him.

He didn't see her for a time. Then, one morning, as he stood on his cabin porch drinking water from a ladle, she walked up the path. "I've come at my father's bidding," she said.

"I've looked for you," he told her. "At the creek. In the woods." She seemed taller, more blossomed, her dress more filled when she climbed onto the porch next to him.

"I have to do as I please." She smiled, nearly sticking out her tongue.

"What pleases you today?" Robert asked.

"It's a nice enough day for spring," she said. She pointed to the apple tree, full bloomed. "I've been kept indoors too much." She loosed her bonnet straps and gave her hair to the sun. Then she told him her business, to collect his stallion for a stud fee. "And Pa says I'll bring him back this time next week." She looked at where the barn would be. "Do you still work all the time?"

"'Cept when it rains," said Robert.

"Not raining now," she said.

He moved closer to Jo. He wanted to pick her like an apple. *Bud to fruit*, he thought. *Might she already be with child?*

Hoofbeats drummed the bridge across the creek, and Robert moved away from Jo. "You're welcome to take the horse," he said. "Even more welcome to bring him back in a week. Then you'll stay? I'll get a halter." He went to the corner of his cabin, where he'd built a temporary shed. "Someday my barn will be full of fine horses." By the time he'd fetched the halter, Jo's brothers flanked their sister.

"Pa sent me here," Jo said to them.

"And we're taking you home." Randolph turned his horse to the cabin porch and held out his arm to her. "Manny can bring the horse, if Mr. Johnson is willing."

"He seems willing." Jo smiled at Robert and took her brother's arm. He hoisted her up on the saddle behind him. She put her arms around his waist. Randolph clucked and his horse started away.

"Don't get no ideas," Manny said to Robert. Like his brother, he had a patchy beard and eyes set close together. His teeth were yellow, his long hair oily.

"Since when are you all speaking to me?" Robert asked. Their land dispute had been in court for a year.

The Bensons considered themselves hoodwinked when old man Johnson deeded the forty acres to Robert, complicating their claim to it by creating legal papers where there had been only shouts of dispute. Robert had spoken once to old Benson. "You raise horses, I want to raise horses. Neighboring will be a convenience for our interests."

"Your *interests*?" Benson had spat on the main street of Pleasant View. "My Randolph is at the courthouse right now. He'll find the way around your pa's trickery. Then you won't have any interests."

"I'll have The Stud," Robert said. "You won't find a better one in these parts."

"I'll remember that." Old Benson had tipped his hat and walked away.

Randolph and Jo disappeared down the lane, and Robert stepped off his porch. He put his fingers to his lips. His rising whistle brought his horse up from the creek, lean rump over long legs that danced into the corner of the corral.

"Got him trained real good," said Manny.

"Some horses you don't train. You just come to an understanding." The Stud put his elegant head over the fence and Robert secured the halter.

"I suppose you got a mind of your own, too," said Manny.

"I'm twenty-two," said Robert.

"She's just sixteen," said Manny. "She's her papa's jewel."

"I can see why," said Robert. He opened the gate and his horse came to him. He handed the halter rope to Manny. "She said she'd bring him back in a week."

"I'll be the one seeing you," said Manny. He spurred his horse and pulled the halter rope. The Stud stood still, and Manny lost the rope.

Robert picked it up and handed it to him. "Might want to let him know what you want." He patted the horse's rump.

"I want to move." Manny tugged the halter rope again, and this time The Stud followed.

Next morning, Robert Johnson walked to below the barn on the Benson place. The door was open, lighting the long interior, horse stalls on each side. The Stud would be in one of them. He walked in, whistling softly.

"Here," she said. Robert saw no sign of her, just followed the whispered "here, here, here," until he found her in a stall, standing in the darkest corner. "You found me." She walked toward him and put her hands on the slatted boards between them.

"I was looking for my horse." He wanted to pull her to him.

"I thought you'd come to see him." She climbed up the boards, sat on the top one. "Maybe you want to see me, too?"

He climbed up next to her. "Your pa? Brothers?"

"They're deep in a whiskey sleep." She touched his arm, held on. "I heard them. They thought I was asleep. They were making plans. This time, with your stud."

The Bensons were rumored to be horse thieves, stagecoach robbers, men who preyed upon opportunity instead of answering its knock. "Tell me."

"Nashville stage line. Lonely Creek Bridge. Tomorrow night."

"What are they after?" Robert tipped her chin and looked into her eyes, fishing for glimmers of deceit.

"I don't know," she said. "Manny's always in front. They don't want to be traced back to Manny's horse. So he'll ride yours. That's all I heard." She took the hand at her chin and pulled it to her face. She kissed it.

He exhaled sharply, then jumped down into the stall to wait for her.

She climbed down to the other side. "That's the stall they've put your stallion in," she said. "You came looking for him, and all you found was yourself." Off she ran, with long strides. Robert couldn't tell if she was running away from him, or whether this was her way of running toward him. He searched their pasture. No sign of The Stud. He went home to make his own plans.

trouble

obert Johnson blackened his thin face with chimney soot. His best horse after The Stud was a lanky mare, Julia. He'd bred her to The Stud but she'd never been with foal. She did not have the speed of the stallion, but had the endurance of three horses. He'd once ridden her to Nashville and back in a single day, over fifty miles. They'd both fallen asleep in her stall immediately after he unsaddled her and brushed her down, and the next morning he rode her into Pleasant View to brag about their adventure. One of the Bailey twins had offered him thirty dollars for her, and even though Robert knew she'd never foal, he shook his head. "You don't sell a horse like this," he said. "You take care of her."

He saddled her and started into the dusk. If the stage was on time—and usually it ran behind—he would have an hour to scout Lonely Creek. He rode along a deer trail, keeping Julia at a quiet walk. He prayed for the moon to give him light, but clouds thickened above the ridge. As he came out of the trail on top of a rise, his heart hammered in his temples. He dismounted and led Julia to a stone outcrop to see what he could see. Below him, through the trees, the black meander of Lonely Creek. The Bensons would wait south of the creek, he thought, in the bottom just below the covered bridge. Or they'd be inside the bridge, perched in the rafters, horses tethered in the grass. Robert started down through thin-leaved hickory, ears cocked.

Julia followed, as light of foot as he. Both black-coated, they were dark as the shadows of trees. Near the bridge, Julia snorted, nickered. The low whinny of The Stud answered her. Then gunshots flared, boomed toward him, and Robert threw himself to the ground. He jerked on Julia's reins but she reared, screaming in a nearly human voice. She'd been hit by the shot that had whizzed by Robert's head. The Stud answered Julia's cry. Hooves clattered on the bridge, and a voice cursed, "Get that Goddamn horse!"

Robert lifted his fingers to his lips and whistled for The Stud. More rifle blasts. Julia thrashed in the grass. Robert had decided not to bring his old flintlock rifle—only mischief comes of carrying a firearm. Now he wished for just one .45 ball to put Julia out of her misery. Hooves pounded across the bridge, and down the road. The Stud appeared, reflecting sudden moonlight.

"You'll stay where you are," said a voice Robert didn't immediately recognize.

"Don't shoot. I'm not armed."

"That's 'cause I have your rifle," said the voice. "You'll be coming with me. Stand up. Nice and easy now." The man—McFall, the sheriff—appeared above him.

"They shot my horse," said Robert. "Listen to her." The horse snorted, then sighed.

"She won't need another ball," said Sheriff McFall. "She's as dead as the man you killed at the bridge."

"I killed no man!" Robert stood up.

The sheriff backed away but held a double-barreled pistol at arm's length. "Steady now," he said. "Hold up your hands."

Robert did as he was told. The Stud moved to Julia, smelled her, turned his head, pawed, snorted.

McFall took hold of the stallion's bridle. "You'll both come along with me," he said. He led the horse toward the bridge. As they reached the road, the hoofing clatter of the Nashville stagecoach approached, lamps dimly riding swells and ruts, then hurried by, soon fading into a distance far from Lonely Creek. Even in waxing moonlight nobody on the stage would have seen the sheriff, nor Robert, nor the dead mare, nor The Stud, nor the body of the man next to the road. The corpse was not one of the Bensons, as Robert had assumed, but Archibald Krummer, a Pleasant View man usually so drunk he might as well be dead, face down as he so often was. This time, he had a hole in his brain, and not from drink, but from a rifle shot.

Robert had seen dead animals. Two dead humans, first his brother, then his mother, peaceful in their pine boxes. "At rest," his father kept saying, as though that was the goal of death. Archibald Krummer was neither peaceful nor at rest, his face covered with dark stains of blood. Robert's bile came, and he knelt by the road and retched. By the time he was finished, he rose as if in a dream.

"Your rifle was still warm when I picked it up," said McFall. He lowered his pistol.

"They borrowed my stallion. For stud," said Robert. "They knew I'd come here, looking for him. They were going to rob the stage."

"Careful, boy," said McFall. "There's a man dead here. And *your* horse, with *your* saddle and saddlebags, and your flintlock, and your bandana, too, if I'm not mistaken. And you running away before someone shot your other horse. What'd you plan to rob from that stage that you'd need saddlebags and an extra horse?"

Robert wondered how the Bensons had stolen his rifle and tack, stowed in the cabin when he left. He thought to point out to McFall that if he'd brought his rifle, he'd also have powder and lead, but he said nothing. Soon McFall would holster his pistol. Robert had asked Jo what her father and brothers had been after from the stage. They'd been after him. Because of the land. Because of Jo. Because they wanted The Stud, horse enough to sire a fine bloodline of horses in Tennessee. The sheriff said, "You'll be coming with me until we straighten this out."

McFall secured his pistol and started for his horse. Robert hurled himself onto The Stud. McFall shouted after him. First one shot, then another, winged the trees he narrowly skirted, and then more hollering from McFall, who no doubt threatened him with incarceration, trial, imprisonment, all that would make his life impossible, where once everything had seemed possible. He wound his way through the woods, his head as close to The Stud's neck as he could get it, for his horse could cut deftly through brush and stray limbs. They hurried into the creek draw, where The Stud found a path and raced up the moonlit trail.

He couldn't return to his cabin, though if he had, he would have seen flames eating the logs, consuming all he'd spent the spring building. When they licked up the thick door, the saddle horn handle, his finishing touch, glowed white as a ghost.

letter

robert Johnson could not write much beyond his signature. His only reading had been the halting repetition of the Bible his father had forced him to recite. His life had been all work, to his mother's regret. Before her death, she'd taught him the language of the few bills of sale for the horses he'd bought.

Before he rode away, he would ride the Clarksville Road to his uncle Judson's. The sheriff would not hunt him at night. He could sleep in Judson's barn. His uncle would help write a letter to Jo. Judson and Johnson's father shared a father, but not a mother. Judson, unlike Robert's father, turned to the world with a generous understanding. Last time Robert had been there, Judson helped write up the land deed to the disputed creek bottom between his place and the Bensons'. Robert had signed it, as had his father.

"And what good will come of this?" Judson had asked them.

"It fulfills his mother's wish," said Robert's father.

"I'll make it turn to good," Robert insisted.

Now, he was a fugitive. Only two things would stake him to his life—his horse and his hope of Jo.

God, the horse could run. Robert remembered the first time he'd been on The Stud. Seven years before, and Robert just fifteen. He would often take his father's horses out at night. They were work horses, not fit for racing. But Robert could always push a horse, find the place and the moment to make a horse want to run. Though he only rode work nags to the field along the Clarksville Road where men gathered to race, Robert often finished first, admired not for the horse but for how he rode. On his way to his uncle Judson's, he passed that field. Perhaps the stallion, too, remembered that night when, wild and untamed, said to be untameable, he was led, kicking, dancing, side winding, and offered to the man who could ride him, one dollar per chance to stay on the horse's back. His owner, a gray-bearded, grizzled bear of a man, teeth like rotted corn on a cob, his breath of corn, too—liquor, that is—bragging how he caught the stallion, wild, in Arkansas, "Had to run him for three days, no rest, don't know where in Jesus's name he come from, probably stolen by Indians. You can see his good breeding, but his long freedom from civilization has made him wild as the savage ready to paint for war."

Robert waited and watched. Instinct told him that an insistent man is up to no good. Others were thrown easily by the horse, tethered on a rope gripped tight by the old cuss who made running comment on the short rides of those Johnson knew to be horse-savvy men. The old man would reel in the horse each time, jerk the halter rope down, and force a lump of sugar into the horse's mouth. He'd smile and say, "Next?"

Young Jacobson took a disastrous turn. "Give me that sugar!" Robert shouted as the old grisly reeled the horse past Jacobson where he lay in the trampled grass. Robert figured he was the last of those with money enough to take a chance on the horse.

The old man palmed the small lump and pocketed it. "You think a little sugar's going to help your chances, boy? I haven't seen your dollar, have I?"

Robert fingered in his vest pocket and brought out the coin. He walked to the man. "I'll buy a chance to ride. *And* a chunk of that sugar," he insisted.

The old man jerked the horse's halter rope, bringing the stallion's head down. When Robert held out the dollar, the man's grimy hand reached into a pocket and found another lump of sugar.

Robert followed the halter rope hand over hand to the stallion, humming. He breathed deeply through his nose and let out the air. He reached his hand slowly to the horse's mouth, was surprised when the horse snorted, then ate the sugar. "That was *his* sugar," said Robert. "Now I want mine."

"You think I'm a sweet shop?" asked the man. But he reached into his pocket and handed over another.

Robert fed it to the horse, too. "Another," he said.

"I got no more," said the man, and spat.

"You've got one more," said Robert. "The one you were going to feed the horse. I want that one."

The old man, flustered, reached into his pocket and shook his head. "Empty. Not a damn thing, gentlemen."

"Show it!" someone in the crowd shouted.

"Show us what Johnson wants to see," said Jacobson. He limped toward the man, and the others in the crowd edged closer.

So the old fellow reached into his pocket and brought out the last lump of sugar. "Eat it," said Jacobson.

"Don't mind if I do," said the old man.

But Robert moved quickly to grab it. "Mine," he said, and put it in his mouth. The sugar was sweet and he crunched the small chunk of it between his teeth. "I believe you saved the last one for yourself," he said. He was so close to the man he could smell the sudden sweat. The others closed in. The man held up the halter rope, and Jacobson reached into the old man's pocket and found the last lump. He gave it to Robert, who had never been surer of himself. He saw the grime on it from the man's hand. An acrid smell told him what he knew already, that the lump was laced with something—strychnine, kerosene—whatever it took to juice the stallion enough to make him wild. "Eat it," he said. He pushed toward the old man.

In three strides the man disappeared into a copse of cedar. Nobody could believe how fast he'd left them. And Robert still held the halter rope. He hadn't even had to ride the horse to become his owner. "He still has our dollars," someone said. A few of them ran after the hoofbeats that quickly disintegrated into the night. The man's other horse, a mare, was quick of foot, no doubt the mother of the stud that was now his.

Robert walked the horse home and put him in the barn. He argued with his father for three days. "No good for work," said the old man. "High strung," he noted. "Bred for and by gamblers." His father spat on the floor of the barn.

For days, Robert fed the stallion, spoiled him with carrots and turnips and apples. He scrubbed him, combed him, cleaned and filed his hooves, trimmed his tail. He slept in the horse's stall each night, talking them both to sleep. He didn't try to mount him.

On his dun forehead, the horse had a lighter spot, like a rising sun. His tail was striped with black. Robert memorized every detail of his new stake in life. On the seventh day, Robert mounted the horse with no resistance. The horse was sleek, long, tall, fast. He'd make a fine beginning to Robert's dream of raising horses. He named him The Stud. Others thought the name odd. One said, "That's like naming a baby The Baby."

"If you had the best baby ever born," Robert said, "you might name him that, and you might say *The* Baby, because such a child might as well be what a baby is. Might as well be the *only* baby. That's what The Stud is to me. Not just a horse, or a stallion, or a stud, but *The* Stud."

He set the horse loose then, with his father's other horses, and The Stud set about organizing them, protecting them, establishing himself as stud. His father called The Stud wild, but as soon as Robert called the horse up from pasture, The Stud was his. Did only as he said, followed his directions and his commands. Robert could quiet him with a quick rub of the nostrils. Each night, Robert stood at the fence, and The Stud came to him. They would sneak from the barn as quiet as hunters in the woods. They loped to the fields along the Clarksville Road, where Robert Johnson never lost another midnight challenge.

Now, he was in a race he could not win. He thought of Jo, wishing he'd had seven days with her, alone in his cabin, talking, touching, comforting, planning, counting the hours together like tokens of the future. They had flirted, and they'd courted by the creek, of course. And in the creek they'd given each other everything but vows. Johnson longed for the closeness, the understanding, the agreement that would nurture a lifetime together. Such intimacy took hours, days, years, like those he'd had with The Stud.

Johnson could stay ahead of his pursuers, but what was speed when it took him away from his desire? And when the end of the trail brought no refuge? His uncle Judson's place was over the next rise. Robert turned from the road and walked The Stud through hackberry and elm saplings along the creek. He would come up behind Judson's barn to shadow himself. Find a stall, feed the stallion, wait.

Robert was awakened by the barn door on its track, shoved open to a gray morning, his uncle shushing anything inside. "Funny thing," Judson whispered, moving stall to stall, "to think you'd kill a man.

When you spend all your time building that cabin. Dreaming about your horses."

"Can you write a letter for me? Deliver it to Jo Benson?" Robert whispered.

Judson stopped in front of the stall that contained Robert and The Stud. The older man's hair floundered from under his hat and he scratched at it as though it were infested with lice. "No other reason you'd come here, is there? You know I lied to them for you." He fished in his coat pocket for a scroll of paper, then brought out a stub of pencil.

"Lied to who?" Robert pushed open the door of the stall.

"Lied first to Benson." Judson moved to keep him penned in. "Had to lie to him with my Pomeroy musket in my arms. Helped his willingness to believe me." He held up the roll of paper, sighting down its length at his nephew. His smile was full of crooked teeth.

"McFall has my rifle," said Robert.

"I know that," said Judson. "The law is never far behind old Benson."

"McFall and who else?" asked Robert.

"Small posse. Five men. McFall made me identify your old flintlock, as if I needed to. And your bandana. Stupid thing to lose near a dead body, boy. Especially with your initials sewn in it by your dear dead mother."

"My mother never did that," said Robert.

"Well, it was *R* and *J*, sure enough. The law don't have dogs with 'em yet." Judson swung the stall door shut and sat down on the straw. "Stud's looking good," he said. "Now let's write this letter, though I'll not be the one to deliver it. I'll find somebody to get it to her. Though why you want to poke a stick in that nest I'll never know."

Robert cleared his throat. "Jo Benson . . ."

Uncle Judson held up a hand. "Keep quiet if you're going to talk about love. Heard all I need of that for a lifetime." He flourished the pencil. "I'll hear enough whilst you dictate this letter."

Robert hung his head, his face still blackened with soot. He spoke softly and slowly. "*My dear Jo. I am disgraced wrongly, but am alive and determined to find justice. Not here, and not now, because all have turned against me. I will return. I will think of you every minute until then. Think of me, I beg you to. With all my love, Robert Johnson.*"

"And she'll just wait for you, however long you're gone?" asked Judson.

"I believe she might be carrying my baby," said Robert.

Judson whistled. "You're in a real stew, son. And liable to be boiled down to your very essence." He folded the paper and put it in his waistcoat. Then he went to an old trunk, half hidden under hay, and brought out a horse pistol, his old G. H. Daw .60 caliber. "Ain't much," he said. "And it'll be even less in your hand. But it might be a help."

Robert took the Daw, held its curved handle, felt its weight. Judson put lead and a bag of powder in his other hand and pushed him toward his horse. Robert led The Stud from the stall. He packed the pistol, powder, and balls in his saddlebag. "You see she gets my letter."

"You trust her, do you?"

"Of course I trust her. I love her."

Judson shook his head, then shook Robert's hand. "Love. Trust. Go do some growing up, boy." He swatted The Stud's backside.

rode

he Stud's hooves matched the beating of Robert Johnson's heart, the racing of his mind. He knew nothing of the trail south and west. He was wary of fellow riders, field hands, the lonely cabins where someone might stare out and later report his progress. By nightfall he was weary, his food and water gone. In the span of one moonrise to the next, his home, love, and reputation had been lost. Time and distance would have to dull the law's desire to pursue him.

Robert stopped at a creek and drank deeply, then washed himself. The Stud found ample grass, and Robert a low spot in the brush. He slept. Next day, he stood before what he knew must be the Tennessee River, the thick current cutting its way through verdant, tree-lined banks. They plunged in, The Stud swimming hard and Johnson thinking, *If this is the Tennessee, what must the Mississippi be?* For that was his destination, and then Arkansas, and maybe even into what they called No Man's Land. Robert wanted to be in the land of no man—with nobody to find him.

Robert rode two more days before his hunger overcame his fear of being seen. A cabin sat half hidden in the woods on a rise above the trail. Wood smoke carried the tangy thickness of meat. Pork, if Robert's nose did not betray him. He left his horse in the woods and walked into the small clearing that surrounded the cabin. A man sat on the porch in a straight-backed chair, a book in his lap. His chin jutted forward. "I'm a traveler," said Robert.

The man nodded. "Those with mischief try to hide. Come forth, traveler."

Robert walked to the porch. "I'm John Roberts," he said.

"You running or seeking?" The man's eyes were milky. He closed the book in his lap, a Bible from the heft and black cover, and set it on the porch floor.

"Have my sights set on Arkansas," said Johnson. "But I sure could use some food."

"If I thought you'd been in my smokehouse . . . You ain't, have you? Damn it!" The man stood and pulled a derringer from his vest. "You and every other varmint in west Tennessee. A man can't have anything but what someone else wants it." He waved the small pistol.

"I've had the same problem," Johnson said. "I was run off my land. Just getting my start and someone wanted to take it all."

"You fight 'em?"

"Best I could," Johnson said.

"Fight 'em," said the man. "You don't stop 'til they beg for mercy. Good Book says vengeance belongs to the Lord. But sometimes He needs our help."

"Tell me what's happened to you," Johnson said. "I'll just sit on the edge of your porch."

The man raised the derringer. "I could kill you right now," he said. "Don't think I couldn't."

Johnson squatted to make himself a smaller target. "I'll leave if you want. I'm just begging for food. But you could tell me what the sons of bitches have done to you, if you've a mind to. My pa quotes the Book, too. A man wronged unjustly might expect the Lord to bring His wrath upon the sinner. The righteous have the power of the Lord."

The man leaned forward. "Where is that in the Bible?" He lowered his derringer.

Johnson stood up and turned to the man. "It's in the *spirit* of the Bible. Chapter and verse, ask my pa. He has it in his mind from begat to begat. I just hold it in my heart."

"You said you were hungry, John Roberts?" The man put his pistol in the pocket of his vest. "You smell food, John Roberts?"

"The Lord said to feed the hungry, I do believe," said Johnson.

"And you shall be fed. Name is Thomas." The man wiped his hand against his pants leg and stuck it out.

Johnson reached up to give the dirty hand a shake. "The Lord will reward you," Johnson said. He hopped up on the cabin porch. A dog stirred himself from under an old carpet piece, yawned, then snarled. He moved slowly toward Johnson, his mouth open. The dog had no teeth. Still the dog latched onto Johnson's boot, all wag, no malice.

"I'd say his bark is worse than his bite, only he don't bark," said Thomas. "Let's go inside."

Johnson shook his foot until the dog turned loose, then followed Thomas into a dark and filthy cabin. A chair was offered, and Johnson sat at a cluttered table.

"We've been eating pork," said Thomas. He went to the stove, which smoked slightly with a dampered flame. He lifted a lid from a large iron pot. "With beans," he added. He took a bowl from the stove top and ladled it full.

Johnson ate, happy that Thomas was too blind to see his ravenous spooning. He burned his tongue with eagerness. He'd expected the beans to be tolerable at best, but once he slowed down he marveled at the taste. Rich chunks of pork, beans peppered and vinegared, with enough molasses to keep the dish one shade from sour. "I haven't eaten in two days," he said. "But I haven't eaten this good since my momma passed."

"Most women will leave you," said Thomas. "So you learn to do for yourself."

"You're a remarkable fellow, Thomas," said Johnson. "You live by yourself, then?"

"I live with the Lord," said Thomas. "And Ezra, he who humbled himself before the Lord." Hearing his name, the dog thumped through the door. Thomas ladled out another bowl of pork and beans and set in on the floor.

"Lucky dog," said Johnson.

"Hand me your bowl," said Thomas. "I hear the need in your voice." Thomas filled the bowl and sat down to weave a story of betrayals. He was the prophet of old, to hear him speak, his blindness giving him the second sight. He could hear the difference between the truth and a lie, straight from anyone's tongue. "As if your name is John Roberts," he said. "Or know the Good Book excepting what your daddy read out loud at the table, or your momma recited before you went to sleep." Thomas had been scorned for telling the truth. For he was compelled to speak, even in church, even to the preacher, loved by so many, when that man uttered falsifications and pieties and comfort where there should not be comfort. Thomas was pushed away by unbelievers who called themselves believers. He was shunned by family and church and the very people who bore him and taught him his letters. He'd found one loyal woman, but then even she had been corrupted by lies. And by her own flesh. Don't think he couldn't see behind her every word, her longer and longer absences. "I can smell impurity just like a vulture can smell the putrid flesh of death. The smell of her man's adulterous jism reeked between her legs." He drove the woman away, then set himself to exile, walking into the woods for forty days before he built the cabin by the sweat of his brow, learned to do for himself, learned to accept all he couldn't do. "The Lord taught me patience, and it was hard won." The righteous, he said, are often reviled. Boys from the town came to mock him, to steal from his smokehouse, to destroy the very crops in his field. "But vengeance will be mine," he declared. "You want more beans?"

Johnson did, but his hunger was bested by his desire to leave. He didn't want to hear Thomas rant as though he was pulpit and Johnson pew. "I'm full," he said.

Thomas, full of his own invective, did not hear the lie on Johnson's tongue.

"Can I leave you some money?" asked Johnson.

"The Lord will bring me my reward," said Thomas. "Though two bits in the meantime wouldn't hurt."

Johnson tossed a ten-cent piece onto the table so Thomas would hear it.

"I asked for two bits," he said. "But ten cents is better than none."

"I thank you, Thomas," said Johnson. He headed for the door.

"Whatever you're running from," the blind man shouted after him, "remember that's what you'll end up running toward."

"I'll remember." Johnson hurried off the porch and went for his horse. He didn't want to whistle, so he plodded through the trees and finally found The Stud in a small stand of oat grass. He also found Thomas's smokehouse. He walked to it and opened the door. A bucket fell, clamoring into the small building, and Johnson heard a shout from the cabin. Then the whanging shot of a derringer ball. The smokehouse walls were lined with moonshine. Johnson hurried a bottle into his shirt, ran for The Stud, mounted, and rode away before the blind man could reload his derringer.

The pork and beans, with swigs of moonshine to warm his belly and drown his growling hunger, sustained Johnson for another two days. He had yet to sense any breath at his neck, so when the thin trail he'd ridden intersected a broader thoroughfare, he took the easier way. The few people he met were talkative but not suspicious. Some men atop a wagonload of timber told him he was on the Jackson Road, the town maybe ten miles ahead. "Jackson is young, but thriving, just like the man she's named for. Looking for a place to settle?" they asked.

Johnson shook his head. "For a night, maybe." After food he most missed a bed. And a bath. Only Jo would be actual balm—to satisfy hunger, to make rest easy, to strip him clean as a Cheatham County creek, their bodies finding each other in water.

"Got money?" One of the men broke Johnson's reverie.

"Not to speak of," he said. He wondered if they would think it strange, his traveling without bedroll, gear, or money to ease the way.

But the man leeward of the load leaned over and said, "Barnaby. He's my cousin some way or another. You tell him Bob Jenkins recommends you. You work for him, he'll give you food and a bed. You work hard, he'll keep you on, like he did me."

"Where will I find this Barnaby?" Johnson shifted in the saddle and The Stud skittered. "It's okay," Johnson said, leaning against the horse's neck.

"Hotel Andrew Jackson," said Bob Jenkins. "He don't own it, but he works the stable there." The other man snapped the reins and the four-horse team started away. "Fine horse you got there," said Jenkins as he passed by.

Johnson patted The Stud. "Powerful fine." They trotted down the road toward Jackson.

Such became his days. Barnaby in the stable, where Johnson was allowed to board with his horse for a couple days' rest in exchange for shoveling horse turds, and Barnaby a nice man, eager for the prospects of west Tennessee. A nonstop talker, in fact, and Johnson soon tired of the wonders of this man's country and his vision for it, farms and horse ranches, canals and highways and byways, churches and schools.

Johnson longed for his tiny cabin, his small ambition to create a line of horses, each to reflect the virtues of the flesh and character of The Stud. And he longed for Jo, who might create another lineage. He lived among strangers. Yet he himself was a stranger.

So he rode for Memphis, where, Barnaby assured him, he'd find "enough people to make a real city some day, aloft of the Big Muddy as that place is. A city on a hill, fit for a king."

Barnaby and the others in Jackson seemed to know the country well, to note the comings and goings. "Where to, Stranger?" was always on their lips. They would remember him, taciturn as he'd been, shoveling and cleaning, currying horses and mending harness, eating his grub, feeding his horse, bartering his labor for powder, lead, a bedroll, and a canteen full of whiskey. He had to prepare for a trip long enough that pursuit of him would be folly. And at folly's end, he'd make whatever plan he needed to make.

After two days of rain, the land soaked, himself soaked, Johnson reached another river. The Hatchie was swollen, roiling, dangerous. A young man, whose woman peeked out of a nearby tent, had strung a rope across the river. The man stood on a substantial raft of logs tied together. A pulley wheel attached to the rope kept the raft from drifting in the current. Though the man was soaked clear through, he wore an undiscouraged determination. "Headed to Memphis?" he asked, and when Johnson nodded he offered to cross both man and horse. "Four bits."

"Got no four bits," said Johnson.

The young man took off his hat, tipped water from the brim. "Then you'd best just turn around. Find yourself a destination that don't include a river crossing."

"How many days you had rain here?" asked Johnson.

"Too darn many, I can tell you." The man jumped onto the bank and reached for The Stud's bridle.

Johnson jerked it away and the horse moved backward. Johnson pulled off his saddlebag and tied it firmly around his neck.

"You can't swim the river," said the young man. "You can try, but ain't no way to survive it."

"I could promise you double the four bits on my return."

"Promises float on a river and disappear, just like the folks who make them."

Johnson let the reins hang loose in his hands. The Stud would know where to enter the water. Johnson gave him a slight nudge with his boot heels, then began speaking encouraging words.

"You want to drown?" fumed the man.

Johnson continued to whisper in his horse's ear. The Stud walked slowly up river, then back down.

"You're going to die, sure enough!" shouted the young man. He stomped on the ground. Finally, when the horse found his way down a grassy slope, the young man yelled after them. "Stop now!"

"You'll ferry me?" asked Johnson.

The young man shook his head. "Maybe you can work some, earn the passage? I'm building me a cabin."

Johnson, remembering his own hard-built cabin, turned and waved. "This is where you should have put your ferry!" he yelled.

"You shut up!" the man shouted back.

The woman, whose head still jutted out from the tent, suddenly barked at her husband. "Get in here, Charles Onnen. You'll catch your death again." She pushed open the tent flap and stood, waving him toward her. She was small and thin, like Jo, and pregnant, a protrusion of child borne directly in front of her.

The young man did as he was told. Charles Onnen would miss The Stud's crossing: the first loss of footing, the powerful swimming, the horse's head jutting forward as though pulling the rest of his body, the relaxed negotiation of the current to help him move to the place he'd already calculated on the other side. Johnson laughed in his fear and delight, standing as tall in the stirrups as he could to keep his powder dry and his whiskey from disappearing anywhere but down his own throat.

Johnson had forded many rivers. His horse was a strong and fearless swimmer. In this current The Stud swam like he ran, with a force akin to the power of wind, with the certainty of lightning striking the ground, with the grace of a buck vaulting a dead tree in the woods. And the horse's power was *his* power, as when they raced. When the stallion finally came to the other side of the Hatchie and found purchase in a small patch of grassy bank, Johnson hollered his victory over the river as he might have screamed his joy in a horse race. When his shouts didn't rouse the young Charles Onnen from his cloister of a tent, Johnson bid the horse upriver to where the ferry rope was tied around an oak. Johnson took his knife from the saddlebag and cut the rope. No sense in Onnen carrying a pursuer, should Johnson have one, across the river soon. Johnson threw the loose end of the rope into the river where the current caught it and stretched it toward where Johnson would head next—south and west to Memphis. He turned then, and paused on the small bluff over the Hatchie River. Charles Onnen stomped on the riverbank, shouting words Johnson could not hear. He took off his hat and threw it down. A sudden gust of wind carried it into the river, where it floated after the ferry rope. Once the man regained his composure, and when the swollen river proved its banks again, Johnson knew where Onnen would restring the ferry rope.

Days were clear, nights warm and musky. Stars became friends, constant as they were in a landscape that went from wooded to meadowed, rocky to loamy, where few travelers hailed Johnson with more than a nod or a wave. He'd found a byway, off the Jackson to Memphis Road, away from those like the young ferryman who would try to find any small advantage in a region of travelers. Hunger became his companion, constant as the stars. Water was sometimes cool and clear, sometimes brackish, depending on whether it ran over rock or chalk. Johnson looked for it where it ran down from bluff instead of where it bubbled up from grass. Occasionally, he managed to shoot one of the abundance of rabbits and squirrels. He'd make a fire but find himself so ravenous he could hardly stand to let the flesh cook before devouring the meat down to the gnawing bone. Wild greens helped him stave his appetite, dock and lamb's quarter especially, plants his mother had taught him to recognize when he was a boy. Her small hand would point toward an opening in the path, where sunlight streamed over a stand of lamb's quarter. Her utterance: "Abundance." This was after they'd lived the past month on salt pork with wrinkled carrots, molding onions, potatoes reeking with rot. Traveling, Johnson remembered the power of simple appreciation. One unlucky rabbit, one stand of dock, one sip of whiskey after water, one day spent without mishap or apprehension, one night of clear sky luminescent with stars.

nerve

emphis was a sore spot above the Mississippi River. A fledgling town, only half feathered, but bustling with the energy of clearing, hauling, staking, building. Men, mostly, with their loads of timber, rock, tools, supplies. The place was like the bottom of a funnel, and people swirled toward it from every direction.

Robert Johnson led his horse toward its center, surrounded by the chunk of axes, the ring of hammers, the calling to horses to pull, to steady. Most everything was but the skeleton of what it might become, buildings and streets paralleling the river, with its commerce of flat-boats, longboats, paddlers, steamboats—all docked at the bruised bank of the Mississippi.

Men paused from their labor, nodded, appraised Johnson and The Stud, but nobody spoke with the usual loquaciousness of Tennessee. Perhaps here at the edge, men were hell-bent, as his father always called it. Perhaps, like him, they were camped at the edge of the Mississippi with the notion that they could cross, and lose themselves to the world when occasion demanded their escape. The Stud prompted the first conversation.

A thin man stood up from inspecting the broken spoke of a wagon wheel and when he rose Johnson thought he might just be the tallest man he'd ever seen. The man wore buckskin breeches that must have been four feet from waist to boot heel. When he moved forward to the team of mules hitched to his flatbed wagon, he so towered above them he turned them miniature. He wore a bandana on his head. Any crown of a hat might have poked into the clouds and broken loose some rain.

Johnson wondered how he might feel if he stood next to the man. Like a boy again? The man looked to be maybe ten years older than Johnson. He wore fine boots and a calico shirt. He hopped onto the wagon seat and took up the reins. "Never seen such a fine team of mules before?" the man said, his voice as high and thin as he was tall and slight.

Johnson was not sure the man was speaking to him.

"You prefer fine horses, such as your own?" The mules started forward, though the man had not slapped the reins. He jerked them back. "Varmints," he said. "Been a while since that stud saw some oats."

"Or anything but singed rabbit for me," Johnson confessed. He led his horse toward the wagon and looked up at the man.

"Hiram William Gillian." The man reached out his hand. "Say that three times."

Johnson smiled. "Johnson." He shook the man's hand.

"Just Johnson?" asked Hiram.

"Robert Johnson." He'd meant to use a different name, but had been distracted by the man's height, his friendliness, his admiration of The Stud.

"Robert Johnson, if you want to follow me I know where a man can eat some pork. And cornbread. Should he be hungry." He held the reins, ready to snap the mules to service.

"I'd see to my horse first," Johnson said. He wanted work more than friendship, and this Hiram had already tricked out his name.

"Oats is what I said," Hiram reminded him. "Where there's meat and corn, there's oats, you might figure." He clicked his tongue, raised the reins. "Now," he said.

"I'm low on money," Johnson shouted, following the wagon.

Hiram turned toward him. "You're low on everything," said Hiram. "Everything but breeding. Your horse has that, even if you don't." He snapped the reins and headed down the street.

Johnson mounted The Stud and followed. When the Mississippi opened into fuller view, Hiram stood in the wagon and pointed across the river. "Arkansas Territory," he said. "Half the men here are looking back to where they came from and half to the West. Never know who will stay to make this place a real city."

"The territory for me," said Johnson. He rode beside the mule-drawn wagon. On horseback, he was tall as his new acquaintance.

"You won't want work?" asked Hiram.

"Not beyond food, rest, a few supplies."

"Men are restless creatures." Hiram pulled on the reins. "Varmints," he called out, and the mules stopped in front of a newly constructed house. He climbed down from the wagon and tied the mules to a post.

Johnson dismounted and had just begun to tie his horse to another post when Hiram disappeared behind the two-story home. Johnson led The Stud around the building to discover a large stable. Hiram strode through the door to become obscured by shadow.

Inside, washed in sepia light, two men led horses from stalls to the back of the barn. They turned into the glow of light from an opening in the side of the stable and disappeared. Somewhere in the distance, horses ran, hooves pounding the ground in rhythm, as though a man with a hollow mouth was chewing an apple and the snorting breaths between bites meant the horses were running hard. "You said the horse eats first?" Hiram's arm waved from one of the stalls.

Johnson led his horse to the stall, freshly cleaned, floor covered with straw. In a grain box, oats. In a bucket, water. The stall rails were built high, a full foot more than most, and well over Johnson's head.

Hiram stood in the back of the stall, smiling. "You might want to unsaddle him," the man said. "Unless you're fixing to run over to Arkansas right after you eat." He stepped to the door of the stall and came out into the stable. "Once he's settled we can feed ourselves."

Johnson unsaddled The Stud, threw the saddle over the top rail of the stall. He shook out the saddle blanket and hung it neatly next to the saddle.

Hiram, whose nose reached the highest rail, wrinkled his face. "Needs washing," he said, and took the blanket off the rail. "Or is that you?"

"I expect me and the horse and everything to do with us are a might ripe," Johnson said.

"I'll have the blanket washed. And your stud, too, after the boys have run the other horses and sprinkled them down."

"You have a track." Johnson led The Stud into the stall and the horse drank half the water in the bucket before coming up for air.

"Better than Nashville," said Hiram. "And I suspect you know that one?"

"Heard of it. Wanted to race there someday," said Johnson. He let Hiram close the stall door. "Until my bad luck." He followed Hiram out of the stable.

"Luck is what you make of it," said Hiram. "If you ever won a race with your horse, it was likely luck." They went inside a mudroom at the back of Hiram's house and removed their boots.

"Township roads. Pastures. I've *never* lost a race with this horse, to tell the truth."

Hiram pushed open the kitchen door and Johnson's stomach nearly caved in. The air itself seemed edible—thick, rich, aromatic. "Run him here," said Hiram, "and you'll lose your share of races, I can guarantee you."

They sat then, at a long table. A woman, short as Hiram was tall, brought two plates heaped with pork chops. Beans, in large bowls, were dark with molasses. Cornbread was served with a scoop of butter. Johnson closed his eyes and breathed deeply.

"Elizabeth, this young man of the gamey smell is Robert Johnson. Recently arrived. Not much, I know, but you should see his horse."

"You can clean up a man and see improvement," said Elizabeth boldly, curtseying at the same time. "But a horse is going to be what it is."

Hiram looked not at his wife but at Johnson. "And his is a fine horse. We haven't run out of soap, have we? Might have a fine young man, as well."

Johnson sat before the food, grinning with anticipation, enjoying the smooth banter of Hiram and Elizabeth, but unsure when he could actually eat. Hiram made no move toward the food. Some folks, Johnson knew, prayed over victuals such a long time a meal turned cold or soggy. "Knew a preacher once," said Hiram, almost reading Johnson's mind. "Said, never bless food for so long that butter won't melt on warm bread. So, amen." Hiram took up fork and spoon.

Johnson was not far behind. The meal tasted even better than it smelled, and when he scooped the final spoonful of beans, Elizabeth brought him another helping. Same with the pork, same with the cornbread.

"I'm hungry, too," complained Hiram.

"You don't have a single excuse for your gluttony," said Elizabeth. "Mr. Johnson here has been traveling."

"It's a fine journey that finds this kind of food, ma'am," Johnson said.

She brought out more for her husband, then more for Johnson, then more for her husband, as though each man would not be outdone in appetite by the other. Finally, Johnson pushed the dishes to the middle of the table. "I'll bust," he said.

"Good," said Hiram. "My pappy always said to eat until company quits, so they don't feel bad about asking for more."

"He gave you a lifelong excuse," said Elizabeth, clearing away the dishes.

Hiram pulled out cigars then. "Tobacco of my own growing," he said. He cut two of them, handed one to Johnson. "Let's get acquainted," he said.

Over cigars and coffee Hiram described his ambitions. He'd have the best racetrack in west Tennessee. He'd breed the finest, most unbeatable horses in all the West. He admired Johnson's stallion. Even travel-worn, the horse looked fit for fine running. They'd rest him up a couple of days. Clean him ears to hooves, exercise him enough to get him used to the track. They'd clean Johnson, too, give him a bunk, let him rest, then put him to work in the stable. He'd race his own horse. For every race he won, he'd keep a quarter of the purse. For every race he lost, he owed Hiram two days in the stable. And he had to stay in Memphis long enough for Hiram to use The Stud as stud.

"That's only a good deal should I *win*," said Johnson.

"You said you'd never lost a race," said Hiram.

"You said if I'd ever *won* a race it was luck," said Johnson.

"Maybe you'll get lucky." Hiram stubbed his cigar into what had once been the bell of a bugle. He extended his hand. "Shake on it?"

"Guess I have to if I want that bath." Johnson stubbed his cigar and took Hiram's hand.

"I took you for a racing man first thing," said Hiram.

"I took you for a mule driver," said Johnson.

"The horses I raise, you don't use them for work." He stood. "Elizabeth," he called. "Don't spare the soap." He left through the kitchen door.

In the tub room, as Johnson scrubbed dirt, grime, oil, and stink, he saw that his attempt to disappear was coming true in loss of weight. Not so long before, he had stood on his cabin porch next to Jo, nearly swollen with pride and confidence. Now he was scrawny, fearful, almost feckless. Elizabeth borrowed clothing from a boy for him to wear while she washed his clothes, which he hoped would not disintegrate in the washtub as he had. He and The Stud needed a rest.

When he went to check on his horse, he studied the other horses. All were bred to the race, slender legs under large haunches. Although his horse had been washed and groomed, The Stud didn't have the polish of these horses. They looked molded, glistening even in the close air of the stable. The bunkhouse was not as clean as the stable. In the evening, the men smoked, played cards, traded whiskey and stories. Some were Spanish, some Indian, some just rugged country boys. Although they swapped stories, they did not tell their own stories, nor ask Johnson to explain himself. He became one of them, no questions. One said he hoped The Stud ran better than he looked. Another told a story of a farm-bred stud and its owner's extreme pride. A true horseman thought to whittle the owner's pride by several shavings. Offered him a hundred dollars as stud fee, but when the horse was turned to pasture he couldn't catch up to the fillies. Of course they weren't in heat, but the farmer took the message.

"When they're in heat," one man said, "they come to you." So the stories took the turn to sexual conquest, then circled back to horses, then to tales of hunting, fishing, drinking, then back to sexual prowess and horses, as though the men were riding around the same track, and would continue, with no clear winner, exercising their mouths and wits as they exercised the horses each day.

Johnson took to his bunk and nothing prevented sleep, not the raucous laughter, the coughing, farting, sneezing, the shuffling of cards, the clinking of glasses. In the stable, The Stud slept, too, and both travelers found comfort in a roof overhead, company around them, the prospect of a tomorrow without miles and hunger.

Johnson's first race put him two days in debt. He finished last, and Hiram greeted him with equal parts glee and advice. "Fine horse. Good first race. Don't *ride* the horse, just let him run."

"He *was* running," said Johnson, still sweating deep from the race.

"Look at him," said Hiram. "The horse is breathing like he never ran. You're all tuckered out. You ride like it was *you* in the race. Make *him* tired."

"How?" asked Johnson.

"You'll figure that out," said Hiram.

His horse had speed, but better speed on the trail or the open road than on the track. The other horses—or was it the riders?—had been trained to push into open spaces, to race fearlessly side by side. The Stud had never had close contenders. The men whipped their horses ferociously. Johnson had never inflicted pain to push his horse. The men jostled one another, elbows, shoulders, even occasionally flicking the whip to snap another man's neck or knock his hat to the track. Johnson wanted his horse to win by nerve and blood, not by intimidation or crooked violence. But with each race he owed more days to Hiram's stable.

"Your horse runs well," Hiram told him after a faster run. He sat on the low fence that surrounded his track. "You'd win if you were the only one out there."

"How do I win against the others?"

Hiram shrugged himself off the fence and approached Johnson and The Stud. He put his hand on the horse's mane, slid it down The Stud's withers. "I believe your horse is more aggressive than you are," said Hiram. "Smarter, too. Let him make the decisions."

"You just want to keep counting the days I owe you," said Johnson.

The next day, Johnson woke up tired. He didn't want to race. He didn't want to run The Stud, or let The Stud run. He didn't want to spend the day shoveling horse turds, lining stalls with sawdust and straw. Though he wasn't hungry, he enjoyed Elizabeth's company. She bantered with the men as she served huge breakfasts of eggs, beans, bread, and potatoes. And gallons of coffee to keen the edge of these men who nearly drowned in whiskey each night. He ate what he could, nursed the mug of coffee that showed his name. Then, as he'd begun to do, he cleared the plates and spoons and cups off the table.

"You didn't sleep?" asked Elizabeth.

"Am I such a book to be read?" Johnson asked.

"But you don't read, yourself," Elizabeth said. She dried her hands on her apron and took his cup. She pointed to his name. "I spelled your name wrong, did you notice?" She traced the *JONSEN* and the letters looked strange even to this man who did not know how to knit letters together into words.

"I don't do much very well," confessed Johnson. "I thought I was good at racing, but now I can't even brag about that."

"If you're racing away, instead of toward, your journey will be long," said Elizabeth. She went to a shelf in the corner of the kitchen. "I have paper," she said. "I can mix ink. Sometimes I write letters for the men."

"Thanks, ma'am." He left the kitchen as quickly as if he'd burned his hand on the stove. He forced himself to the stalls.

Hiram came into the stable shouting his name. "Got one I think you can win. This afternoon. A man in town who thinks he knows horses. I told him I have a horse nobody has ever beaten." He winked at Johnson.

"Liar." Johnson shook his head. "If you're talking about The Stud."

"Ain't your horse lying. Ain't your horse losing those races," said Hiram. "You're the one said he'd never lost a race."

"Well, I learned different, didn't I?" Johnson leaned heavily against a shovel.

"You're sick," said Hiram. "Go to your bunk. I'll come get you when it's time to run. Carl can get The Stud ready."

Johnson collapsed on the narrow bunk, flies buzzing, heat pressing him down, and in his head the beginning of a letter. He worked the words, thinking them up, sorting them, rearranging them, throwing them all away and starting again. He fell asleep.

The banging that awoke him might have been the pounding in his head. He stood, dizzy, sat down again on his bunk. "Time to ride." Hiram thumped the door, then clomped away. Johnson stood up again, sat just as quickly as before. Sweat beaded his forehead. He was both hot and cold. He stood a third time and lurched to the door.

"You don't have to ride," Hiram said when Johnson squinted through the stable door and looked out at the track. Carl was on The Stud, loping around the track.

A large man, still unkempt from what looked like days on the trail, stood beside a sleek mare, watching. "He the one going to ride that mare?" asked Johnson.

"Says so," said Hiram. "He don't think anyone else can. He's mighty proud of her." Hiram took a pepperbox pistol from his belt.

"What else is left to a man in this country?" Johnson asked.

Carl approached, slipped off The Stud. "Look awful puny, Johnson. Should I race him?"

"I'll ride him," said Johnson. "I'll let him be the one to race."

Hiram whistled the large man to where two of his crew stretched a rope across the track. When the man tightened the reins to lead his horse to the start line, the mare reared back and came down so close to her owner she set his hat spinning in the dust. "Atta girl," he said as he picked up his hat, "atta girl." He gave Johnson a lopsided grin and pushed out his hand, which was so dirty Johnson hesitated to take it. When he did, the man showed himself to be the kind of man who liked to crush another man's hand.

"MacDonald," the man said.

"R.J.," said Robert Johnson, pulling his limp hand from the man's grip. Carl helped him mount The Stud.

"How can a runt like him own a horse like that?" MacDonald asked Hiram. "Don't seem right."

"Your mare is mighty fine," Johnson spoke up. He felt better, mounted on his horse, the pounding in his head receding like hooves down a trail. "You might try to match her for style."

Hiram laughed. "Four times around, gentlemen. A small purse, but worth it to whoever should win."

"Fifty dollars ain't small," said MacDonald.

Johnson's eyes widened. "Fifty dollars?" he hissed at Hiram.

The track owner removed two small bags, weighing them side by side. "Twenty-five in each bag," he said. "Now let The Stud beat that mare."

"Not a chance," said MacDonald. He stripped off his vest, threw his hat over the track fence. From his belt he withdrew what looked like a club, but was a long-handled whip, split into what looked like dozens of tails at the end. He cantered the mare to where the workers held the rope.

Johnson leaned forward and talked to his horse. "Run like the wind. You're buying your freedom. I'll hang on." He hoped he could keep his promise.

"I wouldn't get too close," said MacDonald. His face was already contorted, as though he were in the final stretch and just about to lose the race. He furled the mean whip, let it slink from side to side.

"The Stud usually runs in front. You don't have to stay close if you don't want," said Johnson.

Hiram raised his arm and fired the pepperbox. One of the workers dropped the rope as the other whipped it away and immediately MacDonald made a liar of Johnson. The Stud thrust forward for his fastest start ever, but Johnson found himself studying the mare's rump around the first turn. He leaned forward, urging The Stud, but lost ground. On the back straightaway he dropped to a length behind. Johnson flailed his heels into his horse's flanks and did not lose more ground through the turns.

Hiram waved his arms from the side of the track. "Let him run!" he shouted as Johnson approached.

Johnson was exhausted after the first lap. This race was like any other. He was sick and tired and running. And why? He'd become another victim of another trap, hoodwinked by Jo Benson's brothers and father, hoodwinked now by Hiram William Gillian. And all the time riding and riding and getting nowhere. Through the turns, the back straightaway, the turns again, and Hiram waving and shouting, and though The Stud had the nerve, he ran almost as though he sensed Johnson's discouragement, lethargy, homesickness. They took the turns again, The Stud moving closer to the inside rail, which the mare hugged as though she'd raced all her life. "Get her, boy," said Johnson, and then he made himself as small as he could—the runt that MacDonald had called him. He leaned forward lower than he ever had before. He took his feet out of the stirrups, nearly folding them under himself. He felt small, almost nothing but thin air, just enough weight to hold on, body floating above his horse as though they could both fly. The Stud flew. By the end of the third lap, the stallion could have reached forward and bitten the mare's rump. MacDonald turned and raised his whip. The Stud wanted to push by the mare on the inside of the track. Any other day Johnson would have reined him to the outside, but this day they went into the breach. As the mare rocked forward, The Stud surged into the slight space along the rail and they came out of the turn a chest ahead of MacDonald and the mare.

Johnson felt the whip on his back, once and then again, but he did not turn. The Stud surged ahead as though he felt the studded threads of the lash himself. The third blow of the whip missed Johnson's back. The Stud took the blow, and he leaped forward so powerfully Johnson nearly lost his balance. He chanced a look behind him. The mare seemed to be gaining. She took advantage of the straightaway, and by the time they reached the final turns, she tried the same move The Stud had used to best her. Johnson had never been so close to the inside rail, had never felt so imbalanced and precarious, had never held his breath so long. The mare's head pushed into The Stud's side, her snorting breaths closer and closer. Then MacDonald's arm was on Johnson's back, grabbing at his shirt. Johnson shut his eyes against whatever would happen. He felt himself floating, as he'd imagined himself earlier, then he was back on

The Stud, the final straightaway and the finish line in front of them, and they crossed it before he could think about MacDonald and the mare.

Johnson turned in the saddle. MacDonald rode toward him, both fists raised in the air. In one fist the whip. In the other, a piece of Johnson's shirt. Hiram moved toward them, his pistol reloaded and ready. Both men dismounted.

"Bastard!" MacDonald raged. "He wanted to tangle with my mare, going inside like that on the turn." He strode toward them, not stopping even when Hiram leveled his arm and aimed the pepperbox at his chest. "I should horsewhip you."

"You already did." Johnson pointed to the bloody rag MacDonald held in his hand.

"Tried to pull this boy off his horse," said Hiram. He cocked the pistol.

MacDonald stopped. "I should have my money back," he fumed.

"You were beat by a better horse and a better rider," said Hiram. "I want you off my track. By tomorrow, I want you out of Memphis."

"You don't own this town," said MacDonald.

"I own the racing in this town, Mac," said Hiram, "and that's the last time you'll string me along with one of your new horses." He uncocked the pepperbox and returned it to his belt. Carl mounted The Stud for a cooldown.

MacDonald turned to Johnson. "Maybe we'll race again somewhere," he said. "You'll be moving on soon enough, from what I hear."

"What do you hear?" asked Johnson.

"I hear you lost your little place in Cheatham County. Burned to the ground." MacDonald spat on the track, turned to lead the mare away.

"You're lying," said Johnson.

MacDonald turned to him. "You're a wanted man, with a right reasonable price on your head. Did you tell that to your friend here? Did you tell him what you done?"

"I did nothing wrong," said Johnson.

"Why you running?" asked MacDonald.

"Because of bastards like you," said Johnson.

"Well, you'd best keep running then," said MacDonald. He threw the piece of Johnson's shirt on the track. "What I just lost? I'll get it back when I help you with your homecoming. I'll be well paid."

Johnson stomped forward.

"Take it easy," Hiram hissed.

"You don't know what you're talking about!" Johnson yelled. "Name me the sheriff."

"I don't need but one name," said MacDonald, "and that's Benson."

Johnson hung his head at the name of his sweetheart's pa on such venomous lips. He'd have to leave again, and soon. Race to where this man could not find him.

Carl rounded the track at a slow run. Johnson pushed his way past Hiram to his horse and hurried to the stable. Whatever illness he'd suffered earlier in the day was no match for the sudden energy that pulsed in his veins. He unsaddled his horse and combed his coat. "Eat well," he told The Stud. "We leave at dusk."

At the bunkhouse he gathered his things. Hiram found him there. "You'll want to eat. Have Elizabeth pack you enough to hold you a couple of days, at least."

"I owe you some days," Johnson said.

"You won the race," said Hiram. "You got out of The Stud's way." Hiram patted him on the shoulder.

Johnson turned and took Hiram's hand. "You keep that purse if it'll buy back those days," said Johnson.

"One thing you can't buy back. Your horse was going to share some of his lineage."

"On our way back through," said Johnson.

"And when will that be?" asked Hiram.

"I don't know. But please trust my word." Johnson thought of putting his initials to paper, anything to create trust where he had no right to expect it.

"Then trust *my* word," said Hiram. "Be careful of MacDonald. He knows every hill and valley from Nashville into the territories. He's a hunter. Doesn't matter what. He hunts game, men with rewards on their heads, fugitive slaves. He finds every opportunity to bring profit from his meanness."

Johnson threw his things on the bunk. "Elizabeth busy, you suppose?" he asked Hiram.

"You want to write that letter?" Hiram strode toward the house.

Johnson went to the stable, secured his things in his saddlebags. Then he went to Hiram and Elizabeth's warm kitchen. Elizabeth sat at the small table where that same morning she'd cracked eggs and whisked them in a bowl. In front of her was a sheet of paper, an inkwell, and a quill. She smiled.

"You must not judge me. Nor tell a soul of my business," Johnson said.

"Calm yourself," said Elizabeth.

Johnson let the words pour out as fluid and fast as The Stud had raced. Elizabeth slowed him to get the words down accurately. When Johnson finished, she blotted the ink and moved next to him. She put the letter before him and pointed to the words as she read them back:

April 21, 1825
To Sheriff McFall and my accusers:

> *I am wrongly judged. Yet I cannot explain the events at
> Lonely Creek Bridge. I agree that you have evidence against me.
> You witnessed the presence of my horse who now speeds me away
> from you. You have my handkerchief. You have my Hatfield.
> I do not deny that I was in that nearby field. I believe Old
> Harmon owns that land. These are hard facts against me, but
> I will overcome them. You may think I write them to accuse
> myself against myself, but I do not.*

> *I am innocent. I am in love with Jo Benson, which is no
> crime. Her brothers despise me, as does her father, for the reason of
> my love for her and for many reasons that came well before. Our
> land has been disputed, and that question of ownership hangs
> over my family and the Benson family. Would not that be enough
> for them to take their revenge upon me? They borrowed my horse
> as stud. They no doubt stole my flintlock from my cabin and my
> saddle from my shed even as I left home that night. They ripped
> from my dear Jo the one token of our love that she might still hold
> against her bosom, my handkerchief. She, not my mother, sewed
> my initials there. She overheard her father and brother in their
> rough talk and came to warn me of the foul purposes of their
> mission that would involve my horse.*

> *I repeat. I went to observe. What other motive might I have?
> I built a cabin and sought a settled life. I own the best horse in
> Tennessee and plan to raise others. I am in love and I believe I am*

loved in return. I want nothing but to enjoy my land, my cabin, and my woman. I want to marry and settle down.

I am falsely accused. I am fugitive while the true criminals try to steal my land and with it my hope for the future. They have all I do not have, except for my horse and my strong love.

I am innocent. My love will prevail. My horse will prevail. I will return. Not to be shamed, but to shame. Be ready for me with understanding of my plight. Or be prepared to fight. Should you have anything for me, I might be reached through Hiram William Gillian of the Gillian Track in Memphis, Tennessee.

I am, Robert Johnson

"I'll see it gets to Pleasant View," Hiram promised. "Elizabeth, let's feed this young man as much as he can eat, though not so much he sinks crossing the Mississippi."

mighty Mississip

uring his week in Hiram's employ, Robert Johnson had made trips to the water's edge, staring across as though trying to fathom the future. Spring rains had swollen the river, but not to flooding, though everyone called it "The Flood."

"I'll haul you down," said Hiram after they ate. "Put the bridle on your horse, nothing else." He held up his hand. "You'll see." In the stable, Hiram hitched the mules to his wagon. He loaded Johnson's saddle and saddlebags into a large wooden box in the wagon bed. Elizabeth appeared with a jug, a bucket, and a slab of meat wrapped in paper. "Ham and beans," she said. "Enough to give you a start." They tucked the food into the box, along with the jug of water. Hiram brought the box lid to the wagon. "Put your boots and your hat in here, too," he said. Johnson did, and Hiram nailed the lid down. A leather thong was fastened onto the box top and Hiram tied a length of rope to it. Elizabeth pointed to the writing on the lid. "Says to return it to us," she said.

"You'll swim it across with your horse."

"How will I open it?" asked Johnson.

Hiram pulled a small pry bar from behind the wagon seat. "Don't lose it."

Johnson buttoned it into the back pocket of his pants.

"You'll open the box, put the pry bar inside. Secure the lid as best you can and then tie it to a tree. Somebody'll find it."

"Somebody'll steal it."

"This box has made three crossings," said Hiram. "Always finds its way home. Just like you will."

"You sound confident."

"You owe me the stud service." Hiram climbed onto the wagon seat and Johnson climbed up next to him.

"Fare thee well," said Elizabeth.

Johnson bowed his head. "Thank you for everything, ma'am."

He said the same to Hiram as they parted on the banks above The Flood.

At dusk, a full moon rose, pouring itself across the water. The river stretched in its banks. One yawning whirl, one unseen log or limb, one sudden barge or boat not apparent when he started into the water could be the difference between life and death. But with the Bensons, McFall, and now MacDonald behind him, he had to cross. On the bank, Johnson tied the box rope around his waist and lifted the box into the water. Then he urged the stallion forward. The horse, with more courage than his master, plunged in readily and began the swim. Johnson concentrated on helping him, a couple of times leaving his horse's back and swimming alongside him, pulling at the box. Soon, task took the place of fear. They stayed in the swath of moonlight. The Stud swam strongly. Johnson did not tire as he thought he would, after the morning's sickness, the race against MacDonald.

Halfway across, a surge of strength possessed him. He had made a friend in Hiram, and in Elizabeth. They had not judged him. Wherever he ended up, he'd find people like them, folks who understood injustice and hard luck, folks who put a man's dreams ahead of his past. His mother had once told him that though he'd find many kinds of people in the world, each could be sorted into those who help and those who hurt. "I don't tell you this to make you suspicious of others," she said, "but so you might steel yourself against hurt. The hurt others inflict on you, but also the hurt you might inflict on others. You must always be the one who helps."

He was in the middle of the Mississippi, injury behind him. He had stolen whiskey, cut a ferry rope as he'd escaped a world of hurt. He would do better. Johnson returned to The Stud's back, but held onto the box rope. The box bobbed jauntily next to them, dragging them to the side, but not down, as the extra weight would have done had it ridden on their backs. Crossing they were, into something new. On a bank of the river, in front of him or behind, he wasn't sure, a dog howled. Or was it a wolf?

The box pulled itself out of the swath of moonlight into darkness. It became the shadow of a box. Rectangular. The same size as a baby coffin. They had laid James into just such a box, the boy not even two years old, when Robert was five. His brother had crawled, walked, talked, fevered, and coughed himself to death. Robert watched his mother swaddle James in an old sheet, lay him in the box his father had fashioned. The old man had nailed it shut just as Hiram had nailed this box. Robert remembered his mother's extravagance of tears, how she could not leave the hump of earth after the burial. And his father's anger. First at nothing. Then at Robert's mother, until he demanded she leave the grave and get inside and cook. "Life goes on. God took what he wanted. I don't like it no more than you do." He spat on the ground and went inside. He stood at the one small window of their cabin that looked out to where his wife lay on the ground next to the disturbed earth. He cursed God. He cursed her. He cursed Robert when he asked for bread. Finally, he took down his Bible and read. All night he read. All night Robert's mother lay outside, as though she wanted to enter the earth with her child. And Robert's father burned one sputtering candle after another. And Robert? He went to his small room in the rafters of the cabin and imagined he was a bird, that he could fly away, that he was God's sparrow, the one He looked after. Then Robert slept. He lay in bed all the next day. And then the next evening his mother came inside, called him down, and they ate. At supper she said, "I don't believe God takes what he wants. I believe He receives what we are able to give Him." She never spoke of James again. When she died thirteen years later, they opened another hole in the ground, next to James. Robert's father said, "God takes what he wants." Robert did not correct him.

The Stud drifted with the box into darkness. Johnson was pulled from his reverie by a boat so small he'd not seen it riding the current. A deep voice shouted, "There!" and, "Bring it around." A lantern sputtered light. "It's a horse all right," said another voice. "Rider, too."

"Nigger or white?" asked the deep voice.

"White," Johnson called out. "Swimming my way to Arkansas."

"At night?" asked the second voice. The boat came closer.

"Time went faster than me," said Johnson.

"That a box?" asked the second voice.

"Coffin," said Johnson. "My baby boy. Died before I could get to the doctor."

"Sorry to hear it," said the deep voice. "You an Arkansawyer?"

"Trying to be," said Johnson. "I just want to be home."

"Won't be much longer," said the deep voice. The boat moved into stronger current, followed the river southwest.

"Much obliged," said Johnson. The force of the current lessened. He mounted The Stud. He scratched the horse's head. "Soon," he whispered. "Soon."

But soon still meant the slow push toward the darkness of the bank, with trees rearing up, and the pools of debris that swim in the eddies near the shore. They had to find where the bank would be level enough for a horse to climb up in the muddy brush. Johnson felt as if he were indeed dragging something dead behind him. When the bank looked inviting, Johnson climbed onto land and helped The Stud up, too, and pulled in the rope and lifted the box. He lay in the dark, breathing hard, wet not just from the water of the Big Muddy, but from the sweat of exertion.

As the moon climbed to the top of the sky, and the stars began their wheeling, Johnson took the small pry bar and opened the box lid. Some river water had seeped through, but not enough to ruin the wrapped ham, the jar of beans. He took the jug of water and drank deep. The meat twanged his nose, and he unwrapped the paper enough for what he promised himself would be just one mouthful.

A hissing startled him. He stood still. A movement in the brush. Then another hiss. "You the man with the food?" asked a husky voice.

"I have food," said Johnson. "But I don't think I'm the man with the food. Not if you're expecting me. Because I'm not expecting you."

"They said a man would come with food," the husky voice insisted.

"Who are you?" asked Johnson. He grabbed his saddle blanket, his saddle, and began to prepare himself to ride, if he had to.

"Nobody, if you not the man with food."

Johnson cinched the saddle and threw the saddlebags over. "Show yourself, if you want food," he said.

"I'll wait," said the voice. "For the man with the food."

"You a runaway?" Johnson asked. He couldn't leave The Stud while he secured the box lid and tied the rope to a tree on the riverbank, as he'd been instructed. "Some men in the river, they asked me if I was black or white."

"I heard 'em," said the voice, closer now.

"Well, I ain't one of *them*," said Johnson. "I'm running away myself. Soon as I tie this box to a tree down by the river."

The black man appeared next to him, so close Johnson was surprised he hadn't heard him or felt his presence. He was a thin man, with a hatchet face. "But you not the man with the food?" he whispered. He, too, had swum the river, his shirt clinging to a miserably scrawny frame. "He said there'd be a man. A box. Food."

"Who said?" asked Johnson.

"Don't have no names," said the black man. He shook his head. "A mighty tall man. Good with horses. Like your horse there. But he don't use no name."

Could the man be Hiram? He'd packed Johnson elaborately, the box and more food than he could eat. "I have a name. Robert Johnson," he said. "What's yours?"

"Jackson. Like the president."

"Jackson, I believe I *am* the man with the food. Come take your share."

Johnson unpacked some ham and beans, wrapped them in some of the paper. Jackson disappeared. Johnson stowed the rest in his saddlebags, then threw the pry bar into the box and slammed down the lid. He tied the box to a sapling and let it drift to the end of its rope. Then he mounted The Stud and rode slowly into Arkansas, away from The Flood, away from Tennessee. When he stopped back with Hiram to honor the claim to The Stud as stud, he'd tell him his plan had worked.

He found ground high enough to see a few winking lanterns across the river in the gathering town of Memphis. Then he turned away, riding through brush and small trees until he discerned a snaking trail—deer, Indian, military, settler, he didn't know. But he followed it half the night until he figured he had a good jump on MacDonald or anyone else who might be interested in his whereabouts.

Arkansas

Days passed, though the longer Robert Johnson was on the trail, the more he lost track of which day, or how many days. Was he yet halfway across Arkansas Territory? What distance was enough between himself and any pursuers? He could ride all the way west and south, through Texas, a place some were already hoping would become a state of the Union. The Spaniards had lost the country to Mexico. Who knew if Mexico could long keep it. Johnson had heard tales of grasslands, flat lands, deserts, and of Indians who inhabited these places.

He slogged through woods, through muddy creek bottoms, sometimes on a clear trail, sometimes finding his own path. The food Hiram and Elizabeth had given him had not lasted but three or four days of sparse eating, since he'd shared it with Jackson. In a week's time, Johnson was all hunger, weariness, bone-crunch tired. Birds, squirrels, and rabbits often eluded his pistol. He ate anything that looked tender enough to digest, even flowers. Water was still plentiful in the creeks that veined this hilly country.

When he was hungry, pushing forward to stay ahead of pursuit, he thought about Jo. Did she imagine him in these pine woods, head nodding to his chest with each of The Stud's strides? As Elizabeth had said, love should be a moving toward. Regret was in moving away. Absence was the thin connection that might end in either love or regret. Sometimes he saw Jo doing the simplest things—feeding the chickens, currying her mare at dusk, stacking a few stove lengths of wood onto her thin arms

to carry inside. He imagined her thinking of him, whether she was fling-
ing feed, brushing the coat of her horse, gathering hickory. Each time
he imagined a slight swell puffing her dress. And her mare, Molly? The
Stud had been with the Bensons for a week. Old Benson would soon
see the evidence. The mare first, of course, when she stopped going into
heat. His daughter not so soon, unless he kept track of her bloody rags,
scrubbed each month. Johnson imagined the clothesline in her yard,
only her sunny dresses hanging, each one as empty as his chance to be
with her. Surely she would put rags on the line to keep her father and
brothers from knowing she was with child, at least until she could no
longer hide her body's changes from them.

His father would be submitting himself to his steady chores, to the
same Old Testament that allowed him no way to understand his son
except through the violence of eye for eye, of stonings and smitings, of
vengeance is Mine sayeth.

His uncle Judson had surely delivered the letter. Johnson could see
the grimy paper, worn and soft now with the folding and unfolding of
Jo's long fingers, perhaps stained with tears, perhaps now folded tight
and resting in her undergarment, close to her heart, proof that he might
someday be with her. He longed to reach into her dress and draw her
close to him once more. He longed to drink again from that aching well
where he could forget everything but the two of them together.

A crow cawed, and Johnson lifted his head from his chest. Someone
else must be on the trail, ahead or behind. He slowed, and another rider
appeared behind him, riding fast on a roan horse with a powerful chest.
The Stud's ears perked, but Johnson kept him reined, knowing the natural surge of his competitive horse. When the other rider slowed, Johnson
stopped, turned, waited.

"You want by?" he asked.

The rider approached. "Don't know as I want to pass anybody on
this trail," the man said. "A man has to watch his back. Like you were."
He was burly, four or five days of beard on his face, with a leather vest
that hung on his chest like shingling. "What's your business?" he asked.

"Just riding," said Johnson. "Know where I've been, but not where
I'm going."

"See what I mean about my back?" said the man. He took off his hat
and slapped it against his saddle. His hair hung in lanky blond ropes,

which he combed with his fingers before replacing his hat. "A man with-out no destination can be a dangerous man."

"I'm not a dangerous man," said Johnson.

"Then you've left dangerous men behind you?" The big man took a pouch from his vest pocket. He reached in and fingered some tobacco into his mouth. "You want a chew?"

Johnson shook his head. "I've left *everything* behind," he said. "Dangerous and not."

"It's a lucky man has something to leave behind." The man took his first spit of the chew, a quick spurt of brown into the brush. He wiped his mouth with the back of his hand. "How long since you've seen any-one in this country?"

"Days," said Johnson. "Seems mighty lonely."

"Your first time coming this way?" The man chewed vigorously. His cheek puffed, and he spat again. "Always seems lonely that first time through. Like you're the only living creature. Like you're the one mak-ing the trail. But lots of folks come this way. Coming. Going. Running. Hiding. Hunting. Being hunted. A few want to settle down somewhere. Which is it, young man?"

"Just my first time through," said Johnson. "And not a soul for days."

"You'll get used to it. Your own journey, that is. To the rest of us, this trail is old hat." The man reached for his saddlebag.

Johnson turned abruptly and dug his heels into The Stud's flanks. The Stud compacted his back legs and shot forward. Soon enough, Johnson stopped. He heard no horse or man behind him.

A day passed, and then another. The Stud's ears always led them to the trickling of water from a spring, a freshet, a small creek. Johnson's constant and overwhelming hunger meant loading the old pistol and trying again. His shooting improved. The squirrels and rabbits weren't much, but each night Johnson roasted the meager meat and The Stud found grass. They rested off the trail, neither sleeping as soundly as at home, where fence and cabin had protected them from what they heard in this wilderness—wolf? bear? bobcat? Here, each sound might mean a reach for Uncle Judson's Daw, always at hand. A couple of nights, Johnson saddled his horse in the dark, so afraid he was of pursuit, whether by man or beast.

Occasionally, at the beginning of a day without rain or clouds, after a quiet night, Johnson found the land to be something more than territory to cross. Once, on a rise above one of the many rivers, in an open meadow full of wild strawberries, he sat, enjoying a cool breeze, the small red fruit tart and seedy, but reviving his tongue after days of scorched meat. A great stream of birds flew overhead, south to north. Though humans weren't migratory, surely they were meant to cross into new territory, to find new homes, new opportunities, new settlements. Surely that was the same human fever that had settled Tennessee, making it a state fewer than thirty years before. Louisiana joined up when Johnson was a boy. Arkansas would be a state, and all the territory beyond. Johnson had been born on the same day as the Louisiana Purchase, a day that the territory of the United States expanded so far that perhaps dozens of states could be carved out of land the French and Indians used only for trapping and trading.

Along the river valleys, where a man could grow cotton and tobacco and corn, where hogs and chickens could root and roost, people would settle. Johnson imagined the towns, the farms, the pasture, the crop land, the timber to be cut, all in the hope that the harvest would pay the labor of it all, that the towns would prosper as much as the dreams of the speculators who claimed the land and touted its prospects.

But nearly as soon as Johnson had any thought of settlement, he remembered his troubles. He pushed on, through bright days and storm-laden skies and cold mornings and hot afternoons and birds so thick they erased the sun from the sky, nights so dark he couldn't see his horse, though he could hear him breathing next to him. He moved through hunger and thirst, wishing for the moment when he could turn, unpursued or not caring if he were pursued, and face the direction that led back to Jo Benson. Godspeed the letter he'd spoken to Elizabeth.

Red River Valley

*j*ohnson stayed mostly in woods, pine and cedar so thick the ground was covered with needles. The water, tinged with pine sap, had a smoky tang. Four or five days passed before he reached bottom land. Later, he would learn he was in the Red River Valley.

The opening of landscape foretold prairie and humid-hazy sky. The land lay thick and rich with grass. As he abandoned the trees, he felt as though he'd finally thrown himself ahead of any other living creature. The Red was a wide river, and he moved north and west, in line with the bluffs, hoping to spot a cave in the rocks for shelter. He and The Stud needed to catch breath, to rest, to fatten for a time in this good grass.

Overhead, two buzzards floated in lazy circles. A ways upriver, Johnson discovered why. A deer lay dead, shot in the head and matted with flies. As Johnson approached, the carrion fouled his breath. The Stud snorted, so Johnson dismounted to approach on foot. The deer's flank was gashed as though a bear had clawed for meat. The buzzards would soon descend for the feast.

In this country, Johnson thought, a man wouldn't shoot a deer to leave it dead. He was hungry enough to consider cutting away some of the flesh, but the smell brought bile into his throat.

Rocks split the bluff ahead, and Johnson led The Stud up for a look. They entered woods. A crow cawed. A squirrel scampered up a tree. Johnson climbed to an outcrop. Below, through the grass, a figure approached the dead deer, a young girl from the looks of her, frisky as the squirrel in the tree. The girl circled the carcass. With the knife in her hand she sliced back the dun hide of the deer's shoulder and gouged out some meat, shaking her head with the stink. If she'd killed the deer, she wouldn't have the strength to butcher it properly, carry it to wherever she was camped. Where were her menfolk, that they'd leave her to the meat, a slight girl, sunny hair the color of The Stud's coat? She wore no bonnet, no shoes, no more than a gray rag of a dress. As she hurried from the carcass, Johnson headed down the bluff without thinking he would pursue her, but even as he mounted his horse he thought how the girl reminded him of Jo. Slight, golden hair, quick.

He caught up to her as the meadow turned to scrub oak and cedar. When she heard him, she turned, revealing a swollen silhouette. She said nothing, just scampered up into the bluffs above the river valley. Johnson trailed her easily up a path, headed to what must be home. The cabin appeared, ill-built from the beginning, foundation stones as loose as bad teeth under unevenly split logs, cracks between the logs stuffed with mud and smooth river stone. Only a small can filled with dogwood blossoms on the leaning porch distracted Johnson from the cabin's dishevelment.

If the dead deer smelled, the cabin downright stunk, even against the wood smoke of a fire. Johnson stood his ground, unsure who might be inside. At the edges of wilderness he was certain to find two kinds of people. Some, like Hiram, came to new places to make them fit for civilization. Others, like MacDonald, went there because they were not fit for civilization themselves. The latter, Johnson knew, might just include himself. After a time, the girl came out on the porch to sit, gnawing at the meat that would now be venison, since it was singed enough to call it cooked. She ate hungrily, like a dog fed every other day. Johnson dismounted, left The Stud to find grass. He tied his handkerchief around his nose and walked toward her.

She jumped up. "No you don't," she said. She put the piece of meat in her mouth, hopped over a porch rail, and disappeared.

When Johnson cornered the cabin, she stood on the opposite end, still chewing on the hunk of venison, one hand on the side of the cabin, ready to run again like a child playing tag. "I won't hurt you," Johnson said, but she vanished. He went around the cabin, its smell so rank he gagged. The girl was not on the porch. He heard a giggle, and looked up a path. The girl sat on a rock outcrop, still gnawing on the meat. This time she didn't run when he approached. "I won't hurt you," Johnson repeated.

"So you say." With her free hand she lifted a tattered scrap of her dress to cover her knees.

Johnson's nose found peace away from the cabin. "Where's your people?"

She looked down to the cabin. The place looked even more dilapidated from a distance.

"Daddy don't eat," she said. "Not a solitary bite." She tore another thread of meat from the venison.

"He sick?" Johnson asked.

"Not that he said." The girl stared at the small bit of meat in her hand. "I should offer you food," she said, her voice deeper, like the woman she would become.

"Think I'll pass," said Johnson.

"It's good enough when you're hungry," said the girl. She smiled then, revealing small teeth. She patted the rock next to her. "You could sit beside me," she said.

"Your daddy build the cabin?" Johnson asked.

"My uncle Mac," she said. "The bear hunter."

"MacDonald?"

"Jonathan D., himself," said the girl. "He's right known when people begin to swap stories." She put the last bite of venison in her mouth.

Johnson was glad to see it gone. He was hungry, but for meat less close to putrefaction.

"My daddy," said the girl, "he's not known for much at all." She chewed, then spat gristle. "No. He ain't never going to be known!" She lay back on the rock, then rolled into herself as though protecting the protuberance of her womb.

Johnson sat beside her. She smelled almost as sharp as the meat he'd refused. "You and your daddy need anything?" he asked.

"Daddy don't need no help," she said, her hands still holding her head. "No help at all."

"And you?"

The girl shook her head. A burble of laughter broke from her mouth.

Johnson looked for The Stud.

"I'm Nancy," she said. "Do not hasten away." She sat up and put her hand on his shoulder.

"How'd you know what I was thinking?" asked Johnson. A jay landed in a nearby tree to scold the world. "About riding away."

"I always know," said Nancy. "Everyone leaves. Least as much as they stay." She pointed. "See that jay?"

Johnson nodded.

"See it fly away?" The bird cocked its head as though listening, then hurled itself into air and flight, skimming the trees for a new perch.

"Do you have water?" asked Johnson.

"Down to the river," said Nancy. "You'll want to drink. Wash up." She jumped off the rock, again the little girl, fairly skipping down the path.

He followed her, and so The Stud followed him. She would run, then turn to be certain he was behind her, then bound ahead again, until they were all the way to the river. He stood on the bank, but he did not see her. Was she hiding? He waited. Maybe something had frightened her. Who else might be nearby? Her uncle? Was Jonathan D. MacDonald the same man he'd raced in Memphis? Might her father rouse himself from his sickbed?

Her laughter cut the quiet. Upstream, the river bent against a small rise. He climbed up. Below, the river ran swiftly over a shallow of rocks. Nancy stood in the water up to her small orb of a belly, which seemed to float in front of her. She waved.

He shimmied down the bank. He took off his boots and put his feet in the water. "Red River's best crossing," Nancy said. "Sweetest water in the valley. Best for washing away your loneliness."

Johnson waded toward her. She turned away, and he could see the welts on her upper back, the bruises blooming on the sides of her arms. He shook his head. Her daddy might be known in these parts for beating her. Johnson bent for a drink of the fast-moving water. Sweet, yes, but not enough to wash away the homesickness in him. He whistled, and The Stud found a switchback down the steep bank to the river. Johnson unsaddled the horse.

"I'll bathe him before I bathe myself." Johnson followed his horse into the water. His clothes would need washing. The Stud drank deeply, then moved downstream into deeper water, shaking his head. He knelt, until only his head remained above the surface.

"Can he swim?" Nancy splashed her way to the riverbank.

Johnson did not turn around. "Best swimming horse in Tennessee. Ain't no river he can't cross, and believe me, we've crossed many of them. This one, we'll stay in for a time."

"So you're from Tennessee? But who isn't in this country? Uncle Mac says Arkansas clear into Texas is but an outpost of Tennessee." Nancy climbed up the bank and disappeared.

Johnson followed the horse into chest-high water and pulled two ticks from just below The Stud's mane. When he tugged the horse's ear to lead him toward the shallows, The Stud paid him no mind. "Got to check the rest of your hide. Sometime," said Johnson. He moved upstream into the shallows and stripped off his clothes. He lay on the rocks and let the current flow over him, head to toe. He wished Nancy were right, that he could wash away his loneliness. He closed his eyes against the sun.

When Nancy hollered from the bluff above the river, Johnson covered himself and opened his eyes. He waved her back. "I'll be to your cabin soon," he yelled. "You just give me time to dry."

She disappeared.

Johnson stood and let the sun take the water from his body. He slicked back his hair. When he whistled, his horse simply looked at him from the deeper water and shook his head. "Can't stay in the river forever," said Johnson.

The Stud fluttered his lips in a snorting raspberry. Johnson's clothes were nearly dry. He shook them out and put them back on. He pulled on his boots, put on his hat, and stood next to the saddle. "C'mon, boy," he said.

The stallion simply stared at him.

"Lazy good for nothing," said Johnson. "You'll find me at that cabin, such as it is." He wet his bandana and tied it over his nose and mouth, then lifted the saddle onto his shoulder and walked away. Whatever waited for him when he found Nancy could be no worse than all he'd suffered these past weeks. Only it would smell worse.

Nancy sat on the sagging porch. She had braided her wet hair. She let him walk past her into the house, where what had once been a man sat in an armchair, face black as a stove and so swollen he seemed to have no eyes, no nose. Flies swarmed the room. The man's hands looked like stiff, cracked gloves. Johnson did not know enough about death to reckon when Nancy's father had died, but when he saw maggots crawling in the rank hole in the man's chest, he turned quickly and fled the room, the porch, the cabin. When he could breathe again, he turned.

Nancy walked down the porch steps toward him. "He can't eat, but he can be eaten," she said.

Johnson shrugged. Was this gallows humor, or was she half crazed? Half everything? Girl and woman, child soon to be mother, innocent and flirtatious, weak and violent?

"He doesn't look too good, does he?" She turned to face the cabin.

"When did you shoot him?" Johnson moved next to her, though it hurt his nose.

"He shot him that deer. Thought he might find another, so he loaded up his rifle. He had no luck, so he came back here and woke me up in my bed, to help him carry the deer. He was not a gentleman, my pa. After he was finished with me, he went to get his clothes off the floor. I let him dress. I should have carried the deer up here with him. But I couldn't wait. He sat in his chair. He was waiting for me to bring him his boots. I aimed for his heart."

"He responsible for your condition?"

"He was a man to hate. Everyone hated him. Even his own brother. Only flies can bear him." Nancy turned to Johnson. "Where's that big horse of yours?" she asked. "I'd sure like to ride him."

"Nobody rides my horse. His choice, not mine," said Johnson.

"You have a name?" Nancy asked.

"Roberts. John Roberts."

"Well, John Roberts, from Tennessee. I've been waiting for Uncle Mac. He comes this way on occasion. He's strong enough to do something with my pa."

"Every man deserves a decent burial." Johnson moved toward the cabin.

She followed him. "We could lift his chair maybe."

"First you have to have someplace to take him." Johnson stepped onto the porch. "Where do you want him buried?"

"In Hell," she said, crossing her arms over her chest.

"Hell's a long ways off."

"Not when you've had to live with *him*." Nancy pointed to a stump-handled shovel, more her size than a man's. "Anywhere."

Johnson searched for a stretch of meadow near the house, close enough to haul rocks to top the grave with them. His stomach growled with hunger, then turned with the pervasive smell. As always, he ignored it. He began to dig. Three feet deep, a couple wide, maybe five feet long, just big enough to dump the body. He worked for well over an hour before she appeared behind him with a small bucket. "From the river," she said. "Your horse is fine."

"He let you near?" He reached for the water.

"I got on his back. Then he slipped out from under me."

Johnson took a long drink. "Let's bring your pa out here. In the chair, like you said."

They climbed the porch stairs into dense air buzzing with flies. Johnson gagged but set his teeth and breathed through his stinging nose. "I'll lift," he said. "You steady." He reached from behind the chair to lift it by the arms.

Nancy gripped the front legs, helping him some, but as they moved toward the door Johnson nearly slipped in a puddle of leaking fluids. A pestiferous drool, accumulated on the chair seat, dripped to the floor with each step he took. Johnson thought to hold his breath until they were outside, though they now carried the smell with them. So Johnson breathed a scent so horrid he wondered if he would ever inhale again without the memory of it. When they reached the shallow grave, Johnson directed Nancy to the foot of it. She set the chair legs on the ground and Johnson heaved the body forward where it landed face down, a glob of damp-stained clothing, like a long burlap sack full of rotten potatoes. Nancy fled.

Johnson shoveled earth over the body, then covered the grave with a layer of rock, though he doubted any digging animals would have the man. This hasty burial would be the only small dignity given this father survived by his child and her child, both from his loins. What a sad lot human beings could be.

When Johnson returned to the cabin Nancy had the fire blazing. She was sweeping with a wet broom that she'd dipped into a bucket of ashes. The floor had turned gray where she worked. Already, the smell was diminished. Johnson took the broom from her. "You might go wash now," he said. "And put on fresh clothes."

"I don't have a thing else but my nightshirt. Uncle Mac is bringing a dress. Something fit for me, he said."

"He know you're with child?"

She shook her head.

"You might put on the nightshirt long enough to wash what's left of that dress."

She rummaged in a small chest in the corner of the room, then ran out the door.

He finished sweeping the cabin floor. He found the water bucket and a rag and wiped the death stains from his boots. He sat on the porch to wait for her. The Stud was probably still in the river, drinking, cooling himself, resting from the long ride down Arkansas. The horse would watch as Nancy stripped off her clothes, as she waded into the river to wash them, as she washed herself, her small breasts swollen to a size she'd never known before, her belly swollen, too, above what would be a wisp of pubic hair.

Johnson thought of Jo, and felt a pang so deep he might have been shot in the chest for the hole that was there. In the cabin, he opened Nancy's small trunk. Not much to call her own. A scarf, a pair of leather gloves, a musty hat, a matching necklace and brooch, on the brooch a shadowy silhouette—probably her mother, and probably dead, like so many women on the frontier, of tuberculosis, ague, childbirth, infection, fever, accident. Or worse, violence.

Johnson searched the cabin and found worm-infested meal, a bag of salt, a dipper of lard in a bucket. He mixed together what he could stand the thought of eating, and set it in a skillet on the fire. When The Stud whinnied, Johnson went to the porch. The horse stood at the steps, Nancy on his back, the two of them still wet from the river. "I've made something to eat," Johnson said.

She slipped off the horse, her nightshirt riding above her waist. Johnson turned from the sight of her small buttocks. "I'll bring more water," she said, and took the bucket from the porch.

Johnson turned the skillet to even the heat. His johnnycakes were burning brown, but they'd be half sufficient until he could hunt.

Nancy had a fine supply of lead and powder. Her father must have enjoyed casting balls when he wasn't up to no good with his daughter. Johnson set the man's Kentucky rifle next to the door.

He bedded down on the cabin porch, thinking to lengthen the arm between himself and the girl. Nancy didn't argue. When he woke to a darkness just edged with what might be dawn, his horse stood with his head over the porch rail. He buzzed his lips for what must have been the second time, the first being the sound that had wakened Johnson. "Thanks," Johnson whispered, and stood up. He stroked his horse's forehead. "You stay here," he said. He took the rifle from just inside the door and went to hunt.

Sometime later, he stood at the edge of a small meadow that was just beginning to wash itself in sunlight. Two does grazed on the other edge of the trees. Johnson's heart wanted the larger one, but his mind told him small, something easy to carry. He went to one knee, rested his elbow on the other, and steadied the rifle. He needed to make a heart shot. He calmed his breathing and squeezed the trigger. And missed the doe. Both deer raised their heads, then raced into the woods.

Johnson went to where they'd been grazing. He found the matted grass where they'd slept. Just as he was ready to turn away, he saw the blood spores. He ran into the woods and found a thin trail, and more blood splattered on gooseberry and buck brush on either side. They'd be hard to follow, but Johnson would pursue until he was certain they had outrun him.

Behind him, hoofbeats pounded into the woods. He jumped aside as Nancy and The Stud bolted past, down the deer trail. Johnson was surprised the stallion would take Nancy as rider, and stunned when moments later his horse trotted back up the trace, riderless, and stopped in front of him. Johnson jumped onto the horse's bare back and let himself be carried to where Nancy stood above the larger of the does. Johnson had put a hole in its lung. Blood seeped out of its open mouth. The hole sputtered blood as the doe breathed laboriously toward its death. Johnson jumped off his horse. He took the small packet of powder and another ball from his pocket and loaded the rifle. He put another shot into the doe, this time the barrel to its ear, the bullet to the brain.

Johnson gutted the deer. After, he touched his horse's right knee, and The Stud knelt and let Johnson and Nancy lift the deer onto his back. They walked to the cabin. Johnson was eager to skin the deer, cut up the meat, eat until his stomach was as swollen as Nancy's womb. They'd smoke the rest. In the chimney, since he'd not seen a smokehouse. Nancy would have decent meat through her wait for her uncle Mac, if the man came as she said he would.

The smell of death diminished with the roasting of venison in the banked fire. Nancy spoke of all her uncle Mac was soon to bring her. Meal, bacon, lard, sugar, salt, coffee. "Maybe even a piece of fruit," Nancy said. "He knows how to get what he needs."

"What does he look like, your uncle Mac?" Johnson asked.

"As big as the bears he hunts," said Nancy. "Blond hair, but his beard turning to gray."

"And his horse?"

"Different horse every time I see him. But always a mare. Pa said he never knew a man liked to trade horses as much as my uncle Mac. Maybe he just keeps trying to find a horse as fine as yours." She left off cutting venison into strips. She put her hands in a bowl of water, then came close to him. "You could stay until he gets here."

"Your uncle Mac been up to Memphis, or where?" Johnson asked.

"He travels is all I know. Memphis sometimes. Then he'll take off into Texas." She took his hand.

Johnson flicked her hand away and sat down at the table.

"You aren't like most men," she said. She put the bowl of water in front of him. She took the chair across from him. "Most men would have taken me by force. Most men are more animal than you are."

Johnson smiled. "I'm animal, all right," he said. "But the human part of me remembers a girl back in Tennessee."

"You love her?" she asked.

"I do," said Johnson. "She's the only sunshine I have left in this world."

"Your stud is sunshine," she said. "He shined this morning when he woke me up whinnying. Soft. Like he was calling just to me. You're a lucky man, John Roberts. How lonely it will be when you take yourself and your stud away." She set her hand across the table, in front of him, as though asking him to take it.

Johnson stood up and poured water in a cup. "Let's eat," he said.

They ate venison until they were gorged. They hung meat in the chimney, pounded some to dry. Johnson salted pieces to take with him when he left. By nightfall he was content. He sat on the porch, wished for sugar, or whiskey, or coffee, for any small luxury. He would leave at dawn.

That night—or was he simply dreaming?—she stood above him on the porch, a blanket around her. She let the corner fall from her shoulder. "I could love you. I know how," she whispered.

Johnson did not look at her exposed breast. The father who had taught her some distorted rudiment of love was buried in the ground. The dead man's clothing and bedding, along with his chair, was burned. The ramshackle cabin was clean, smelling only of lye and wood smoke. The venison still hung above the gray coals.

"I could come with you."

"Wait for your uncle. Someone to care for you," he said.

"No man will treat me fine as you have. They're all like my daddy. Make a slave of me, then have their animal way. That's how men are."

Johnson knew he must flee this girl, swollen with bruises and child, before he did her wrong and saw no harm in it.

Nancy was up before him, sitting on the porch stair in the earliest light, arms and legs crossed. When he sat next to her, she took his hand in hers, then pressed it against her thigh. Her bruises were turning to yellow, moving back under the skin. She looked up at him. "I've grown so fond of you it will grieve me to have you go. I could love you so true, I know I could." Her legs squeezed his hand to her sex.

He pulled his hand away. "I reckon you could," he said. "But I have to leave." He stood up. "I have pursuers. Unlikely as it seems, your uncle Mac might be one of them."

"Do not hasten away." Nancy stood up. "If it's Uncle Mac after you, ain't no place he hasn't been, and no man or bear he can't find. You'd best just let him come, because he'll find you sometime. If your choice is between sooner or later, why not let it be sooner?"

Johnson lifted his saddle onto the porch rail. "He'd blame me for your condition. Before he'd blame your pa." He whistled. He would pack the salted venison and ride away.

The stallion did not heed his whistle, nor his impatient shout. Johnson hurried down the porch stairs and to the meadow. His horse faced away from him. Johnson heard a whinny from the woods and The Stud jumped toward a mare, who ran into the meadow, stopped to stretch her legs, exposing her sex. There would be no controlling the horse now.

"Might just be Uncle Mac's," said Nancy from behind him. Johnson spun in time to see her disappear into the woods, back toward the cabin.

Was her uncle there? The Stud whinnied and ran to the mare. She cantered away, and he followed, nipping at her flank, her shoulder, trying to stop her long enough to mount her. She ran, and he ran, a flurry of hooves, tossing manes, bared teeth. He was certainly determined. *Love*, after all, might just be a dignified way to say *lust*. But Johnson had said *love* time and again, thinking of Jo Benson. And he had not defiled himself with Nancy.

The Stud would soon run the mare to exhaustion, raise himself above her, hooves at her shoulders when she finally settled into him. Perhaps the horse was right to take what was there for him. What did either of them have but this very moment?

Johnson strode toward the cabin, alert to possibilities. An eager Nancy, an uncle enraged by his niece's pregnancy, bounty hunter MacDonald ready to capture him? Had Johnson worn his pistol, he'd have lifted it from his holster and cocked it to the ready.

The cabin was empty. Nancy nowhere to be seen. No bounty hunter sat on the porch waiting for him. The place might have been abandoned except for the plume of smoke that rose from the chimney. Johnson called out. Nobody answered. He walked up the path to where he'd buried Nancy's father. Rocks covered the small patch of earth, but the sky, cloudless and nonchalant, told nothing of what had transpired. Johnson hurried toward the Red River, alert and ready, but he saw nothing untoward, heard nothing but an occasional songbird, the deep drip of a cardinal's voice, the trill of a finch. A jay scolded a chuckling squirrel. He should have been able to hear the horses, for they would not procreate without snorting, squealing, even screaming. When the path opened into the river bottom he hesitated. Was someone waiting for him to reveal himself? Might Uncle Mac have him in his sights, the barrel of a musket trained to his heart? Johnson stopped. He ran to the meadow where he'd left his horse and the mare.

The Stud was alone, and trotted toward him, nickering. "You ready?" Johnson asked. He put his arm around the horse's neck. "Where's the mare you found so important?"

The stallion wrestled his head away. He lifted his front hooves from the ground, came down with two thuds.

"Still frisky?" Johnson asked. He shook his head. "Let's go."

He ran, The Stud behind him, to the cabin, still empty, as though Nancy had never existed. Or had she taken her uncle somewhere to give Johnson time to escape? He grabbed the saddle from the porch rail. The hairs on the back of his neck bristled in sudden fear. He saddled his horse and ran into the cabin for the sack of meat he'd readied earlier. He raced back and tied it around the saddle horn. He reached in his saddle-bag to retrieve his pistol. He mounted The Stud and cocked his gun.

The Stud whinnied as Johnson turned him down the path. "Quiet," Johnson said through gritted teeth, and kicked The Stud's flanks. "And speed."

He rode away so fast nothing could catch him, not horse, not hound, not Nancy, not Uncle Mac, not even his own thoughts. He did not take a deep breath until he'd crossed the river shallows and climbed the bluffs on the other side. He stopped to look back. He could not see trail, cabin, even the thinnest wisp of smoke. Nothing but remembrance: the musky scent of rotten death, the lure of temptation, the narrow escape from Nancy, from her uncle Mac.

After several days, the venison turned rancid and he threw it on the trail for the flies. He rode away from the smell of death, what his father would have called "the wages of sin," putting distance between himself and the Red River Valley.

drifted

everal days into what some people called Texas and others called No Man's Land, Johnson woke in a wash of sweat. The heat had not yet risen with the sun, and he feared he might be taking sick. The last river he'd crossed smelled of rotten eggs, and the whole country had a brackish yellow tinge to it. Compared to Tennessee, even to Arkansas Territory, this land looked faded, the rich brown of earth turning sometimes to gray, sometimes to ochre, the vegetation pale, as though covered with dust.

He mounted his horse and rode. With the growing heat the insects rose. A persistent horsefly followed him like a bounty hunter intent on blood. He swatted and swore at it, then settled on patience. He let the fly land on his horse's neck and ready itself for a stinging bite. The fly took hold in spite of The Stud's twitching flesh. A hawk had been swooping overhead, riding the currents of air. Johnson had been waiting for it to gather itself, collapse its wings, then strike prey—snake, mouse, lizard. The drama unfolded, the hawk's snapping descent, then the climb back up, some small thing in its grip. Johnson remembered the horsefly, now tasting The Stud's blood. He slammed down and felt the small victory in his palm. He dropped the fly to the ground, wiped blood on his horse's mane. All the flying, crawling, creeping, hopping, biting, burrowing, stinging creatures, some even too small to see—their kind would probably kill him off before he was hunted down by Benson's bounty hunter MacDonald, or someone else looking to claim the sheriff's *right reasonable* reward.

The country had opened up, and Johnson rode along the fringes of creeks among scrub oak and willow, close to shade, water, and shelter, and obscured from sight. When the landscape crumpled again into a range of hills, he felt more at home. The sweat of the morning, he decided, had been the breaking of a fever rather than the beginning of sickness. He would find something to eat soon. He knew he would survive, after all. *The long run, in the end, after all*—these phrases defined the distant prospects of his life.

He came through a stand of elm, cottonwood, and sycamore to look down onto a clear creek that ran over smooth pebbles. Surely the water would be fit for drinking. He nudged his horse forward, but The Stud balked. Johnson leaned forward in the saddle, shook his head, rubbed his eyes, and looked again. He had not expected to see bears so far west, but in the shallow creek a brown bear and her cub were fishing or bathing, maybe just playing. They studied the water, then splashed their front paws. They took turns standing up, rolling into the water, snorting back into air, mouths open. The mother's teeth might have been knives, but when she playfully bit her cub's neck and he swiped back with his small paws, the two did not look ferocious—they looked domestic.

The Stud was backing away, his head lifted. Johnson dismounted, rubbed his horse's nostrils, and turned him into the woods. Johnson walked to the rise above the creek, kneeled down, and crawled to where he could watch the bears.

They played in this interlude between whatever had concerned them last and whatever might concern them next—food, shelter, enemies. The cub was a comical version of his mother. She rose on her back legs, looking around her. He stood, too, listing like a drunk, then wobbling until he fell on his back into the water. She crouched in the water, completely still, one paw raised. He tried the same posture. When she swooped her paw at something—fish, crawdad, frog—he slapped his paw, splashing his mother until she splashed back. The water churned to foam.

Johnson nearly laughed, but the bubble of glee he suppressed brought him sadness. How long before had he shared a light moment with his mother, one day when he was a boy and she'd been making soap, and the pot of viscous liquid blew bubbles that sounded like polite burps, and she'd taken one of his father's old pipes and dipped it into the pot and blown gently through the stem to make a soap bubble big as his head, and he'd poked it with his finger, the liquid still hot enough that he quickly put his finger in his mouth, and then the vile taste, the slimy thickness that he thought he'd never be able to rinse out, though she brought him cup after cup of water to rinse and spit into what was soon a bucket of foam. "My rabid son," she'd called him, the bubbles sticking to his lips and cheeks, and he thought she'd said *rabbit*, and he took to hopping, legs together, across the room and back, his hands held above his ears, and she had put her hand over her heart and laughed and laughed, saying "Rabid rabbit, rabid rabbit," until he forgot the taste of soap and fell to the floor in a fit of giggling because his mother was laughing, and she so rarely did.

The mother bear grasped her chest at the same time Johnson heard the shot. The cub did not imitate her. Another shot followed, this one to the mother's head, and both wounds gushed with blood beyond stanching. Red threads stained the water, and the cub backed out of the creek and started up the bank. His mother staggered after him, then buckled into the creek.

Two men tumbled down the opposite bank from where Johnson hid. One of them hurried with a rope toward the cub, circling around it as it screamed hoarsely. Twice, the man tried to lasso the cub around the neck. The other man locked his arms around the mother bear's neck and heaved her toward land. The cub, torn between mother and flight, wheeled around until the man with the rope finally wriggled the noose around his neck, pulling tight until the cub nearly flew backward into the water. "Got the little bastard," the man said gleefully. He let the cub swim up to find its footing again.

"You make me proud," said the other. He dragged the dead bear onto the bank of the creek, then sat beside her.

"Whooey!" said the man with the cub. "I'll tie him behind my horse, run him out of juice." He climbed the bank upstream from the mother's corpse, jerking the cub after him. Johnson heard him shout to his horse, curse the horse's fear, then whip the poor creature to run from its fear while what it feared followed right along behind it. He was the kind of man, Johnson assumed, who could abuse anything.

The other man turned the bear onto her back. From his pocket he took a flask and drained whatever it contained. *Courage*, some called it.

This man seemed to be drinking greed, disregard, meanness. The man removed a knife from a sheath around his boot and cut from the bear's gullet down her chest—Johnson could see she'd been nursing the cub— and then to her anus. Next, he cut lines down the insides of her front legs, then her hind ones. Johnson knew he would remove the paws because of their valuable claws—he'd be trading with Indians, no doubt. He would finish skinning her, then maybe cut some of the meat from the bone, maybe not, then go and find his partner. Soon enough, they'd trade the hide and claws for food, lead, powder, and whiskey.

Johnson went back to his horse, found a small copse of trees and hid. He'd been powerless to change what had happened. He'd remained in hiding because hiding was what he had to do. These men might ask questions, might know Nancy's uncle Mac. Such men were too common in Nashville and Jackson, where others gathered to become stupid with drink. They would train the little bear, put a hat on its head, and it would bow and take sips of whiskey and remove its hat, dance a short jig to the hoots of a crowd who were too drunk to imitate either its grace or politeness.

Johnson could not stop such things from happening, not even here at the side of the creek, for he was someone who had been called villain, someone running from what he wanted to be, someone on the edge looking in. And worse? He knew what he would soon do. After these men left, he would cross the creek and cut strips of meat from the bear's haunch and shoulder, dry them over a fire, and continue his journey. He would be nourished not by the moments of playful domesticity he'd seen, but by disruption and death.

no man's land

Days passed. A man on a roan horse threaded his way down a bluff. Probably not the same man he'd seen on the trail so long ago. Another day, a thin man on a small horse appeared above a creek, in dappled shadow. Johnson almost shouted out, so happy he was to see another human being. If the man was real, and he shouted back, Johnson would be flooded with relief. But he'd also risk pursuit. He stayed quiet.

Once, Johnson had just crossed a river whose name he would never know. He climbed up out of the river valley and looked back. A large rider on an Appaloosa was just starting across. The man seemed to know the territory, for he'd found a gentler place a quarter mile downstream from where Johnson and The Stud had swum. The stranger and Johnson might simply be heading the same direction on parallel paths. But as long as he felt like prey, he had to assume anyone could be predator. Johnson changed course, loping along the river bluff south. When the smell of sulphur drifted into his nose, he thought affectionately of his father. Was the old man right, that Johnson was headed to Hell, fire and brimstone licking at his stirrups as he rode deeper into hot, dry prairie grass? Surely, he would be alone in this country. If the large man on the Appaloosa showed up on his trail again, Johnson would assume he was pursued. And if pursued so persistently six weeks from Pleasant View, Tennessee, then how might he ever stop long enough to find his future?

If he saw the man again, he told himself, he would confront him, lose his fear, quit running. He took his uncle Judson's Daw pistol from his saddlebag, loaded it, and stuck it in his belt. He kept it there for a couple of days, until the sighting of nothing became the something that reassured him.

No Man's Land meant it was anyone's land. Crossing it, Johnson named creeks, rises, stands of trees, rock outcroppings, as though his own vernacular might fix these places in his memory and make the return journey more familiar. He turned often, not only to see if he was being followed, but to see what the country he crossed looked like from the other direction. "Every tree is a different tree from the other side of it," he'd once been told by his grandfather. Johnson supposed the same might be true of people.

Robert's mother had raised him with a tender touch, with gentle correction. Often, she seemed sadly delicate in her movement and demeanor. But put her in the garden with a sharp hoe, and she attacked the weeds around her carrots, potatoes, peas, and beets like the enemies they were. Any errant plant fairly flew into the air, loose dirt crumbling from exposed roots to wilt between her neat rows. She could numb a deep cut with a bay leaf poultice and stitch a wound with mere pinches of a needle and boiled thread. But put her in the henhouse and she'd snatch the one she wanted for dinner and dispatch its life with a quick twist of her wrist. Feathers were soon plucked, guts spilled from her forceful cut, sternum to anus. Yet she served the meal with such demureness Robert might have thought the chicken sacrificed its own life to her and her family.

What sides did Jo Benson have to her? She had seemed shy when a young girl. He'd seen her in town with her mother, trailing in a dress that nearly hid her. But he'd seen her ride past his place with her brothers, not lagging behind, but forcing them to chase her. When Jo's mother died, Robert's mother had taken him in tow to offer the family a loaf of bread, a chicken, a fresh bowl of peas. Jo had appeared behind her father at the door to their cabin. Benson was unshaven, eyes red with grief, his mother later told him. "Not with drink?" he would ask her now. Jo had outgrown her dress, and it fell to just below her knees. Her shins were bruised, as his often were. Her bare feet were grimy. She would not look at him directly, and when her father snarled a thank you and turned, she disappeared as quick as a weed in his mother's garden. "No doubt she'll have the most difficult time," his mother said of Jo. "I don't think a living soul has ever sung her to sleep." Then Robert had seen her around his place, and then in the creek, both forward and shy, both giving and withholding at the same time. Was she innocent of her pa's plan or part of it? Had she been forced by her brothers to get his stud, or did she suggest it? Had she sewn his initials into his handkerchief as keepsake or clue?

He traveled through meadows rich in flowers. A gray-green plant, shaped like a candelabra, was growing what looked like peas from the top stems that bent with their weight. God how he wished they were peas. How he wished for something fresh from his mother's garden. How he wished for her voice, singing about oats, peas, beans, and barley, asking, "Can you or I or anyone know how oats, peas, beans, and barley grow?"

Can you or I or anyone know? Not when you are the no man, pushing farther into an unknown world. *Dear Jo*, he began. *I hope*, he thought. *I wonder*, he began again. *Did you*, he started over. *Please*, he decided. He'd start with *please*. *Please keep me in your thoughts. Please wait for me. Please know that I will return. Please be innocent. Please.* He begged for the future he wanted, yet he rode away from it each day.

Indians

robert Johnson traveled south and west, and the country opened up until he found himself surrounded by nothing but sky above and grass that reached nearly to his stirrups. Miles stretched before him. His eye followed the shadow of a cumulus cloud playing with light on the landscape. Spring rain must have been good, interlaced as the grass was with yarrow and spiderwort. Clover waved purple fingers.

When Johnson saw smoke curling to the west, he skirted south. He pitched down a ravine and was swallowed by brush. He'd ridden prairie crests all day. Now, he rode a couple of miles in the scrub oak along the draws. When he felt like he'd been at the bottom of a bowl long enough, he spurred The Stud back up to the rim.

More smoke joined the threads in the west, two plumes on the southern horizon. Two camps. Travelers? Soldiers? Indians? Trees wound between the wisps of smoke. He spurred The Stud back down the bowl among those trees, to meander with the water to the other side of the camps.

The scrub trees were joined by stands of willow, their drooping branches dusting the air with wormy flowers. When the creek widened into a stream, cottonwoods released a snow of seed. A redwing blackbird sounded its ratcheting call and another answered. Where the water accumulated into a small pool, Johnson and his horse drank sweet water, as though all the flowering prairie, all the dense pollen and seeding of the trees had become cool liquid.

Johnson sat and watched a hawk glide. Grasshoppers clicked in the warming grass. No doubt this land was harsh in winter, wind and ice slicing the air with bitter knives. And summer heat might soon suck the water from this small pool, ephemeral as Johnson's reverie.

They rode the creek bed, rock and mud, until the water deepened. Snapping turtles slid off gray branches where they sunned themselves. Beavers had begun a dam, then given up, a few trees fallen, others chewed to a rough hourglass. When Johnson rode up the shady bank again, through loose shale and onto a grassy ridge, the bright sun hammered his eyes shut. Before he opened them, shouts, and a thundering of hooves, startled him. He jerked The Stud's reins and the horse reared before plunging back into the scrub oak. Three bison thundered past at a rocking run, tails upraised, nostrils snorting. A dozen Indians chased after, those in front with rifles, the others with spears, tomahawks, knives. Johnson listened for shots. After they'd made their kill, they'd think of nothing but turning the animal to meat, to hide, to everything else they needed. He'd heard that these nomadic Indians could turn bone to needle, gut to thread, bladder to canteen or ball, shoulder to hoe, horn to spoon. The buffalo was their commissary.

Two shots, then what must have been the whooping of victory, though the sound curdled Johnson's blood. The only Indians Johnson had seen were civilized. The others had been run out of Tennessee by Andrew Jackson, with men like David Crockett at his side. These western Indians, he'd heard, were savage. Any of them would be happy to cut an enemy's scalp, wear it in his belt. Johnson's head tingled. He reined The Stud into the creek brush. His half-hidden lope startled rabbits, set squirrels to squabbling, gave flight to thundering quail. And then ahead of him an Indian. Another Indian, on a paint pony, came from the side.

Johnson's whoop sounded like a hoarse coyote, drunk on bad whiskey, baying at half a moon. But the force of it, with a quick spur to the flanks, made The Stud perk his ears and head for open country as though it were a finish line. Johnson ran his horse at a slant, between the man in front of him and the one to his side. By the time Johnson reached open grass, he had an Indian on either side of him, neither more than thirty yards away, both with rifles lifted. Johnson crouched in the saddle to make himself as small as he could, whooped again, and headed up the prairie. He shut his eyes, waiting for gunfire.

Gracious, how The Stud ran! He was half again as big as the Indian ponies. Though the Indians tried to squeeze Johnson between them, they soon fell in together behind him.

He crested the rise, bluestem swelling like the ocean, and felt a small victory. But below him was the Indian camp—a swarm of people, horses, huts of bent willow saplings covered in hide and blankets erected in a circle along a draw that led to the creek and the stream beyond. Squaws were already flaying bison carcasses.

Behind Johnson came such a whooping that the Indians in camp turned to fix their eyes on him. Johnson jerked the reins and The Stud turned. As his pursuers crested the rise, he rode straight toward them. They warbled their glee.

Johnson had outrun them once. He calculated his second chance. Below him, Indians swarmed toward hobbled horses. Who knew how fast one of those paints might be? Johnson turned along the rim above the camp, and the two Indians turned with him. Savages below mounted their ponies and ran them up the hill to intersect him. Johnson nudged his horse forward, as though to meet them, then suddenly reined The Stud to a tight circle and steadied him. Two Indians were behind him, a band of them were running their horses to the ridge. Johnson surveyed the camp below. The Indians yelled, turning their horses toward him.

Johnson touched his heels to The Stud's flanks. The horse shot like a ball from a cannon, straight down into the Indian camp. Wailing Indians turned their horses after him, women and children dove into their wickiups. The Stud jumped a campfire, broke through three snarling dogs, hopped over a log, and headed into the brush along the creek.

Although the Indians were after him, he did not cross the creek. He wound his way upstream at the side of their camp, and then took to open country again where his speed could win any contest except with a rifle ball. Yet he saw no rifles, no knives, no tomahawks. When he stopped on a ridge, the Indians were in their camp, some already dismounting. Were they content to have run him off?

Still swollen with excitement, Johnson raised his arm and yelled bloody murder. He readied his horse for one more gallop across the rim, just to show these riders what a Tennessee horse could do. Several Indians, still mounted, started back toward him. Their horses must have been the best in camp, for they came with surprising speed. Johnson ran down the prairie swells away from their camp into open country, giving The Stud his head. When he reached a creek draw and turned, he saw five Indians on the top of the rise, pointing at him and laughing. One of them lifted his arms as though he carried a rifle. "Bloom," he shouted, and his companions laughed.

Johnson took their message. They could easily have killed him. Maybe they respected his horse and horsemanship. Maybe they valued their bullets for game more than grudge against a lone white man trying to cross their land. He raised his hand and saluted them. They turned their horses and disappeared.

Johnson yodeled with joy, blood rushing. He moved toward the draw, which he aimed to follow to the river. He'd cross as far from their camp as he could, avoid the smoke he'd seen farther south, wind his way slowly and cautiously. He would remember his luck and not count on it in future sightings of Indians. He gave The Stud his head and they galloped into lucky freedom for half a day. As his excitement waned, he felt stupid. In challenging these inhabitants of the prairies, he'd simply created more to run from.

He slowed The Stud. They both needed rest after such an adventure. He wished for someone to talk to. He imagined Hiram Gillian. He imagined Elizabeth at her kitchen table, writing down what he wished he could speak to Jo, back in Tennessee.

My dear love, Jo: They call these Indians savage, and they are, but they have a beauty in their wildness. Their dark skins glow when they ride, their bodies and their horses wet with sweat. Their small ponies charge forward graceful and turn in the smallest space. They ran me good, enough to put fear in my heart and then joy came soon after when they could not catch me on The Stud. Only their voices followed me, stronger than the howling of wolves, or the yipping of the coyote. They are natural men, untethered to one home, unchained from plow and chores. I do not want a life like theirs, but they are suited to this country and I doubt they will be easily routed from it . . .

He paused in his composition to conjure Jo. She was reading his letter, sitting in a chair at her father's table after he'd left for town. Or she had stolen to the barn, perched herself on the top slat of a stall, notched her feet between two lower slats and pulled the letter from its hiding place. Or she had taken it to the creek where they'd first met, taken off her shoes, sat on the bank, and let her feet dangle in the riffling water.

Johnson wondered if Jo imagined letters to send to him. *My Dear Robert, Even as a new life grows in me and I await the first movements of our child I hope you will stop running and come home. I have set my mind to a plan.* Johnson could not imagine anything that would allow him to give up being fugitive and return home. Perhaps she would simply write, *Dearest Robert, I miss you but know you will fly home to me when this trouble . . .*

The Stud shook his head. Two Indians on horseback charged through a stand of trees toward Johnson, tomahawks raised. He stopped himself from reaching into his saddlebag for his pistol. He might kill one Indian, but not both. One of the Indians dismounted, and Johnson held up his hands. The Indian pulled a knife from his belt and strode toward him. These men would no doubt steal his horse, and were sure to treat him well. But Johnson had no value to them. He would not survive a scalping, or worse. Weren't these Indians known to castrate a man, eviscerate his organs slowly enough that he might have a fine look at his stomach, liver and guts, all twisted into knots? Well, he'd have thin enough guts to look at, no more than he'd found to eat these past six weeks. He breathed deeply as they came closer.

The Indians muttered in their tongue, a garbled stuttering that might be the last sound Johnson ever heard. One of them jerked the reins from his hand and motioned to Johnson to dismount. The other placed his horse so close to The Stud they might have been harnessed to wagon or coach. He took the reins from his savage brother, and urged both horses forward. The Stud turned his head and gave Johnson a baleful look as the Indian on horseback led him away. The native still on foot grunted at Johnson, motioned for him to take off his hat. Johnson did so, and handed it to the man, who put it on his head. Then he imitated Johnson taking off his boots. Then pants, then shirt, everything. Until Johnson stood before the Indian, naked. Hat, boots, clothes, then evisceration, while The Stud was led into another world.

The man grunted, and held up his hand. Johnson stared back at him. "Go ahead and kill me," Johnson said, shaking his head.

The Indian grunted again.

"If you won't kill me get your wild self to hell!" Johnson shouted, but naked as he was, he knew he looked more like a chicken clucking over an insect than a man bent on defending himself.

The Indian put on Johnson's boots, wadded up his clothing, mounted his pony, and left, hooves throbbing the earth. Johnson was a fool to think he could survive in this country, so familiar to these people. To Johnson, the prairie was a landscape more formidable than he could ever have imagined, especially without his one familiar, The Stud. For seven years they'd lived side by side, shared most every moment, put their ambitions together—work, speed, a future of land and horses. And now he was in No Man's Land, with no horse. Separated from The Stud, Johnson tried to imagine his horse's captive life, just as he imagined Jo's captive life. But he could not conjure anything but loss.

His thick despair overtook him. As a cloud shaded the sun, his mind blackened, too. He did not expect to survive. The brush was abuzz with insects. On the grasslands, the sun beat down sharp as a hatchet blade. He would trudge toward his inevitable death. The Indians had not scalped him. Not killed him. They *would* kill him if he went after The Stud. Might that be better than wandering, slowly starving to death? He could not have followed them anyway, without knowledge of the land, of their wanderings, so quickly pacing ahead of him in whatever direction they might have taken.

When the sun slanted in the sky, heading west to the horizon, Johnson put his right shoulder to it so that he faced south. *Dear Jo,* he began, and took his first step.

San Antonio

a man with no horse. No pistol. No knife. No shoes, pants, shirt, hat. A man scratching for beetles. A man reaching for grasshoppers. Turning over rocks for crickets. Finger-seining for minnow, tadpole, crawdad. A man whose thirst was rarely slaked. Whose belly never stopped growling with hunger. Whose piss stung, whose feces strung off him, feral. Such a man was hardly human.

Johnson had only a remnant of hope tucked away in his heart to counter the suffering that each day told him to give up, lie down, put face to the sun and drift into rest, sleep, then death. Since the Indians had stolen The Stud, the fear that he was being pursued had turned to the hope that he was. He longed for that someone who would haul him up from a creek bank where he lay to drink. Or a voice behind him saying, "Looks like you've covered a lot of ground." Such a joke, given how he had no cover.

He foraged prairie, staying close to water, sleeping when tired or so hungry his stomach coiled like a rattler ready to strike. Sometimes an entire day might blur into another and another and he would lose the passage of time, forget how he had spent his day. He would shake his head and realize he was on all fours, combing the grass for anything that moved, whatever he could put in his mouth without thought—a crumple of jagged legs, a bitter taste, an abrasive swallow.

He could not have told anyone how much time had passed. Nor could he have spoken. Nor did he think of his name. The name of anything. He remembered his brother, and his mother. He wanted nothing but to lie beside them. Finally, he fell. Into what, he could not have said. Soporific. Thick. Fluid. Settling.

He came to a groggy consciousness, head pounding. Someone was prodding his side. He kept his eyes closed, not wanting to know who his tormentor might be—Indian, outlaw, bounty hunter, trader, soldier, fugitive like himself. Johnson certainly had nothing, so could offer nothing but humility and vanquishment. And ask for the simple mercy of food, water, rescue.

"*¿Quién es?*"

Johnson moved his hand to show he had heard.

"*¿De dónde viene? ¿Dónde va?*"

Johnson opened his eyes. He tried to sit up, but his head throbbed.

A man sat next to him. Spurs. Boots of fine leather. Chaps, the hide tooled and embellished with leather thong pinned by silver. Leather vest. Skin the color of the leather. A hat ludicrous in size. The man offered him a bag, wet and dripping in his calloused hand. The man's eyes were black as a beetle's.

Johnson drank. Then turned to vomit the water. "I'm sorry," he said.

"*De nada,*" said the man. "*Más.*" He motioned for Johnson to drink again. "*Sólo un poco.*" He brought his index finger close to his thumb.

Johnson understood to take only a sip. His tongue was swollen. He swallowed with difficulty, breathed deeply, determined to keep the water in his belly. Perhaps more would follow. And food.

A horse nickered. Johnson rolled up onto all fours. His rescuer laughed, and Johnson couldn't blame him. Who could imagine an animal scrawnier than himself, nothing but blotched skin, protuberant bone, wild hair, filth no animal would tolerate?

But Johnson found such pleasure at the sight of a horse that he didn't mind laughter, even ridicule. The Spaniard—Johnson had decided the language was Spanish and that he had been discovered by what folks called a *vaquero*—had the finest horse Johnson had seen since leaving Tennessee. Blacker than black, tall, broad, thick headed, full maned, large hooved, with fine musculature. He wondered what The Stud would look like next to the animal. Surely not as pitiful as Johnson looked next to the vaquero, whose laughter seemed natural.

"*Caballo,*" Johnson said, using one of the few Spanish words he knew.

"*El Primero,*" said the vaquero.

"*Sí*," said Johnson, though he might have argued the boast had he known what he was agreeing to. After all, he knew *The* Stud, lost as they were to each other.

The man loosened the saddle cinch enough to remove the blanket. He handed it to Johnson, then mounted the horse and motioned Johnson to him. "*¿Viene conmigo?*" the man asked.

"*Sí.*" Johnson took the offered hand. He was hefted behind the man, on the croup of the horse. He held onto the back of the vaquero's saddle. Dizzy, he slumped against the man's back and nearly lost consciousness.

The vaquero kept a steady pace. Whenever the man said anything, Johnson said "*sí*" and hoped he was headed toward something better than sun, grass, insect, slow-moving water.

The smell of the horse, of leather and rope, even the smell of dropped turds was tonic, but also brought back his mourning for The Stud. For half a day, Johnson dozed. Surely the vaquero could not be so far from camp. Yet no other vaqueros appeared, nor the cattle they'd be herding. Mercy might be tricky—the good luck of being rescued meant Johnson was completely vulnerable. Once again, he did not know what lay at the end of a journey.

Johnson dozed, sipped water, dozed again. When the horse raised his hooves higher with each step, keen for food and rest, Johnson peered over the man's shoulder from under the shadow of the sombrero. They approached a stone wall. Behind that a bell tower, topped with a cross. A dome, also topped with a cross, rose above a building that must be a church. Johnson had never seen stone built up so high, to make such monument.

The vaquero eased him off the horse, then dismounted. They walked through the gate—a thick wooden door swung open to them—and into the courtyard. Against the inside wall leaned one long, low building, with door after door. As they walked toward the church, Indians appeared in the doorways to stare at this man robed only in a saddle blanket, with bony legs and matted hair, who followed the Spaniard across the courtyard to the stable. More Indians—too many for Johnson to count—worked in garden plots.

At the stable door they were met by a man in black robes. The vaquero spoke rapidly to the man who, to Johnson's relief, turned to him and said, "Please come with me."

The robed man led Johnson inside an arched doorway. The stone floor cooled Johnson's feet. How he wished for another sip of water. Suddenly he felt cool, then his knees and head found the stone floor.

He awoke in a narrow cot in what seemed like a cool cavern. Water filled an earthen cup on the floor beside him. He turned onto his side and drank. Sandals paced toward him. The man in robes said, "*Bienvenidos.* Welcome to San José y San Miguel de Aguayo." He held a pitcher of water.

Johnson finished drinking from the cup, and the man filled it. This time the water, sweet and cool, calmed his belly. The man smiled. "You are well enough to eat?"

"You bet I am," said Johnson. He threw off a sheet and lifted his legs over the side of the cot.

"Stay seated." The man picked up the sheet and covered Johnson's nakedness. "I am Fray Antonio. I will serve you here. Then we will clothe you."

"I have nothing," said Johnson.

"Of course. We each of us saw your arrival. You have tested our Savior's words."

"Savior's words?" asked Johnson.

"Do you not know the Holy Bible?" asked Fray Antonio, more disbelief than question. "You are a stranger and we welcome you. In your hunger we feed you. I bring you water for your thirst. You are naked and we clothe you. But first, since you come to us with such dirt and smell, you will have a bath."

"Where am I?" asked Johnson.

"I will bring you food," said Fray Antonio. "Then we may talk."

The friar disappeared. Johnson lay down. A miracle that he was alive. And in a bed—his first since Memphis. And clean water. Food. Bath. Clothing. He savored the words one at a time.

Fray Antonio woke Johnson with a bowl of stew, beef with vegetables. The first spoonful brought tears to Johnson's eyes. He shook with relief. Warm bread brought more tears, the substance and sweetness of grain, the texture of home and hearth. He ate the stew in small bites, with gulp after gulp of water. When he finished, Antonio poured a snort of brandy, which lifted his skull. "This is about as close to worship as I've been for a long time," Johnson said.

"Still, you did not ask a blessing, nor did you acknowledge the God who has made you and this food." Fray Antonio retrieved the bowl.

"My father mumbled over his food so long it was cold before he put it to his mouth. Suited him. He could not take pleasure in anything but his own prospect of salvation."

Fray Antonio smiled faintly.

"You teaching the Indians to pray? To love God? I thanked God when some savages didn't scalp me. They stole my horse, the best horse Tennessee ever saw. And my clothes, and my pistol. Everything. God bless them, they didn't steal my life."

Fray Antonio left the room. Johnson thought he had offended the brother, if that's what he was. But the man soon returned, carrying a stool and a pitcher of water. He sat down near the bed.

"You supposed to watch me?" Johnson asked. "Because when that food hits my blood I'll drift for a good long while. I've been eating nothing but grasshoppers, beetle eggs, grubs. Drinking anything wet, no matter how sluggish. Been sick. Feverish. Real close to death. But you don't have to watch me."

Fray Antonio crossed his arms. "I fear I must listen to you," he said.

"A man can get as hungry for words as he is for food and water. I haven't talked to a soul since I crossed into Texas."

"You are not in Texas," said Fray Antonio. "You are in what was New Spain, what some now call Mexico. We Spanish have built missions along the Rio San Antonio, though none of us have the strength in numbers or in troops as we used to. Our time is short here. The Comanche and the Apache raid our cattle. Destroy the crops we plant outside our walls. Only a handful of Indians remain with us."

"Looked like a lot to me."

"Only the few," said the brother.

"Are they Comanches? Apaches?"

"No, Coahuiltecan. We have protected them from the fierce tribes. Still, they abandon us. They return to heathen practices. You say you encountered Indians? Had they been Comanche or Apache you would be dead. For death is all they understand."

"They were hunting. Buffalo. A few of them had rifles and muskets, but most of them carried tomahawks and knives. They had these little huts."

"Wickiups," said Fray Antonio.

"I was northeast, near as I can calculate."

"Tell me of your journey." Antonio leaned forward with the pitcher of water and poured the cup full. "I will tell you then what they say of you."

"What who says?"

"The Indians who stay with us. But first, your journey."

Johnson had not been invited to pour forth any account of himself since he'd been in Memphis, at the kitchen table, with Elizabeth acting as his hand. Johnson told the intricate machinations of all he had once had, all he had hoped for and lost. He had encountered strangers, strangeness, violence. He had learned new landscapes. Mostly, convinced he was followed, he had run from the false accusations of Sheriff McFall and the Bensons.

"And your flight, what has it brought you to?" asked Fray Antonio.

"Here," said Johnson. He stood up from the cot, still wrapped in the sheet. His head reeled, then settled. He paced to the wall, touched it, came back to the cot. "At least for now."

The brother stood up. "You are running from your past. You are running from your future, as well?" He started from the room.

"What do the Indians say about me?" asked Johnson.

Fray Antonio turned. He was a silhouette in the arched doorway. "You are a spirit. Wandering. In you they see themselves. Once they hunted. They gathered their needs from harsh surroundings. We have shown them civilization. Agriculture. Settlement. Government. The one true God. They barely comprehend these things, but they will someday become men. And you?" He turned to leave again.

"What about me?"

The priest turned once more and stood in the doorway. "You appear to them today. Hardly a man. Wrapped in a blanket. You are the remnant of who they were. You are a prisoner, following one of our vaqueros into the mission. Tequan says they want to help you return to the world to wander."

"Are you holding me prisoner here?" asked Johnson.

"From what you have told me, you are prisoner." Fray Antonio walked away, and though Johnson shouted after him, the brother did not turn back. Johnson paced the room. He could leave any time. But here was the prospect of food, water, a bed. At least for a time, he would be like the remaining Indians, trading freedom for comfort and protection.

For several days he rested. His stomach loosened its tight coil. He bathed and was clothed and booted. Johnson asked to go to the stable. There the Spaniards kept well-bred horses, mostly Arabian—black, bay, chestnut, gray—with thick chests, long manes, tails that flowed gently when running. Their ears perked forward, as though listening with attention.

Days passed, and Johnson worked among the horses. The vaquero who had found Johnson was Juan Francisco de Padilla. He had not been tending mission cattle that day, but scouting for the Comanches and Apaches who kept the missions under a loose siege. The vaquero had sighted a band of Coahuiltecans who had meat with them. Johnson asked after The Stud. Fray Antonio, who carried the information between Johnson and the vaqueros, said these men would have noticed such a horse among those ridden by what they called the *Tecans*. They had no report of the horse.

After a fortnight of hard work, Johnson went to Antonio's chamber. He interrupted one of the brother's meditations. The vaqueros were preparing the horses for some kind of excursion. Johnson wanted to accompany them.

"Well timed," Fray Antonio said. The men were to cut from the herd a good-sized yearling to slaughter for the feast of Saint Thomas.

"That the one they call Doubting Thomas?" Johnson asked Antonio.

"The apostle, yes. One time of doubt and he is known forever as doubter. Would you like such a fate?" Antonio touched the Bible that lay open on his lap.

"I'm doubted by all but myself. You know that."

"Then why can you not be as Thomas?" Fray Antonio turned the pages of the Bible. "Have courage. Christ determined to go to Bethany, near Jerusalem, after the death of Lazarus. There, Jesus would face nearly certain death." Antonio put his finger on the words. "Still, Thomas said to the other apostles, 'Let us also go to die with him.' That is John 11:16."

"Did Thomas die with Jesus?" Johnson asked.

"None of the apostles did. Would He have wanted such a thing?" Antonio shut the book.

"I don't expect any of us want to die," said Johnson. "That can't be the only way you can call yourself courageous."

"Yet how many times have you risked death in your flight from Tennessee?" Antonio stood up and placed the Bible on his desk. His room was cool in spite of a punishing sun.

"I catch your drift," said Johnson. "But such thinking is easier in a sanctuary like this. I can't say I'd have these same thoughts out on the trail." He folded his arms over his chest. His heart pounded.

"You may go with Juan Francisco and the others. They say you know horses. They will give you a mount. They will be thankful for your offer of help." Fray Antonio raised his arm, as though giving a blessing, but Johnson did not see him, loping as he was toward the stable.

Johnson did not object when the vaqueros pointed him toward the naggiest horse of the bunch, a dun mare. They gave him a badly worn saddle and tack, too. "Her name?" he asked Juan Francisco.

The man shook his head.

Johnson pointed to himself and said, "Roberto." He pointed at the vaquero and said "Juan Francisco."

The man smiled. "Isabella," he said. Johnson thought he was saying, "Is a bay," though she was not a bay horse.

The Spanish saddles had no horn and sat him deep between cantle and the ridge above the gullet in front. Still, he seated well and his horse, though old, was as eager as he was to ride. Juan Francisco nodded and the rest of them mounted and rode to where two Indians stood at the open gate. Johnson was the last to trot through. Several Indians squeezed toward him, each touching him as he passed.

The vaqueros spurred their horses and ran away from Johnson, but he knew Fray Antonio would have given them orders to watch him. Was he the help he promised to be, or the young man who simply wanted to ride? Perhaps Antonio did not believe his story. The West was full of men who were not as they appeared, not as they said they were. In a lawless land, each man had to take charge of himself. Many were not capable of such a task.

Johnson, indeed, wanted to ride. He nudged the horse with his boot heel, suddenly realizing that her name was Isabella, Spanish for Elizabeth. He shouted her name as she strode after the others. She caught them. The vaqueros laughed, speaking ever more quickly in their rolling, rollicking tongue. Raucous or gentle, commanding or coaxing, the Spanish was like music. After their outburst, the vaqueros ran their horses ahead once again, splashing across the irrigation ditch Fray Antonio said watered each of the missions along the Rio San Antonio. They urged their horses into short grass prairie. Isabella had no trouble catching the others. Perhaps she'd been cooped up as long as he had. She looked like the nag, but who could know her heart? The vaqueros seemed to agree. As soon as they were out of sight of the mission, Juan Francisco circled back to Johnson. He clicked his tongue, raised up in his saddle, and leaned forward. His young stud tossed his head, eager to run. Johnson whistled through his teeth and Isabella stepped up her pace, not ready to run, but not willing to be left behind. Johnson could sense her hesitation. Juan Francisco snapped his quirt and his horse shot ahead. Johnson leaned forward, no quirt, no spurs.

He could not have anticipated Isabella's speed. For an old horse, she had genuine run. Perhaps she felt Johnson's eagerness. Perhaps she appreciated the lightness of his body, his gentle touch. Perhaps she was one of those spirits who liked a challenge. Juan Francisco lowered his shoulder, ready to turn to see if Johnson was close. But when he heard Isabella's hooves he sat forward and whipped his horse. Johnson laughed, then yodeled, not because of the competition, but with the joy of freedom.

From behind Johnson a vaquero shouted and soon hooves thundered past him. The man they called Diaz, sitting easily on the horse they called Rayo, soon caught Juan Francisco. The two of them slowed, as did Johnson, and the brief competition over.

From then on, the day was work. One of the vaqueros rode forward as scout. Often they could see him, a tiny dot on the prairie. Sometimes, the land rose to swallow the distance. Sometimes, they dipped into small washes. Yucca sent up straight shafts, some rich with white flowers. Gourds vined the rocky ditches. Small green buttons where flowers had been promised autumn fruit. Occasionally the riders scared up a jackrabbit, huge legs pumping fear into distance. The grass was short and wiry. Thick, too, against the penetrating sun.

Each time they found a male calf born in the early spring, they roped it. Many fought. All were pursued by the cow who had given them birth, for they were unweaned. A couple of vaqueros were armed with long poles—*garrochas*, they called them—to avoid the sharp horns of the cattle, and to drive the cows from their bawling calves.

Antonio wanted the fattest yearling sacrificed in their feast of Saint Thomas, and Juan Francisco appraised the cattle as they culled the calves. "Feast days are plentiful," Fray Antonio had told Johnson. "Both the plenty of a feast and the very number of feast days on the calendar. The Indians have grown to respect our abundance." Johnson's mouth watered with thoughts of the Thomas feast. He had been fed well, though mostly on corn and squash. The beef had been tough, dried from previous slaughters, suitable only for the occasional stew like the one he'd been fed when he first arrived.

The herd was not as large as Johnson expected. Under two hundred, he guessed. Nor were there as many calves. Occasional scatterings of bones might mean predators. And surely Indians stole from the herd. The vaqueros quit their search after roping and separating a couple dozen calves. They drove and dragged them toward a distant clump of trees growing in the cut of a dry creek bed. Juan Francisco followed behind with the yearling he'd roped. When they reached the trees, they hobbled the yearling's front legs. They tied the rest of the calves to trees. Two vaqueros gathered wood. Juan Francisco and Diaz unpacked metal skewers, their knives, and several flasks. Juan Francisco offered Johnson one of the flasks. Though he hoped for something strong, Johnson swallowed warm water. He pointed to the other flasks, shrugged his shoulders, reached out his hands. Diaz threw him another flask. He uncorked it, lifted it to his mouth, but a sudden silence kept him from drinking. He poured some liquid from the flask into his hand. An intense heat spread quickly across his palm and he shook his hand, wiped it on his pants, and still it burned. He corked the flask and tossed it back to Diaz.

They built their fire, then heated their knives to glowing. Two vaqueros wrestled a calf to the ground. A third spread the animal's legs and a fourth vaquero cut the *cojones* from the calf. The man who made the cut poured the fiery liquid into his gloved palm and doused the wound. "*Chiles*," Juan Francisco said, "*y hierbas.*" The disinfectant stung the calves to their feet, sent them rocking and bawling back to their mothers. The cojones, tossed in a bucket, would soon be a meal, popped out of their membranes, skewered, roasted over the fire, and eaten with sips of the third flask. Johnson's mouth watered.

Such rich meat, fresh and tender, was the feast before the feast day. The calf testicles were spongy as steaming cornbread, still juicy even after the fire sputtered with the dripping of their fat and blood. The men squatted with their skewers, making jokes Johnson could not comprehend, followed by laughter that he could. When one *cojón* was cooked, cooled, popped in the mouth and followed by a snort of brandy, a man would go to the bucket for another.

Johnson did so, along with Diaz. He fished out a testicle the size of a chicken egg, Diaz a smaller one. "No," said the Spaniard. He handed the small cojón to Johnson. "*Hombrecito*," he said. "*Pequeño por pequeño.*" He took the large cojón from Johnson's grasp. "*Grande por grande.*"

The vaqueros laughed. Johnson felt as small as Diaz wanted to make him, standing with his skewer hanging, the small piece of viscous meat bloody in his hand.

He shrugged. "It ain't what you eat," he said, hoping none could understand him. "It's what you *are*. You're just wishing that cojón wasn't bigger than your brain." He lifted the skewer and ran it through the small testicle. "Even *this* one is bigger than your brain." He started for the fire, muttering. "You don't get half what you could out of your horse. Probably don't get half what you want out of yourself. And only half of that to a woman." Johnson smiled, rich in insults nobody else understood. He held his skewer just above the glowing coals.

Juan Francisco put a finger to his lip. "*Suficiente*," he said.

Johnson didn't know how much English Juan had picked out of his words, but he was a guest. Pride and bravado had not always been his helpmates. But his strength was returning.

They finished their cowboy feast, pulling on the flask of brandy until nothing was left, then stretching out in the shade for half an hour before Juan Francisco stomped down what was left of the fire. Two vaqueros rode ahead as scouts. Diaz untied the hobble of the Saint Thomas yearling. He shouted to Juan Francisco and led the cow to Johnson. He handed him the rope. "*Rápido*," he shouted, and spurred Rayo. The others urged their horses after. Isabella tossed her head and started after the others. Johnson was pulled so forcefully he had to drop the feast cow's rope. He tightened the reins until Isabella turned her head, circled, and stopped. By the time Johnson rode down the startled yearling and recovered the rope, he was alone on the prairie.

No matter, thought Johnson. They wanted him to limp in behind, wanted him slow so he could not exhibit prowess even on a horse they all thought to be nag. He'd slow them even more, since they wouldn't rush too far ahead. He rode back to where they'd castrated the calves and eaten so heartily. He filled his pocket with ash. Then he let Isabella find the mission. She walked, only running to stay ahead of the yearling when he frisked alongside her.

Diaz had given him a blessing. He would enter the mission leading the feast, bringing the substantial yearling to Fray Antonio. This action, small as it was, would ensure the brother's trust in him, any doubt evaporating like water in this dry country. Alone and alert to the danger of attack—outlaw, Indian—he was intent in his thinking. He had been rescued, fed. He had worked, he was horseback. He had feasted on cojones and the brandy that still sputtered in his head. The next day, he would feast again, with Saint Thomas, he who had doubted yet still found courage. Fray Antonio wanted him to emulate the saint, to find sureness and purpose.

When Mission San José rose from the landscape, bell tower and dome each topped with a cross, he patted Isabella. Of course she'd know the way home. He stopped the horse near a lone cottonwood and tied the yearling rope around the trunk. He uncinched the saddle and dropped it on the ground. The bridle, too. He put the saddle blanket over him. He untied the yearling, grabbed the horse's mane, and jumped onto Isabella's back. She trotted toward the mission gate. "Whoa, girl," Johnson chanted, "whoa, whoa," and she approached the gate in the kind of procession Johnson wanted. He hoped the Indians were watching, but the gate remained closed. He whooped and screamed like the Indians who had left him with nothing.

One head, then another, peered at him over the mission wall. Voices rushed from the courtyard—shouts, calls, a whole weather of sound. The gates opened before him. When Isabella started forward, eager, Johnson chanted his "whoa, girl, whoa, girl." She strode calmly through the gates, the yearling now spooked and bawling behind them, the Indians touching Johnson, as when he had ridden out with the vaqueros. The man who was gatekeeper nodded, and Johnson turned to him and tried the Spanish he had picked up from his stay at the Mission de San José y San Miguel de Aguayo. "*Vaca*," he said, and pointed to the yearling. "*Comer*." He pointed to his stomach, and then at the Indian's. "*Dormir*," he said, putting his hands together as though to pray, then tilting them as a resting place for his head. He closed his eyes. "*Noche. Voy*," he said finally. He pointed behind him, out the gate, then put his finger to his lips and shook his head. "No, no." He turned then to the people who surrounded him, and hollered in triumph. The feast was home. Isabella trotted to the stable, nearly dragging the yearling behind her. The feast was tired, hanging its head as though ready to be sacrificed.

In the shade of the doorway, the men waited for him, some smirking. Fray Antonio walked forward and took the calf rope. "Your saddle and bridle?" he asked Johnson.

"They left me." Johnson swept his arm at the vaqueros. None would understand his whispered English. "Probably thought you'd have to send out a rescue party. Make me look bad. Sure enough this is a Godforsaken hellfire of a country. But this here's a fine horse. Led me right home. Me and your Saint Thomas Feast. My tack is out by a tree. Wanted to show I could ride in like an Indian. You can send one of them for the tack. Seems like I've done my duty." Johnson patted Isabella.

"A man talks most when he is lying," said the monk.

"You want me to get the tack?" asked Johnson.

Fray Antonio looked over Johnson's shoulder. "Tequan has brought them already," he said.

The gatekeeper carried the saddle, bridle draped over it. He heaved his load onto a stall slat. Johnson shrugged the saddle blanket off his shoulders and approached Tequan. "Gracias," he said.

Tequan put it next to the saddle.

Johnson left the stable for the room where he slept. He had not looked Antonio in the eye, nor had he acknowledged any of the vaqueros. Still sated from the cojones, drowsy with the brandy, and full of plans of his own, he wanted to sleep if he could. Night would fall, then a day of feasting, then another night. *Comer, dormir, ir?*

The Feast of Saint Thomas the Doubter, Johnson discovered the next morning, was July third. His sense of time had been lunar—full moon to full moon—rather than the calendar of days and months. The feast day was given over to the slaughter, the parsing of meat, the cooking, all hot work in a place where summer seemed the only season, the best part of the day just before the sun rose, and then again just after it sank.

At dusk, the bells tolled from their towers and everyone gathered at the center of the mission. The thick yearling had been entirely rendered. Head cheese, blood pudding, a stew of parts Johnson was not eager to name—though the tail was among them—tongue, sausage, ribs, rump, shoulder, loin. After a lengthy bout of prayer and the giving of thanks, all in Spanish, the brothers of the mission found the best meat, the Spanish vaqueros and other workers took the richest of what was left, the mestizos next, and then the Coahuiltecans. Although he was implored to take, eat, by Fray Antonio, Johnson shook his head. He waited, lifted one of the crude bowls allotted the Indians, filled it, as they did, with stew.

When Antonio asked if he had reason to humble himself, he shrugged. "You know my story," he said. "I don't suppose I'm any better or worse than most. But where I come from, we believe in equality." The stew was rich in tomato, so many ripening in the gardens tended by the natives. The corn was tough, dried from the previous year, boiled and added to the stew.

"And yet you own slaves in your country?" asked Fray Antonio.

"I own only myself. And once I owned my horse," said Johnson. "I answer to nobody, and nobody answers to me." He brought the bowl to his mouth.

"Yes," said Antonio, "you in your United States are famous for being independent. But have you no need for others? No obligation to help each other?" The brother speared a cube of tenderloin with his knife, chewed slowly.

"We have laws," said Johnson.

"And that has served you well? To keep you from hurting one another?" asked the priest. "What good are laws without justice?"

"Better than justice with no laws. A king's justice. A pope's justice. A tyrant's rule. A bully." Johnson held up a hand. "Not that I want to be hard on the pope."

"The pope is feeding you now, as he does all his children," said Fray Antonio.

"I heard you giving thanks," said Johnson.

"And you?"

"I thank you," said Johnson. "You've been . . . you are a fine host." He tilted his bowl for more stew.

"And Jesus? And God?" said the missionary. "They, too, are hosts. The holiest of hosts." He speared another chunk of meat.

"I thank them, too." Johnson reached into Fray Antonio's large bowl and took a cube of tenderloin. He plucked it into his mouth. "You've been generous." He walked away to sit in the grass near the Indians, enjoying the cooling evening. Johnson nodded to Tequan, who looked away. A good sign. Johnson ate slowly. He did not know when or where he might have his next meal. All of them ate until nothing was left of the Feast of Saint Thomas. After the feast, the Spaniards—Franciscan and vaquero and mission help—drank a thick wine. Johnson took sips, then quit. Let them drowse. He followed them when they drifted to their beds.

Johnson lay on his cot. The breathing around him elongated into sleep. The restless bodies stopped turning, tossing, adjusting. Coughing erupted, then quieted. Snoring began its shuddering cacophony. Johnson had learned something of patience in the past months, and he waited longer than he needed to before rising soundlessly from his narrow blanket. He carried the boots he'd been given. He looked out a notched window in the hallway. Some of the Indians sat around the embers of a fire. Soon the last of the coals would turn to white dust, like the ash in his pocket. Once he reached the stable he put on his boots, then covered his face with ash. As he approached Rayo's stall, he heard a nicker. Would one of the horses betray him? Rayo was asleep. When Johnson opened his stall, the horse wheeled toward him, hooves raised, attacking so quickly that Johnson barely squeezed through the stall door in time. The clatter of Rayo's hooves against the wooden slats of the stall echoed through the stable. In the silence that followed, Johnson heard another nicker. He found the horse who called him. Isabella. She was already saddled, waiting. A large leather bag, sweating through with water, was tied to the pommel. He did not question why. He had learned that if he had a plan, others might know it. Some might help. Tequan? Antonio? Juan Francisco? Even Diaz? Everyone might have a reason to want him gone, but none more than himself.

He opened Isabella's stall, took up her bridle reins, and led her out of the stable and into the courtyard. There, he hopped into the saddle and let her walk, for the sake of silence, to the gate. On the horse, in the slip of moon, with the ash on his face, he might have been the ghost he wanted the Indians to believe he was. The gate groaned on its hinges even before Johnson saw Tequan waiting in the crack of its opening. Johnson leaned forward as he went through, for Tequan wanted to touch him, to bless this wandering spirit. Then Johnson straightened quickly and nudged Isabella forward. He was not proud of himself, but he was free. Isabella ran into the prairie as though she were the one who dreamed of flight.

Rio Grande

obert Johnson rode southwest. Fray Antonio, after all his sermonizing, would expect him to prick his courage and head back to Tennessee. He had water, horse, tack, and clothing. He had restored that precious commodity, strength. But he had no plan, no firearm, no money. In the desolate landscape that promised Laredo at the end of a hundred-some miles, the trees were stunted, then disappeared as though into quicksand. The grainy soil produced dwarf cactus—yucca and prickly pear. Even the rocks were worn, as though resting with their bottoms buried deep in the landscape to escape the sun.

The forests of Tennessee dwarfed a man. The stands of trees near San Antonio provided some cover. But this desert exposed a man. Johnson was used to hiding. He rode from dusk to dawn, since the sun baked everything crisp each day. The same dark that protected him slowed him down. One night he heard what must have been a bobcat, a fierce shriek so close Isabella's hide shuddered beneath Johnson's touch.

Soon, water disappeared. Moist creek beds turned to dry gulches. He would have to risk exposure to sun and pursuer—the one certain, the other speculative—to get the lay of the land by daylight. On Isabella, he was no longer confident he could outrun anyone. A bounty hunter would have a good horse. And, this country was said to be full of Apaches, the same ones who attacked the missions of San Antonio, who destroyed any who dared upon their territory.

Lizards zippered the ground. A coyote fled with rocking gait. Occasionally a snake slithered a dry hiss across sandy soil. The stolid cacti were the most immobile living things Johnson had ever known. At one gulch, Johnson was lucky enough to dig through sand to create a small hollow that was soon cupped with water.

After a week alone with only the prospect of being alone, Johnson stopped watching for pursuers. One day, he even turned Isabella in a circle. Something worse than pursuit had befallen him—the realization that he had propelled himself almost to the Rio Grande, and that he was likely not being sought. He felt a tug toward Tennessee. Only the fact of water, the Rio Grande closer than the Rio San Antonio, made him urge Isabella south.

The landscape began to bite—both heat and cactus—as he imagined the snakes would, if Isabella weren't so attentive. If she shied suddenly, what looked like gritty soil would begin to undulate ten yards away. Killdeer shrieked, wind shrieked. In the level landscape, Johnson grew bigger in comparison to the vegetation, shrank smaller in the vast distance, which could not be calculated, only survived.

The last of the prickly pear blossoms withered on the edges of those flat, thorn-shot pads, mustard yellow and bruised purple, and tiny buds of fruit had just set. Johnson tried one, so sour his mouth puckered at their sight for the rest of the day. But the pads themselves yielded a viscid fluid. He broke them apart, and, avoiding their thorns, chewed their edges, sucked their stored moisture. He brought some to Isabella, too. In another day, he was removing the thorns and both of them were eating the pads. Neither swallowed eagerly, but both were on survival's edge.

Johnson's thoughts cast behind him, to home, to the cabin he'd built. He imagined it burned, as MacDonald had reported in Memphis. He possessed only a log cabin of dreams. A life of dreams. A mirage of possibilities. He imagined a letter to pass the time:

Dear Jo,

> *I miss my cabin, only for a short time my own home. I hoisted each log, brought together each joining. I meant to bring you there, your true heart and fair face. My happiness was as brief as our time together, away from our fathers and their feuding. Now my cabin is nothing but ash. I sometimes hear it calling me, as you call to me, too, like a bird that warbles in the springtime, like*

waves that ripple in the stream beds, like the whippoorwill that
calls from the hill. Poor me, poor me. My home in Tennessee. My
love in Tennessee. My life in Tennessee. Wait for me somewhere, as
you do in my dreams . . .

The heat, his hunger, and thirst sharpened as he thought of Tennessee, cool and green. Perhaps only mirage shimmered ahead of him in the rippling heat waves. But ribbons of green slaked his thirsting eyes. Isabella hurried forward, sensing the river, too. Each of them bent toward green, yet in the incalculable distance of this country, they spent the rest of the day excited by water that would not come closer. Isabella had too much heart and too much thirst to stop at dusk.

They reached the Rio Grande as the moon rose. Johnson remembered the Mississippi moon shining a path across the water, leading him from Memphis into the territories. He remembered the power of The Stud, a horse he could trust to swim any water, who would know where to cross, all confidence—from the plunge into any water to the rise onto an opposite bank. What rivers had The Stud crossed since he'd been stolen by the Indians, with who on his back? Johnson and Isabella clambered down the bushy banks to drink and bathe in the Rio Grande, happy for the simple rescue of water, warm and sluggish though it was. After a time they climbed up the bank and slept until birds woke them.

streets of Laredo

robert Johnson did not know whether upriver or down would bring him to Laredo. He mounted Isabella and sat stolid. She waited for his guidance, then walked downstream. A trail—cattle, Johnson thought—opened into a discernible path above the shimmering river. Midday, Johnson thought he saw what might be buildings huddled next to the river. He whooped, and Isabella surged forward.

Laredo was a small flourish of stucco and clapboard just high enough above the Rio Grande that it might not flood with spring rain and snow-melt from distant mountains. Johnson rode into the town square, tied Isabella to a rail, and looked for the fair skin that would mean someone who spoke English.

After a time, a short man, as wide as he was tall, came out of a commercial building, clomping shiny boots on the packed clay of the streets. He sat on a bench against the shade of another store. He seemed as tall sitting as he'd been when standing. He took off his boots to adjust grimy socks.

Johnson approached. "Just rode in," he said.

"Just bought these Goddamn boots," said the man. "Lucky," he said. He dropped the boot in his hand and extended it to Johnson.

"James," said Johnson.

"Lucky you found me," said the man. "Not much English around here." He stomped a foot into a boot.

"Your name is Lucky?" asked Johnson.

"Call me that. I'll call you James," answered the man. He stomped into the second boot and stood up, the crown of his hat even with Johnson's shoulder.

"I've got no food and no money," said Johnson.

"I'll call you *un*lucky, then," said the man.

"I know my way around horses. Stables. I can ride any horse and urge it to speed. Faster than any other man can make it run."

"That your nag?" asked Lucky.

Johnson nodded.

Lucky shook his head. "I can see where you might have honed your talent."

"She's hungry as I am," said Johnson.

"Across the river, and just south of the town squares. Find La Concha, the shell. Ask for Carlito. He'll show you where they race."

"I thank you," said Johnson. He untied Isabella.

"Good luck to you," said the man, taking off his hat.

Johnson rode the short distance to the river.

He waited on the north bank of the Rio Grande, repeating La Concha, Carlito, La Concha, Carlito. He had thought a path would show a promising place to ford, but all this landscape appeared worn, as dry as it was, even down the riverbank. Just as he was ready to find his own way, as he would have done without hesitation on The Stud, two men rode to the river from the south. He watched where they put in their horses, where they came up on the north bank. They raised their hats to him as they passed, but said nothing. Johnson followed their path. Isabella balked. Johnson urged her forward with knees, then heels. Soon, the mare was swimming. Johnson cupped the muddy water into his hands, onto his face, into his mouth.

South of the Rio Grande the thatched-roofed buildings were arranged around two squares—*zócalos*, Johnson would hear them called. The dirt streets were stirred into dust as the commerce of the day was under way. The porch roofs of the buildings extended themselves and men gathered under them in the shade. From the rafters of a store, a merchant had hung garlands of garlic and chiles, blankets, boots, tack. Barrels, no matter what they contained, were used as seats. Johnson rode slowly and a few men, swarthy faces under large hats, nodded to him. He stopped at the largest gathering.

"Concha," he said. "Carlito."

The men shook their heads.

Johnson tried for a different pronunciation and a man pointed him down the street.

The same thing happened each time Johnson stopped where men sat together in the shade. Nobody seemed to be working, but maybe it was their time of rest. Everyone at the mission in San Antonio had disappeared for siesta, sleeping or gathering to talk and wait out the midday heat. None of that in Memphis, where the bustle of construction and commerce signaled a belief in the future rather than a reliance on the traditions of the past. Laredo seemed to have been part of the landscape forever—changeless, covered in dust.

Johnson finally saw the crudely painted shell on a small building at the edge of Laredo. Music drifted from the open door, a thick-stringed guitar, Johnson guessed. A small man, thin and wiry, with no hat to cover his shock of black hair, hurried from inside and took Isabella's reins. He led her to the back of the building where other horses drank from a trough. One of them whinnied, and Isabella shook her head and snorted. Johnson unsaddled her, but left the bridle on until he could beg a halter. He leaned the saddle against the side of La Concha and turned to the small Mexican man. "Carlito?" he asked.

The man nodded. He approached Isabella, ran his hand from withers to croup, then down from flank to fetlock. "*Vieja*," he said.

Johnson had no idea what Carlito said. "Isabella," he said.

"*Isabella, la vieja*," said Carlito.

Johnson had no idea how to ask the man for all he needed. Food and drink, first. Somewhere to rest, recuperate from his desert sojourn. A chance to race Isabella, naggy as she was. He might just be lucky and win some money. He was heartened by Carlito's interest in Isabella, which extended to the examination of her hooves and then forward, once she'd slaked her thirst, to her teeth. Did he think Johnson wanted to sell the horse?

Carlito walked to the front of the building and Johnson followed. Inside, La Concha was dark but cool. A man stood behind the bar, another strummed on the big guitar, chords, without rhythm. Three men sat at a table playing cards. Carlito spoke to the man at the bar, who poured a short glass full of a cloudy liquid. Johnson sat. Carlito put the glass in front of him. The smell alone flared Johnson's nostrils.

"*¿No agua?*" asked Johnson.

"*Agua de agave*," said Carlito. "*Tome.*"

Johnson did as he was expected, sipping what he'd never sipped before, the pungent fire lurching to the back of his throat, his tongue burning, and then the swallow. His eyes watered. He took more, for he knew that such distillations improved with inoculation. By the time he finished the glass he was well satisfied with the contents—some essence of the desert, like the sap of the cactus he'd been forced to drink between San Antonio and Laredo.

Johnson bowed his head, breathed deeply. "*Gracias*," he said.

Carlito took his glass to the bar and the man there poured it full. Johnson stood up, and the liquor sat him back down again.

Carlito approached him with the refill. "*Tome*," he said, smacking the glass on the table.

Again, Johnson drank, this time more quickly to the head. The air buzzed as though thick with flies. As he drank his third glass, he lay his head on the table and gave over to oblivion.

When Johnson awoke, La Concha was full of men, several at the bar, all the tables taken, a group of men in a corner tuning guitars. Carlito was nowhere. Johnson stood up, his body heavy, one of his feet asleep, and went outside into dusk. He walked around the building, and, as he expected, saw no sign of Isabella. Nor his saddle. On the other side of the trough, a man sat, back to the building, short legs extended, new boots on his feet.

"They want to know some things, they do." Lucky's bulk sat like a boulder.

Johnson squatted next to him. "What do they want to know?"

Lucky took off his hat, put it over his short thighs. "Like where you come upon the horse. Yours, is she?"

"In a manner of speaking," said Johnson.

"That manner of speaking might get you in some trouble, is what I'm worried about. Might get *them* in some trouble."

Johnson stood up, as though he might search for Isabella right away. "She's all I have. I'd like to race her, maybe win some money."

"So you said, when first you rode in." Lucky waved Johnson back down. "Sit."

Johnson's head pounded from his liquor-enforced siesta. He sat down.

"I saw that horse. Didn't think much of her. Should have looked closer. They tell me she's branded. Mexican army horse."

"That's a lie."

"Carlito says she was." Lucky flicked a fly from his face. "Not that I've seen her since you was on her."

"She's mine," said Johnson. He unburdened himself. From Tennessee, to the band of Indians, and how they'd stolen his horse. He defended the quality and uniqueness of The Stud in such a diatribe that Lucky held up his hand. So Johnson abandoned that ride to tell of his rescue by vaqueros, who took him to the San Antonio mission. He'd left them a week or so before. "They knew I was leaving. They gave me horse, saddle, bridle, water."

"I've stayed with Fray Antonio," said Lucky. "A good host when he ain't *serving up* the host, if you get my drift. Catholics won't be in this country long."

"Where are you from?" asked Johnson.

"A bit of everywhere," said Lucky. "But someday I'll be a Texan. We'll be making a new country here."

"People speak of it in Tennessee," said Johnson.

"First we have to get rid of the Mexicans and pick off the rest of the Spanish. The Indians are helping to get rid of your generous Franciscans. Nice, since we haven't even asked for Indian help. Spanish are getting wary up there. Don't have as much as they once did. I doubt Antonio or his vaqueros would cotton to what you call the gift of that horse."

"They won't ride this direction to find it, will they?" Johnson decided Lucky enjoyed conspiracy. "And if I borrow it for my own good cause, who would care?"

"There's Carlito," said Lucky. "How's it going to look for him when the Mexican army comes for a little visit and finds one of their horses, mounted by an American such as yourself, running for a purse?"

Johnson stood up again. He stomped his boot in rhythm to his pounding head. "Where's Isabella? Carlito?"

Lucky stood up, too. "I'll take you to the track when they say so," he said. "Meantime, Carlito has a little cot in the back of the building. You'll sleep there." Lucky put on his hat and walked away.

Johnson decided on patience, the virtue a powerless man has no choice but to practice. He found the cot. He waited for the raucous drinking to end. The music, too. The last banging of a door. Sleep was patient, too, but finally found him.

raced

"It ain't Carlito you worry about," Lucky said quietly. "It's who Carlito answers to." Lucky held a cup of coffee.

Robert Johnson sat up on the cot and stretched. He took the coffee, blew on it once, then gulped it down. "And who does Carlito answer to?"

Lucky walked to the doorway and pointed into the main room of La Concha.

Johnson followed him. Carlito stood with his back to them. At the table sat three men, tall in their chairs, each with leather pants and white shirts, each with thick, well-combed hair. Their hats, sitting before them on the table, sported silver bands. Johnson returned to his cot.

"They own the best horseflesh around here," Lucky said. "They must like your Isabella."

"That why they lied about the brand?"

"I have to play both sides," said Lucky, "and tell the truth, there's more sides than *both*." He gave the history of Laredo as he knew it, founded sometime in the 1750s, the Spanish in charge then, creating outposts along the trade routes from Mexico up north all the way to the missions. "Where you stayed, that's over a hundred years old," Lucky said. A dozen Spanish families still owned the land, he explained, even after Mexico won independence from Spain. "These people did the same as we did to old King George," said Lucky. "They're like us—they don't want to be ruled from across the ocean. So the Spanish families created their own governments, called themselves Mexicans. You're visiting a whole new country, but with the same old people," said Lucky. "So you've got your old Spanish, who are now your new Mexicans, while your old Mexicans—the natives like Carlito, and the mestizos—work for them and plot against them for the day Mexico will be free of them. And then you've got us Americans. Stephen Austin came in some years ago. And there ain't going to be an end to that until Texas is Texas." Meanwhile, Lucky reminded Johnson, the authority of the old Spaniards, the Catholic Church, the customs of Spain, all had to be lived with day by day. "If you want to race a horse, you do it their way."

"What if you want food?" asked Johnson, since his companion seemed to like talk better than anything else.

"I'll bring you a bowl of posole, the Mexican breakfast." Lucky stomped from the room.

Johnson heard him speaking in Spanish with the men at the table. He returned with a bowl of stew.

"So how *do* I race my horse?" Johnson spooned up the stew, savory with chiles.

"They race when the track is cool. They've already raced this morning. You're not to miss tomorrow."

"Where do they race?" Johnson drank the broth in his bowl.

"I'll take you at sundown. Isabella should be recovered from her branding by then."

"I'll be able to ride her?"

"They expect you to lose," Lucky said. "Their men do nothing but ride their horses. You'll be their little joke. You and that horse."

"I won't lose," said Johnson. He handed Lucky the empty bowl.

"You haven't seen their horses," said Lucky.

The scraping of chairs signaled the end of Carlito's meeting with his bosses. Johnson went to the back door to watch the men ride away. Their Arabian horses, two bays and a gray, reminded him of Rayo, Diaz's horse. The men did not hurry. Lucky stood next to Johnson. "Think you could outrace those horses on your nag?" he asked.

"I could try," said Johnson. Had The Stud been his partner, he would not have hesitated in the challenge.

"And those ain't even the horses built for speed." Lucky trundled down the street. Johnson wondered if the man had a horse, or could seat a horse, or whether a horse would want him on its back. He was that wide.

Carlito showed Johnson where to bathe, fed him more stew, then took him to the stable, south and west of what these people were already calling Nuevo Laredo. Johnson walked the length of the barn. He did not find Isabella. He pretended he was sitting in a saddle. He pointed to himself. "*Mi caballo*," he said, pretending to ride. Carlito handed Johnson a shovel. He led him to a vacant stall. Johnson knew what to do. Shovel manure, lay down fresh hay. Find a bucket and replenish water. Feed the stock. Outside, men washed horses, others dried them, leading the powerful creatures slowly in circles, the coats of the horses shining in the Mexican sun.

Johnson had slept on a cot. He had a belly full of posole. He had nowhere to go, no horse to ride, no plan but to run Isabella when they'd let him. He'd get lucky, no matter what Lucky said. The horses were led to their stalls, and what horses they were. The Stud was a fine horse, but if Johnson had set out to create better ones, these would be them, rippling with muscle, sure-footed, alert. They tossed their manes, exhorted each other in nickers, whinnies, lip-flapping bursts of sound. In the stable, surrounded by the pungent smell of horses and horse turds, the tonic smells of straw and hay, the men laughed and called to each other like the horses—joking, challenging. Dust motes floated in the slashes of light that streaked between boards. Johnson was not home, but he always felt at home with men and horses.

That night, Lucky was at La Concha again. They ate beef stewed with beans and red chiles. When Johnson could eat no more, he began to drink. "*Más*," Carlito said when Johnson finished a small glass of mescal. Then más after that, until Lucky put his hand over Johnson's glass. "Come," he whispered.

They went to the back room where Johnson had slept the night before. "Your horse ain't branded with the Mexican army brand, like they told me. I saw her today. With the brand of Diego Morales de Seville. He's claiming her. Stolen as a young mare, before he branded her, years ago. Good breeding, he claims. I told his foreman you'd ridden her down from the missions, loaned to you by a thieving vaquero."

"So I no longer have a horse?" Johnson asked. "These Spaniards are as bad as those Indians."

"You are in their territory, yes. You'll ride Isabella tomorrow. What have they got to lose? They show you what their horses can do. They'll wager the horse, because you rode her into town. Then they'll watch you lose her. There ain't much sport around here unless there's a new horse, you see."

"A new horse they say is theirs all along?" Johnson shook his head. "I ain't going to lose, then."

"You'll lose, all right. One way or the other. But lay off the mescal unless you want to slim your chances even more."

"I don't get a drink very often," said Johnson.

"Unless it's Carlito's best, you'll wake up with a belly full of snakes. And your head will be full of bees for noise, hammers for hurt. What more could they want, if you catch my drift. I'll see you at the track, just as the sun is coming up." Lucky left the back room. Johnson followed him, watched him order another drink.

Johnson returned to the cot and lay down, wondering for all the world what Jo Benson was thinking that very night, lying as she probably was in her own bed, her hands resting on a swelling belly. He hoped some small part of him had stayed home, and was growing inside her. That small piece was to be another of his loves.

Carlito woke him in the morning. He slapped his face with water, put on his boots, and followed the man to the stable. From one of the forward stalls, Isabella whinnied. Johnson stroked her muzzle. Her eyes were tired, glazed. The seared flesh where they'd branded her was swabbed with a rank unguent. She'd had but two days' rest after the difficult journey from San Antonio.

Carlito pointed to the tack hanging on the back wall of the stall. Johnson pointed to himself, then Isabella. "Ride?" he asked.

Carlito nodded his head, clapping his hands impatiently. Johnson opened the stall door and got busy. Carlito ambled away, greeting Lucky, who sauntered into the barn already talking. Lucky had not changed his clothes, rumpled and dirty as they were, since Johnson had arrived in town. The fat man leaned on the slats next to the stall door. "So you're going to ride, are you? Well, I have bad news."

"Something's wrong with her," Johnson interrupted.

"But you don't know what, am I right? They fed her hay with plenty of hemp in it, and believe me, down here in the sun, the hemp can make you forget who you are. That horse knows who she is, but she's sluggish. Should have watched her appetite."

"I have to run her just the same?"

"I can help you with that. Assuming we can share in the stake, whatever it is. If you win, that is. I won't be responsible for your debts, since I've never seen you do much more than stagger into town on a horse. But I have in my pocket a little something that might help when the time comes."

Johnson knew he'd bring out a lump of sugar, as soiled with grime as the ones he'd seen so long ago, when the owner of The Stud had laced those small hunks with whatever had made his horse wildly impossible to ride. "When do I feed it to her?" he asked as Lucky brought out the small lump.

"Works fast. Right before the starting gun, I'd say." said Lucky. He held up his hand, "And don't ask me what's in it. If it works, we'll use it again. Share and share alike, as I say."

Johnson finished saddling Isabella, and she took the bit. He led her from the stall, mounted her, and reached down for the sugar. "Can't hurt to try," he said. When he urged Isabella forward, she took two steps, then stopped. Then two more. "If I can get her to the track," said Johnson.

Lucky slapped Isabella's flank next to where she'd been branded.

The track, a quarter mile around, was next to a creek. Some men rode toward him, then settled in on either side, nudging Isabella forward between them. They stopped, as Johnson knew they would, in the middle of the straightaway. One of them muttered in Spanish. The other man laughed. They rode away quickly, leaving Johnson and Isabella on the track under a punishing sun. He fingered the lump of sugar in his pocket.

Lucky strode out, followed by five mounted riders. Johnson shook his head. He had not been lucky to find this man, a two-faced player of both sides, with nothing to lose no matter what happened. Lucky told Johnson what he'd negotiated. Four times around the track. The stake, Isabella. Should Johnson win, the horse would be his to race as long as he was in Mexico. If he lost, Johnson would be on foot again.

The horses lined up, and the Spaniards held their quirts ready. The flesh of the horses began to twitch. Isabella snorted, tossed her head, tensed. "There you go, sugar," shouted Lucky. Johnson put his hand in his pocket. The gun would soon go off. Lucky stomped his new boots into the dirt, dusting up little puffs that thinned and disappeared into the air. Which side was he on? "Sugar!" the man shouted. Johnson took his hand from his pocket just as the gun sounded.

No sugar, no quick lean toward the horse's mouth. He could not do it, not after he'd witnessed The Stud's frenzy with laced sugar those many years before. They were off.

The first time around seemed more an assessment than a race. The Spaniards were not quick to spur their horses. They watched Johnson atop Isabella. The horse was equal to the pace, not wanting to push ahead, so no need to go out any stronger than the other horses. They passed the starting point. Lucky sat on the railing of the track, his legs tucked under the wooden slats, perched like a fat bird waiting out a storm. He cupped his hands to his mouth, "Sugar!" Johnson smiled at him. When the other men looked to him, Johnson knew they were part of Lucky's game.

Johnson raised himself in the saddle and notched his knees. He raised his hind end and whistled in Isabella's ear. She startled and quickened her pace. The other riders matched her. Then one edged ahead. A whip cracked. Isabella shimmied, away from the whip, nearly throwing Johnson to the track. He shifted his weight and they took off in earnest. The Spaniards wanted only one horse to win, the one already in the lead. Johnson needed but one horse to win, Isabella, his nag, not muscled like theirs. Without the conformation. But they wanted her. They'd branded her. What had they seen in her? No different from what everyone saw in The Stud. They saw spirit. They saw heart. They saw a pure creature, the same one who had brought him from the mission through the desert to Laredo.

He shouted and stretched forward. Isabella pushed harder, found her rhythm. By the end of the back straightaway, they were to the lead horse's neck. The Spaniard on that stud's back did not dare turn around. He was flailing his horse, flagrant with his whip. Johnson worried he might lose an eye to the fury of the man's flagellations, but he could not break his stride without losing the race. Isabella was eager. Johnson gave himself over to her, the Spaniard's whip at his shoulder, twice stinging his face as they rounded the back stretch for the second, then third time.

Each time that Johnson and Isabella rounded the track and shot into the straightaway, Lucky jumped up and down yelling, "Sugar!" But Isabella could run no faster, no matter what laced that chunk in Johnson's pocket.

Isabella's shoulder neared the shoulder of the lead horse. The Spaniard on that stud turned to look behind him, but not at Johnson. The Spaniard's horse moved away from the posts, nudging Isabella with him. Another set of hooves clamored behind, and Johnson could see it all as though above the track. Another horse, fresh from hanging back in the race, was to take the inside track. Johnson jerked Isabella's reins and she slowed to just behind the lead horse. They surged into the post to cut off the fresher horse. The Spaniard in the lead reined his stud as an impediment.

They wedged into the small space between the two Spaniards' horses. But the inside horse had more reserve, and on the back stretch pushed its lead to two lengths. Isabella kept her pace, her breath expelled with a snorting that might have steamed the air on a cold morning. Not here, where the sun sucked water from horse and man. The race evaporated by the final backstretch, the Spanish horses lengthening their lead so easily that Johnson supposed they must have been playing with him all along.

"The sugar?" Lucky asked as the racers circled back to the start line.

"Lost it," said Johnson. His pocket hid the chunk well enough. He dismounted and a Spaniard took Isabella's reins and led her away. Another spoke softly in Lucky's ear, as though Johnson could have understood what he said.

Lucky nodded and turned to Johnson. "You lost the race, but they like how you ride. They want to see you ride their horses."

Johnson walked to the Spaniard's horse, hardly lathered from the race. The stud reminded him of his own horse, long, lean, something in the eye that sized up a man.

"Isabella is a fine horse," said Johnson.

The Spaniard led his stud away. "But she's past her prime," said Lucky. "It's her name, is what it is."

"Isabella is what the vaqueros called her."

"Diego named her for his oldest daughter," said Lucky. "The one who run off. When this horse came to town, he wanted to have something, if you catch my drift."

"I know what it's like to miss someone," said Johnson.

Lucky started after the Spaniards, toward the trees along the creek. "You'll race tomorrow," he said, "same time, right here. You can give up your cot at La Concha."

Johnson stood still. "Carlito's been mighty nice."

Lucky turned. "Diego Morales has better tequila, better food, better women. You might want to live like they do if you're going to ride their horses. Besides, it's a long way back in this sun." He turned on his new boot heel and began the march to the hacienda.

Johnson caught him easily. "What about the sugar."

"Don't know," said Lucky.

"Why the hell did you give it to me?" A low-slung stable of adobe nestled in shade just ahead of them.

"They wanted me to," said Lucky.

"Why?" asked Johnson.

"I am as beholden to them as you are now," said Lucky. "Will you question their hospitality? Ask them why you have to ride? You going to ask Diego about his daughter? Not ours to ask questions, if you catch my drift."

They moved into shade, and Johnson saw past the stable to the house, adobe, too, and spread out, with room after room, door after door, a porch all along its wide front. The breeze seemed cooler in this oasis. If he was to be stuck somewhere, better in comfort.

The stable had four rows of stalls, maybe twenty stalls in each row, each stall housing a horse. All of the horses looked like they could have outraced Johnson and Isabella. The rows of stalls opened into a corral, where the five horses that had run that morning, including Isabella, were being bathed. After, they'd be led in circles until they were fully dry. They'd be given food and drink, sheltered from the hot sun for the rest of the day.

Johnson walked along with Lucky. "They run them before sunrise," said Lucky. "Sometimes again in the evening, depending on the heat. You'd best learn to bed early, rise early. You're a man who likes horse-flesh, so you'll get along."

Johnson followed Lucky across the corral to a lean-to bunkhouse, where hammocks waited instead of beds, where each man had a box for possessions. Johnson's could be a mighty small box. Lucky led him to the end, where Johnson had to knock cobwebs from the hammock webbing. "They'll bring you a blanket, a plate, and a cup."

"They take better care of their horses than their men?"

"Horses are worth a lot more," said Lucky. He sat on a box, pointed to another. "They'll take care of you, too. Miss Flora is the cook. Best frijoles. Best tortillas. Chickens soaked in goat's milk and chile, then slow cooked until you can pull the meat from the bone in silky threads."

"That how you got so big?" asked Johnson.

Lucky clamped his mouth shut. He took off his hat, placed it carefully on his knee. "I'm a small man who's been well fed. I see that as a difference between us, young man."

Johnson looked out into the sun-drenched earth of the corral.

"And another difference," said Lucky. "I'll stay. You won't."

"Yeah?" asked Johnson.

"You'll want more than what you find here." Lucky stood up. "Get some rest until they notice you." He walked away.

"I can't understand them," said Johnson to his back.

"Start learning." Lucky disappeared into the stable.

Over the next month Johnson worked hard, impressing the Spaniards who gave the orders, working alongside the natives who cleaned stalls, maintained the gardens, crops, livestock and house, gaining the respect of the mestizos who worked the horses, warming them up, riding them hard around the track, cooling them down, washing, drying, feeding, and watering them. Each of the horsemen knew the horses as well as they knew each other, and better than any of them knew Robert Johnson. They would spend hours wrapping a stud's foreleg when, after a race, the horse walked gingerly back to the stable, but would not help Johnson off the track when thrown from a skittish horse.

Johnson spent as much time as he could with the men. He learned how to say "*Cómo se dice,*" and point to whatever vocabulary he wanted. Some things came quickly, the words that ended in that soft a, like *Flora, señorita, tequila, guitarra.* Lucky had been right about the food and drink. And the women and music were lively, the long ballad songs, *corridos,* sung with a passion Johnson had not experienced in the hills of Tennessee.

He soon learned to speak the language as well as Lucky, and perhaps understood even more. Lucky made sure that any Anglo who crossed the Rio Grande was known, was mined for secrets, intentions plumbed, aware of who was in charge. Johnson had a natural distaste for any man who thought he was in a partnership when he was but a parasite.

Nights became cooler, and Johnson knew that once he needed a blanket so far south, they'd be building fires in east Tennessee. Jo would be sitting next to a fire, her belly swollen, no doubt suffering the abuse of father and brothers as to her condition, which she would be long past hiding. Johnson found his mind setting to home, but also descending to desperation. He'd escaped San Antonio by stealing a horse, with half a blessing from Fray Antonio. If he stole one of *these* horses, the Spaniards would not stop until they'd tracked him down and proven to everyone how much more valuable horses were than men.

Johnson was companionable with the horses, the men, and, with the occasional socials sponsored by Diego Morales de Seville, the women. Some of the señoritas asked the men what they knew about him, stood watching him from across the floor where the young people danced. Johnson did not answer their obvious invitations. God knows, temptation was a boil to be suppurated, but such a lancing would bring him nothing but guilt. He did not feel he was keeping himself pure so much as keeping himself focused. He stood by at socials, enjoying the food, the drink. He watched the courtships, the jealousies, the quick flashes of romance and temper. He would remain bystander even to himself, his hair now covering his ears and neck, his beard a nest of curls. How could he be, or remain, anything but stranger?

With the horses, he worked hard. They did not let him ride Isabella. But he found other horses he understood, who seemed to understand him. None could take the place of The Stud in his heart and mind, just as no woman could take Jo's place. When he was on the backs of the mare, Mirabella, and the stud, Nopal, he seldom lost a race. The few times he did, the other riders implored him, "*Azótelos. Comprenden solo la fusta. Azótelos.*" Johnson refused to lash the horses he rode, refused to carry a whip he would not use. The others thought him strange, but he proved to Diego and the others that he could ride well and win races. Each time he did, they gave him silver. Sometimes gold. Soon, he might buy clothing, a horse. But no matter how proud of the money and respect he won, each night the constellations wheeled in the firmament. He watched the same stars Jo watched, and their turning marked the passage of time.

Monterrey

Diego asked Robert Johnson to ride with a group of his men on a buying trip south, to Monterrey, where other landed Spaniards like himself bred and raced their prized Arabians. He trusted Johnson's judgment, he said. Each man could pick a horse he felt strongly about, even if the choice went against the wishes of the others. Diego wanted horses men chose to ride, so gave the men their heads. He liked many kinds of horses in his remuda.

The group set off under a rising moon. They traveled hard each night until the next day's sun wearied them. Sometimes, at daybreak, though horses and men were tired, they'd race toward some feature of the landscape, wherever they might make camp. Johnson let others win those brief competitions. After their fifth night, the huge outcrop they raced toward was too far in the distance. The riders called it Cerro de la Silla, Saddle Hill. They'd crossed rough terrain, but this sheer mountain, with its peaks that jutted a mile above Monterrey, was harbinger of the city and of the mountain ranges to the south.

Though they were a day away, the riders were excited. Johnson's anticipation was muted. Each mile he rode south was another mile away from both his past and his future. He had told no man about Jo Benson, or his treatment by Indians and his loss of The Stud, or the tale of his stay in San Antonio.

He was swept along with the others, riding toward a city marked even from a distance by a cathedral and large buildings dedicated to those in charge. What else for these Spaniards but priests and governors and armies, tendrils setting root far from a rich and powerful empire. In the United States, aside from stray ministers and explorers, people flung themselves into new territory without government or church, more escape and opportunity than missionary for established power. Johnson was happy to be from Tennessee, where a common man like Jackson could rise to power. Here, common men stayed common.

Diego had power—fine land, fine horses, comfort in a home beyond anything Johnson could have imagined. Diego's hands, a ragged group, rode toward a similar hacienda on the edge of Monterrey next to a track with seats built up the length of one side and surrounded by thick trees to break the hot wind, and decorated with pots of golden flowers as plentiful as Tennessee mushrooms after a rain, and everything not adobe was painted in deep red, cobalt, or a turquoise rich as the stone itself. Diego's eager horsemen had been to this place before. Johnson put aside his melancholy. Horses, led by their trainers, moved from the track to a stable twice the size as the one owned by Diego Morales de Santiago. What horses these were.

Two hours later, after water and rest, the horses for sale were lined up. The Spaniards here, as everywhere he'd seen, preferred Arabians. Diego's men dispersed among the offered horses, looking for conformation, sores, signs of either abuse or care. Johnson carried the image of The Stud's perfection, which bled to dissatisfaction with every horse except for a mare he might become attached to, gray, with eyes almost blue, a strong neck. Another of the men shook his head. "*Mira*," and he pointed to the thin hindquarters.

"*Sí*," said Johnson. He wondered why size was always equated with strength. The one muscle that mattered most—the heart—was hidden. Only the best horseman could look inside a horse and discover that. Finally, he refused to pick a horse. Should he choose one not to his credit, he'd have to live with their judgment. The ranch hands, he knew, thought him either simple or too choosey. "*Los gringos*," they said finally, and shook their heads.

"Show me a horse I can like," insisted Johnson. "*Un caballo para gringos*," he bantered. "My kind of horse."

"*Venga conmigo*," said a man, and walked toward the stable.

Johnson followed him. Inside, huge fans were suspended from the ceiling beams. Four boys, one under each fan, jerked pulley ropes to keep the fans turning. They shouted to each other all the while, hurling insults, making jokes. They seemed a contentious group, as though they'd fight if not tethered to the fan ropes, but they united into the same laughter when the ranch hand Johnson followed led a thin, tan horse from a stall. A stud, long and lean, but leaner than Johnson would ever have imagined. Some of his mane hair had fallen out or been clipped to rid him of vermin or clinging seeds. *Goddamn it!* Johnson wanted to shout when he saw evidence of a recent lashing. But he stopped himself. The fist he'd raised quickly returned to his side. The Stud, tossing his head in recognition, stamping his front hooves, seemed to understand what Johnson knew—this was a joke, *una broma*, they called it among the hands, and Johnson and The Stud would play along. The boys laughed, pointing, all the while riding the ropes up and down to keep the fans swirling. Johnson smiled, his first elation in months. Like The Stud, he hid his relief, his joy, his sudden hope.

Johnson followed the hand as he led The Stud into the line of horses to be considered. The man walked bowlegged, slumping his shoulders, letting his head loll. In this exaggerated imitation Johnson saw something of himself. He'd lost much in his long journey. Not his hope for the future, nor his love for Jo and what they would be together, but his will to make that future and that love the immediate focus of each moment. He had run as fugitive and become fugitive, even from himself. He stumbled toward The Stud, clowning his own imitation of the ranch hand imitating him. Diego's crew laughed. When Johnson took the lead rope of this diminished horse, they laughed harder.

"*Mi caballo, por cierto*," he said when they'd quieted themselves. For The Stud was certainly his horse.

They shook their heads, smiled at each other. They thought him *loco*, Johnson knew.

"*Mañana*," he said, and made his proposal. He would ride The Stud, El Semental, against all the horses the men had chosen to take back to the Morales ranch. If he came in last, he'd return the horse to the stable. They agreed.

That night, they were shown Monterrey. They ate well, drank well, and in those moments of forgetfulness, Johnson found a hand who could tell him how El Semental had come to the ranch. A large man, a gringo, bearded and stinking, had ridden onto the streets of Monterrey a week before. He wanted to find a track. He'd been directed to their ranch, but did not want to race. He was tired of the stud, he said. He wanted a horse he could control. He'd been riding the feisty bastard for only one reason, to attract its owner, a vile man, a murderer.

Johnson poured the man another drink and asked where the big man came from. "Tennessee? Arkansas?" asked Johnson, when the man seemed puzzled.

The man shrugged his shoulders.

"Did the man have a name? MacDonald?" Johnson asked.

The Mexican shook his head, threw back his shot, slammed the glass on the table, and left Johnson, who worried he'd said too much. The man would sense he was the owner, the vile murderer. And he'd forgotten the most important question. Where was the large man now?

Johnson left the cantina. He let the cooling air clear his mind. He walked back to the ranch where they would sleep, but he didn't go to the bunkhouse. He went to the stable, quiet now, and walked to The Stud's stall, the only one in which a horse was waiting, the shadow of his head turned to Johnson as though expecting him.

They had the reunion they could not have had in front of the others, a long touching of heads. Johnson ran his hands along the horse, felt for scars, tangles, insect bites, matting. As he smoothed The Stud's coat, Johnson boiled with anger at the man who had webbed his horse's rump with a lash. He wanted to weep and he wanted to kill.

He found a currycomb and brushed the horse for an hour. If MacDonald had been riding the horse as bait, he had also ridden him without thought, without heart, with only one cruelty in mind, to ruin an innocent animal while hunting down an innocent man. Such men spoiled everything they touched—territory, horse, companion.

The Stud had lost muscle, but then his privation had probably been even worse than Johnson's. No matter, the two of them would have a better chance together, no matter what they faced. Tomorrow, a race. "Beat one horse," he said, "and we're together." He shook his head. Since when had he encouraged The Stud by telling him not to come in last?

He found hay and water, made sure his horse had everything he needed, then went to his hammock. The small sack he'd hidden carried his money, but it contained something else. He touched it before he went to sleep. Lucky's sugar lump was still there.

Johnson could not say if he slept. The others returned from the foray into Monterrey. They laughed, perhaps at him, the gringo who wanted to ride the least of the horses offered them that day. They would run their best in the morning, he knew that. If they didn't, he'd be mounted on The Stud for the journey north, and none of them wanted to explain to Diego Morales de Santiago just how such a horse had come into his herd. A man's reputation sat atop a horse, just as a man did. Johnson lay in his hammock, eyes shut to feign sleep, remembering the feel of The Stud beneath him.

Johnson slipped from his hammock before the others. He was alone in the stable, where his horse watched for him, head over the stall door. Johnson found hay and water, brushed The Stud while he ate.

"Let's warm up," he said. The horse took the halter eagerly, then shook his head. Once out of the stall, The Stud pushed Johnson toward the door that led to the track. He was ready, each push told Johnson.

The other men had risen. When they saw Johnson being shoved along by the mangy horse they slapped their thighs, laughed. But Johnson had The Stud, and the lump of sugar in one pocket of his pants, his small sack of money in the other. He jumped onto the horse's bare back. Johnson's legs remembered a fuller girth. The Stud reared, throwing Johnson to the soft dirt of the track. Johnson ignored the laughter. He picked himself up, walked to his horse, grabbed his ear. "It's me up there," he whispered. "We got to trust each other." He ran ahead of the horse, and The Stud followed.

The men headed to the barn to water their horses, brush them, ready them for the race. Those from the hacienda would bring food, tortillas and beans, and turkey eggs if they were lucky. Then the race would begin. Johnson did not join the rest of them. He ran once around the track. The Stud stayed behind him, as though enjoying the sight. Robert Johnson, his boots worn thin as paper, in pants flared at the bottoms, in a shirt already soaked through with sweat, his hat threatening to blow off so that he held it with one hand. Robert Johnson, the seeming clown. He didn't mind entertaining his horse, or the ranch hands who had lost whatever respect they'd had for him in Nuevo Laredo, or the small group of people who gathered along the rail of the track. After his own run, he mounted The Stud again, and this time the horse loped once around the track, no rearing or stuttering, just the steady power Johnson knew so well. He dismounted and led his horse into the stable. Most of the men were outside, eating lazily, unconcerned about the race.

The only man inside was the ranch hand who had led Johnson to The Stud the day before. Johnson asked for tack. "You are not riding bare back?" the man smirked. He went to an empty stall and came back with a ratty blanket, a cracked saddle, a bridle chewed by mice. "*Especial*," he said. "*Exactamente como el caballo*." Johnson wondered what had happened to his own tack. MacDonald had probably sold it off. To such men, everything was calculated in money.

Johnson saddled The Stud, let him take the bit. "Just one race," he said. "Just four times around that track." He took the lump of sugar from his pocket. "But I've got us a little help, too." The Stud stretched his neck, then immediately pulled it back, snorting. "Not for you," said Johnson. He'd already decided which of the horses The Stud was most likely to beat. That horse did not have the same experience with lumps of sugar as The Stud, and took the offering without hesitation. Johnson waited for a reaction. Nothing.

The others drifted into the barn, and Johnson, eager for the race to begin, chided them to hurry. He made fun of them and their horses. They laughed at him. He made fun of their prowess with women, and they fumed. When he started to speak of their mothers and sisters they offered to shut him up. He mounted The Stud and rode out of the stable. The others hurried to meet him on the track. A bugle called.

He did not have time to watch the sugared horse. The Stud was so eager to run that Johnson could barely contain him. Queer behavior for a horse usually so calm before a race. The others gathered their horses in front of the length of rope stretched across the track, most of them high in the saddle, brandishing their whips. The Stud reared and stamped, and when the gun sounded, and The Stud leaped forward, Johnson nearly fell off.

He'd wanted that familiar feeling, the one telling him he and his horse were the same creature, running, not faster than anyone else, but better, more smoothly. But they could not find their rhythm. Even as he tried to calm himself, for he must if he wanted the same for The Stud, he felt doomed to lose, saw himself rag-tagging across the finish line to find not only humiliation, but an aborted reunion with his horse. They were more than a length behind the slowest horse, the one Johnson had predicted would be at the back of the race. The lump of sugar had no effect by the second lap. Johnson was last, he and The Stud still unable to find their pace.

The third time around the track, Johnson saw the cause of his horse's hesitation—the bear of a man, bearded, slouched hat, one leg calmly raised onto the railing. MacDonald returned Johnson's look. Brief as it was, *all* was exchanged. Johnson would finish one race simply to continue the long race he'd been in since the Bensons had framed him in Tennessee. The true finish line was far into the distance, well ahead in time. He stopped urging The Stud.

And then the horse that was three lengths, four, ahead of them, buckled and fell to the track. As Johnson passed the downed mare, the men lining the track hurried into the soft dirt to see what was wrong. Johnson turned to see the rider, a man who had never been friendly to him, stand up and limp away. The race was over, The Stud no longer in last place.

But instead of hurling himself through the back curves and down the straightaway to the finish line—where he would most certainly be finished—Johnson urged The Stud to jump the fence. They took off around the stable and down the road. Toward, then into, the hills. He turned many times to see if anyone followed him. For the time being, he was free. He was on The Stud, and that elation swept him forward. But freedom had the same price he'd paid too long—he was on the run.

gambler

two days in the foothills among blackish boulders, snips of thick grass for The Stud to chew, and only tepid water stolen at night from a nearly empty barrel by the only dwelling he found in this barren land. Robert Johnson's stomach shrank. On the third day, his guts were wringing him double. Finally, he knocked on the door of the shack where he'd been stealing water. He offered to pay for food, and reached into his sack for gold. The poor man soon found Johnson a plate of beans. He crushed dry tortillas over the top. Johnson suggested the man go into Monterrey to buy meat, but the man hesitated. "If I buy meat," he said, "they will grow suspicious. I am not a man to have money."

Johnson understood. What good was money if you could not spend it? Johnson had more money from racing the Spaniard's horses than he'd ever had in his life, yet he'd never been more destitute. "Buy the meat," he said. "Describe me. Tell them you found the gold on my dead body." Johnson gave the man more money than he'd probably held at any time before in his life. "I am dead," said Johnson. "I died at your place, even as you were getting ready to walk to town to tell them about me. My horse ran away. Now, you are buying some of the things you've always wanted. Buy plenty of cooked meat and tortillas. A new bridle. And a cup. A pot. Knife. Pistol, with powder and lead. For each thing you buy, I will give you the same amount for your trouble."

Johnson placed silver and gold in the man's palm and watched him weigh his desire for money against his reputation in Monterrey—a handful of gold against a ruined future. Like most in this country, the man had not had many opportunities to make decisions.

As Johnson hoped, he made the wrong one. He went into town for everything Johnson needed to begin his journey back to Tennessee.

When the man returned, they exchanged money for supplies. Where he'd been furtive, frightened, the man was bold. He insisted Johnson leave the small shack. "I am alone out here," he said. "They gave me this place because I am responsible for the cattle." Johnson had seen the thin herd, grazing desultorily. "I will tell you where you will be safe," the hand said, "for they will hunt you soon."

"You didn't tell them I was dead? That my horse ran away?"

"What I tell them and what they believe will be two different things. I am not a good liar. I have not spent enough time among the people of your United States."

"Where, then, for shelter?" Johnson began packing the supplies.

The ranch hand directed Johnson to an arroyo where he would find shade, where he could light a small fire without detection, where he'd find a small spring. "Sometimes just moisture on the rocks," the man said, "but you will suckle enough to keep from thirst."

The man was specific in his directions. Johnson was sure he'd given the same ones just an hour before. Johnson would soon be pursued. "I will go there," he told the man, "and I thank you for your trouble."

"*De nada*," said the man.

Johnson wished it were nothing, but it was everything. His life had two directions ever since he'd come to know Jo Benson. One was a future—they would marry, he would raise horses, they would have children, free from the bounds of their pasts. The other was the past he created each day, disconnected from Jo, farther from her than he'd ever been, farther from their future. He mounted The Stud and urged him in the direction the man had pointed. Once they were out of sight, he turned from Monterrey and began the journey north toward home.

He rode for two days and two nights before he stopped in the hills south of Laredo. He did not seem to be pursued. He found a niche between some rocks and nearly fell off The Stud. He awoke at nightfall, hungry and thirsty. He'd not found water in a day, and the agave he'd cut into was a thick drink to suck down. Johnson had been spare with his meat, sucking it as he rode. But the iron richness was turning rank, and when he found a jackrabbit sitting nearby, watching him, he shot it with the Spanish cavalry pistol he had held in his hand even as he slept. He built a fire of mesquite. He slit the rabbit's throat and drank as much blood as was left, though in this hot land nothing had enough fluid. He gutted the gangly thing, skinned it, and once the fire was burned to coals he placed it right on top. Watching meat cook, he'd once thought, was one difference between humans and animals. A dog would rip into flesh, fresh or rotten, with full-toothed hunger. Animal as he'd become, Johnson hardly let himself hear the sizzle of what paltry fat this rabbit had stored, hardly smelled the cooking meat before he lifted it from the fire.

As he bit into the thick muscle of the hind leg, a rock scrunched behind him. "Two fugitives," a voice said.

Johnson knew who had found him, but didn't turn around. "You including yourself?" he asked.

"Just you and the horse," said the man. "I return the horse to Sanchez. My journey with you will take longer."

Johnson dropped the rabbit to the fire and turned to face MacDonald. The man was still mounted, but his horse might be outrun. "I've brought you a long ways." Johnson whistled and The Stud showed himself from around a rock.

MacDonald took a small sack from his shirt pocket and pulled some tobacco into his mouth. His horse shifted under his weight. "Memphis. Arkansas. San Antonio. Laredo. Monterrey." He shook his head. "I've pushed *you* a long ways. But no more pushing. This is the end of it."

"Fine by me," said Johnson. "I was just keeping away from my trouble." The Stud reared and MacDonald's horse backed away. In spite of himself, Johnson's eyes wandered to his percussion pistol, now empty, on the ground near the fire.

"You're sure enough in trouble. Right here, and back in Tennessee." MacDonald spit tobacco juice and wiped his mouth.

"Tennessee is my home," said Johnson. He wondered where the man kept his weapons. He backed toward The Stud when the man took off his hat and wiped the sweat from his forehead.

"You got no home," the bounty hunter said. "You been riding so long, I'll wager you don't know a thing about Tennessee."

"You a gambler?" asked Johnson. The meat on the coals burned acrid in his nostrils. His stomach roiled. He backed up slowly until his hand found The Stud's head.

"I do have a bet," said MacDonald. "One that will pay off right handsome when I play my hand."

The Stud nuzzled Johnson's hand, and Johnson moved to the horse's withers. He might well have to make a break for it, bareback. "You bet on horses?" asked Johnson. "For you don't have much of a horse there." He looked behind him again, at the small pile of his saddle, at his pistol, at the saddlebag where he kept powder and shot. The rabbit was black and smoking.

"When you bet on a horse," said MacDonald, "you're never sure what she might do." The man nudged his horse forward, turned her as though to block Johnson's escape. Johnson saw the butt of a rifle in a long holster behind the man's leg. "Now a man," said MacDonald, "a man is more of a sure bet. A man will run when he's in trouble. And the more he runs, the more you *know* he's in trouble."

"My trouble seems to be with you," said Johnson.

"See how predictable the human being can be?" asked the man. "See how you calculate your horse against mine even as we speak? How your legs twitch to mount and run away again?" He removed the rifle, a Kentucky flintlock, from its holster, pulled back the cock, and laid it across his lap.

"What do you want from me?" asked Johnson.

"I want what is wanted," said the man. "I want to take you back to Tennessee. I want the reward that's on your head."

"How much is the bounty?" asked Johnson.

"Two hundred dollars," said the man.

"I'll pay you twice that to leave me alone," said Johnson. He took two steps back, toward his saddle.

The bounty hunter raised his rifle. "You've obviously made a mistake," MacDonald sneered. With the rifle he directed Johnson away from his gear. "You think all I want is money. You're too young to know how much I hate you."

"Hate me?" Johnson asked.

"You learn about a man, tracking him," said MacDonald. "You are in cahoots with that nigger lover Hiram Gillian. You are the despoiler of my niece, a girl too young for defilement. You are a horse thief. A gambler. A drinker. A carouser." The man raised his rifle, pointed it at Johnson's heart. "It ain't just money I'm after."

"Am I wanted dead or alive?" asked Johnson.

"If I shoot you now, you'll be a mighty stink before Tennessee."

Johnson had heard of bounty hunters shooting their prey in the foot, or blowing an arm off at the elbow. Wanted alive didn't say in what condition. "You'll wait until we're in Tennessee, will you?" asked Johnson.

"Haven't decided," said the gambler. He spat a glob that rolled in the dirt.

"You won't be able to kill me," said Johnson. "The closer we get, the more you'll want me alive."

"Dead men are always a hard loss to my reputation," said MacDonald. "But a dead man with money. Well, now, that's *two* rewards. How much do you have? Enough to salve the wound to my reputation? I'd have your little sum. And then the sheriff's. I might have enough to stake myself. Maybe marry a pretty little girl like Jo Benson. Her child will be needing a father."

Johnson had wondered, when the time came, if he'd be able to kill. Now, he did not think at all. He jumped to his pistol, then over his saddlebag, pulling it close for protection, then dragging it and himself behind the rock where The Stud had been searching for grass. The horse moved with him. Johnson scrabbled in his saddlebag, wondering what MacDonald would do. No shot, no movement that he could hear. Just the silence of assurance that chilled Johnson even as he removed powder and shot and, hands shaking, prepared a charge.

"You forget," MacDonald called out. "I'm a patient man. I have a pistol, too. And so two shots to your one. You come out with your hands up, and we'll do business. You come out firing and you're dead. I'll take your horse, your money, your ears, and that'll be the end of it. I'll leave your body to turn black as this jackrabbit."

Charge ready, Johnson steadied his hand. He'd carried firearms most of his life. He'd hunted with the long rifle of his youth, brought squirrels down from trees, lucked onto deer and brought them down. He'd held a pistol to his first horse's head, removed Blaze from the misery of a broken leg upon which she would never walk again. He'd carried his uncle Judson's pistol, the old Daw .60 caliber, unsure if he would use it.

After all the miles, all the hardship, the hunger, the desperadoes he'd encountered and the desperado he'd become, Johnson jerked his cavalry pistol to the level and threw himself from behind the rock. MacDonald had dismounted, was kneeling beneath his horse, rifle barrel jutting out. Johnson found nothing to shoot at but the barrel of the rifle pointed at him—surely the man's head was at the other end of it. He shot. The spark and a double pop told him MacDonald had shot, too.

The man who gambled and lost lurched forward and thudded to the ground, blood gushing from the hole in his throat. The man's horse reared so violently Johnson had no chance at the reins. He saw nothing of the roan mare but her tail, nearly erect as she ran away. The Stud came from behind the rock and whinnied after her, stamping his front feet.

Johnson stood in shock. Then he began to shake. His knees buckled and he put his hands to the ground, where blood waded into the dust from the gushing gurgle of the bounty hunter's last breaths. Johnson's ear buzzed. With a spastic hand he felt his head. His left ear was tattered and his hand returned red to his sight. He pulled his hat low, over his ear, to create pressure, to hide the blood. He still had to haul a body, sweep the area clean of that thick liquid. MacDonald, the bounty hunter, the man who had most wanted to find him, was dead.

His chewed ear under his hat, his hearing dead on that side, Robert Johnson was still alive. He went to MacDonald's thick body and turned him over enough to slip the Kentucky rifle from between his grasping hands. "Two shots," the man had said. Johnson used the rifle to leverage the body onto its back. The derringer was underneath him, and loaded. The man's vest contained a small bag with powder and shot. And a pouch, not heavy with lead, but silver and gold. In a fold of leather inside the other vest flap, a letter. If ever Johnson wished for the ability to read, he wished for it then, for he ciphered the script of his name, written over several times in ink at the beginning and end of the short statement. Because he expected the words, he thought he could read *dead*, and *wanted*, and *Pleasant View, Tennessee*, and *murder, Sheriff McFall, April 1825*. He didn't know if MacDonald could read or if he had traveled all the miles to find Johnson with the same blind instinct that made Johnson put all those miles between them.

He put the contents of the man's vest and the pistol into his saddlebag, then tied the rifle behind the saddle. He stooped down to drag the body into the rocks. He backed down a small ravine, a wash for what little rain ever found this country, and hauled the body as far as he could. Then he lifted a few rocks to the chest, the legs, the arms, to pin the body down. No sense in someone finding a dog with a man's arm jutting from its jaws.

His fire was out, the rabbit burned crisp. Johnson tried to find something edible, but tasted only the charred ashes of the rabbit's death. He threw down the meat, repulsed suddenly by blood, fire, ash. The Stud had already moved down the trail, and Johnson knew that his horse's instincts were probably better than his own. "I'm coming," he said, his first words since he'd killed MacDonald. He set himself for home, well armed, and rich in gold and silver. He took even richer consolation in some of MacDonald's hateful words: Jo was indeed with child.

Johnson kept to hills, bluffs, and ravines, anything craggy. He doubted that anyone would wonder about the fate of the bounty hunter, just another tobacco-stained traveler between Monterrey and Laredo. But Johnson had ridden away from a rich man's track on a claimed horse. He must return there or fear being hunted all over again. He had not truly won The Stud. He had to hope his compadres at Diego's ranch might let him go.

Another two days would bring him to Laredo. Johnson wondered why the whole landscape did not spontaneously combust. Rock burned his hands, water in the few streams shimmered in its evaporation into a sky so blue his eyes lost themselves in its vastness. The small islands of habitation were but outposts in Hell, cool oases that served mostly to remind the traveler what not to expect on the trails between them. Johnson kept the sun to his left in the morning, to his right in the evening, but he might have been marking time. The landscape, unchanging, mocked him.

The dry air sucked the moisture from him. He was trapped under the monotonous canopy of blue sky. Among the rocks and bluffs he was cramped and exposed. The Stud, with rare green eyes, often tilted his head as though to look at the sky. When Johnson looked into The Stud's eyes, they were blue. Had they been green only in forested country? How far they were from home. In the past months Johnson's bland tongue had come to know the taste of skunk, grasshopper, snake, and cactus. His parched mouth had burned with whiskey, mescal, tequila, pulque. His horse racing had brought stakes, purses. He had been pursued for miles, not just around a track. His innocent hands were stained in blood. And now The Stud's green eyes were blue. Blue as Johnson's heart. The Bensons had burned his cabin—again he saw his year of work in flame. The old saddle horn would be there, melted askew, fallen into the strewn fieldstones of his foundation. Johnson imagined it still hot to the touch, plumes of smoke rising from ashes that would soon be dust.

On the third day, Johnson discerned a sparse fur of trees in the distance, where water crossed the landscape. A river, coursing in the distance, glistened with sun. He did not know if he was east or west of Laredo. He could cross the Rio Grande, head straight to Tennessee. But running would mean renewed pursuit, even as his run from Tennessee had brought him nothing but peril. He'd been running because he had so much to lose. And yet in running he had lost everything. When he reached the river, he and his horse plunged in. They drank, they bathed. Johnson cleaned the scabs from his ear and looked at his reflection. His ear was shredded at the top, nothing more.

He guessed Nuevo Laredo was northwest. He tried to form a plan, but when he looked at The Stud's blue eyes he told himself, *No more plans.*

The sparse adobe of the fledgling town nestled among trees. Johnson sat straighter in the saddle and urged The Stud forward. In Diego's stable, he would find Isabella. He approached the ranch, pulling out his pistol, loaded and ready. He rode into the gate, past the track, toward the large stable. The men nodded to each other, began to gather like birds swirling to a dust-leafed tree. All the hands appeared, as though they'd been waiting. Out of the darkness of the stable, stout, bowlegged, his boots still shiny, Lucky marched into the sunlight, pulled off his hat, flapped it against his leg, and put it back on. "Well, well, well," he said, his voice high.

Johnson let the reins fall. The Stud stopped.

"We've been expecting you." Lucky circled his arm to include the hands gathered to watch whatever might take place.

Johnson surveyed the hands, those men he'd run against, drunk with, who had kept him awake when he'd wanted to sleep. They watched him with interest, but not alarm. He put his pistol back in his belt. "This is my horse," said Johnson. "Stolen from me by Indians. Way up by San Antonio. He ain't much to look at now, but he's more horse than any I've seen before or since."

"We wondered that you took to him so," said Lucky, striding toward Johnson now that the pistol was tucked away.

"I have another horse," said Johnson.

"I understand you might feel that way," said Lucky.

"I'm going to pay for her." Johnson opened his saddlebag and reached for MacDonald's small pouch. "More than she's worth." He threw a handful of coins in the dust at Lucky's feet.

"You forget the horse you doctored," said Lucky. "The one that fell on the track? She still ain't recovered." He stooped to pick up the money.

"It was *your* sugar sickened that horse," said Johnson. He pulled his pistol from his belt. "Isabella would be just like her if I'd done what you told me. You have *not* been my friend."

Stooped to the dust for gold, Lucky did not notice the pistol. When he stood up, he shook his head like a horse startled from its feed bag. He grinned. "Lucky me," he said. "For in the dark of the stable behind me, three men have their rifles trained on you. You will put your pistol away. You will turn slowly. You will ride away. Nobody will follow you."

Johnson threw more money to the ground. He turned and swept his arm to include all the hands. "*Dinero*," he shouted, sweeping his arm to include them all. "*Por todo. Cada hombre tiene dinero allá.*"

The men turned to each other, whispered, some of them grinning. Not at the prospect of money. Or his broken Spanish. But because they knew Lucky. Johnson put his pistol in his belt and rode directly into the stable. He braced himself, but no rifle shots blasted his ears, no bullets penetrated his scrawny frame. He was free to find Isabella's stall. He grabbed a rope halter from a nail on the wall. He leaned over to swing open the stall door for a horse that recognized him, and took the halter, and followed him into sunlight.

Impossibly, not a man stood where the whole of them were gathered but seconds before. Of course not, for if they watched him, they'd be to blame. They'd have to tell Diego what happened, and about the money. They'd have to follow him. He and The Stud ran, Isabella as eager as they were, away from the ranch north, toward the Rio Grande.

The lies he faced in Tennessee seemed simple by comparison with what he'd experienced on the road. Surely someone—his uncle Judson or even his father—would help him unravel the knot of the Bensons' accusations. His Hatfield Kentucky rifle? Uncle Judson would know they'd stolen it. He'd see Jo, big with child, and he'd want to make that right, knowing how much his nephew loved her. He'd find out that she was the one to sew the *R.J.* into his handkerchief, the one she'd kept as a token of love. And her father and brothers had found it and forced her to give it to them. Surely they'd tied her up so she could not slip away to warn him of their plans.

These knots tied into knots could be no worse than this country, this exile, where The Stud lost his green eyes in the Mexico sun. Johnson would ride home proudly, tall on his mount, beginning with the streets of Laredo, taking on whatever came his way.

His resolve took him unmolested through Nuevo Laredo, across the Rio Grande, onto the streets where anyone who approached him would note his glare, his piercing eyes. Even the cock of his hat would tell them he was moving through, hell-bent to somewhere beyond what they could fathom. Only one man stood up. "Aren't you . . . ?" the man began, but Johnson merely spurred The Stud, who raised his tail, dropped a turd and, Isabella in tow, ran toward all that awaited them— girl, baby, home.

Antonio

For all of Robert Johnson's eagerness, the days passed slowly. Hot, parched, with little to fuel him but desire, Johnson marshaled his few resources in anticipation of the oasis of San José y San Miguel de Aguayo. After a week of riding, he sighted a cross atop a dome, the one he'd seen in mirage so many times. He felt more wary than relieved. He backtracked until he was certain nobody who might be watching from the mission could see him. He tied Isabella to a tree. He patted her on the rump. "Won't be long," he said.

He rode at a run to the mission gate, half expecting it to open in the face of his hoofbeats. He was forced to bang on the large wooden door. When he had no answer, he took his pistol from his saddlebag and shot it into the air. He waited, impatient, until voices on the other side assured him the place was not abandoned. Two ladder poles appeared above the wall, and Tequan's face peered at him from above, a frowning stare turning to a smile.

"Fray Antonio?" Johnson asked. "*¿Está aquí?*"

"*Sí*," and the head disappeared.

The thick door opened, but only wide enough to allow Johnson and The Stud to pass into the compound. "What the hell? *¿Qué?*" Johnson asked. In the two months since he'd left, the gardens had been burned. Some of the rooftops of the Indian dwellings were blackened as well, cinders crumbling in front of doorways, now mostly empty.

Tequan said nothing while Johnson surveyed the damage. He put his hand on The Stud's shoulder. "*¿Y Isabella?*" he asked.

130

"Isabella?" Johnson repeated, shrugging his shoulders.

Tequan frowned. Johnson took a gold piece from his pocket. "For you," he said, his palm up, gold ready for Tequan to take.

"*No*," said the Indian. "*No necesito.*"

Fray Antonio approached. "*Necesitas*," said Johnson. He reached into his pocket for the five more pieces of gold he would offer as thanks for the brother's care. "For you. For the mission," he said to Antonio.

"Come," said Antonio, "Tequan will care for your horse."

"I can't stay," said Johnson.

"You do not trust us with your horse? As we should not have trusted you with our Isabella?" Antonio turned and walked toward the mission buildings, leaving Johnson with palm outstretched.

"You want the gold?" Johnson shouted.

Fray Antonio turned quickly, his robes rising, then settling. "A man so suddenly generous surely has more than gold to offer."

"What do you mean?" asked Johnson.

"You have stolen your freedom. You have stolen our horse. Terrible things have happened to us since you left." He swept his arm to the damage Johnson had observed, but he included the charred remains of the stable as well. "Our Indians have most of them left. The vaqueros as well. All but Juan Francisco. And now you have no time to sit with us?"

Johnson was about to dismount when hoofbeats pounded to the gate. Juan slipped through, on Rayo, the horse who had been ridden by Diaz. Behind him was Isabella. "I'll pay you well for her," Johnson said to Antonio.

Antonio examined her, running his hand along the Diego brand. He spoke a rapid Spanish with Juan Francisco. "She will stay here. This is her home," the brother said. He checked her hooves, front then back.

"I'll treat her as well as she'll be treated here," said Johnson.

"As well as you've treated her these months past?" Antonio stood behind her.

"I went to Laredo. The Mexicans branded her. Tried to steal her." Johnson still held the coins, bunched in his fist. "I got her back. And looks to me like you need this gold."

"You will not stay?" asked Antonio.

"I wanted to pay you something for your trouble. I hoped for food and water." His hand began to tremble. "Here, take these."

Antonio let him sit atop his horse, arm outstretched.

"You may take what you need. But you may not take what *we* need. You took Isabella from us just as you have taken yourself from the world. When the only thing that pursues you is your own folly." Antonio strode from behind Isabella. He said something to Tequan in the Indian language.

"I was pursued," Johnson said. "MacDonald said San Antonio. He was here."

"I do not know a MacDonald," said Fray Antonio.

"Liar!" shouted Johnson. "Tell me. This fire. Was it Indians? Were you attacked from outside or inside?"

Fray Antonio raised his right hand, perhaps asking silence, perhaps avoiding memory, perhaps blessing what was left of the mission. Tequan disappeared inside the living quarters. Fray Antonio followed.

In spite of the brother's scolding, Johnson hoped Tequan would return with water, and dried beef, no matter how stringy. He flung the coins to the parched ground. "I am pursued no longer!" he shouted. "I am not the Thomas who doubted! I am going back to Tennessee!"

Antonio walked out of the shadow of the doorway. He raised both his hands. "I have instructed Tequan to take care of you. Juan?" Juan Francisco took Isabella's reins and led her toward what was left of the stable. Antonio walked into the mission, darkness swallowing him.

The small bit of gold gilt painted on the edge of the mission dome looked as feeble in the sun as the few coins Johnson had flung to the ground. Tequan returned carrying two skins already sweating water. A leather bag, bulging with food, slapped at his back. Johnson pointed to the coins. "For you, too," he said.

Tequan handed him the water bags and Johnson tied them to the saddle horn. He slung the bag of food over his shoulder. Neither Juan Francisco nor Fray Antonio appeared to mark his departure. Tequan walked to the gate.

Johnson turned his horse and hurried through. When the great door slammed after him, he looked one last time at the dome of the mission. How grand a structure, how failed an outpost. The Stud trotted toward the horizon.

They headed due east, hoping to avoid another encounter with Indians. Days passed without signs of human habitation, no smoke from fire, no pathways trod with more than the hooves of antelope, no fire circles along the creek banks where the thin trees gathered to drink. A few sparse herds of buffalo, no more than a couple dozen, grazed on distant rises. He turned north. Perhaps the Indians had retreated to more permanent homes to harvest their squash, corn, and beans. In the cooling nights, coyotes yodeled to each other over the ridges as they hunted mice and prairie chickens. Owls hooted as if to voice their disapproval as they hunted the same mice. Through those moonlit nights, Johnson thought of Tennessee. He would wrest Jo from her brothers and pa. Together they would find land, make a home far from their troubles in Pleasant View, far from his troubles in Laredo. Between those two points they would find a peaceful life.

After several days, Johnson found himself increasingly unafraid of anyone he might find on the trail. He carried rifle and pistols by his side. Each day, he scared up a jackrabbit, squirrel, or bird. Each night he stopped to cook what he'd shot.

When the flames died and the small brush and limbs he'd gathered broke to embers, and the meat was cooked, he lay his head on the saddle, hands folded on his chest, and listened to The Stud grazing nearby on grass. Always, Jo's voice came next, gentle, like a breeze trying to fan coal to flame. "My Robert," he conjured her voice, "I have missed you. I want to care for you. I want you to care for me. If only I knew where you were." The voice continued from there, sometimes for an hour or more, but always ended with, "They burn all my letters to you."

In his exhaustion, thoughts restless, he actually heard her voice, as surely as if she lay beside him. If he unfolded his hands to touch her, the voice would stop, the coals would smoke sharpness into his eyes. So he listened, motionless, then slept until first bird. He found water, saddled his horse, and rode toward that imploring voice, answering her through the miles. "I come. I will find you, and together we'll ride home."

Home would have to be Arkansas. When he crossed the Red River, he would seek rather than avoid people, except for Nancy, and her ill-fated outpost. He did not want to see how she was doing. He'd continue east, cross south of that place, then veer north, exploring new territory.

loped

Once he crossed the Red River, Robert Johnson felt easier, though he had miles to go. Each time he came to a creek, he followed it for a time, even though he found it hard to meander. But after he found Jo, they would need a place to settle. He rode through piney woods, peered over bluffs above rivers, found ragged settlements mottling the sky with smoke.

He talked to few people, but when a traveling preacher began to follow along, Johnson attempted to find out what the man knew about Arkansas. The preacher seemed bent on saving Johnson's soul. When the preacher would ask, "Do you believe in our Lord?" or something like it, Johnson would say, "I believe *you* must know where the finest people are settling around here," and if Johnson asked, "Have you seen people with horses?" the preacher might say, "We are all beasts, carrying the burden of our lost souls from place to place."

Johnson soon tired of this man who likely carried more sweat in his clothes and grease in his hair than he did belief in his heart. He kneed his horse for distance, but the preacher clopped behind him on what Johnson had misjudged to be a dauncy mare. They stopped at a thin creek, with sweet water, and their horses drank, as did they. "Fine horse," said the preacher. "Runs well." He dipped his dirty hat in the stream and put it on, water cascading down his round face, his chest. "Yet another baptism." He grinned, one front tooth black. "But just what else would you expect from a preacher by the name of John. John Macy. Yours?" He held out his hand.

"Robert Jenkins," said Johnson. He did not take the offered hand, filthy and wet.

"This here horse, Magi, is part of a conversion," the preacher said. "The gift of a sinner brought to belief. Another stray lamb, now in the fold."

"You came out ahead in that conversion, no doubt," said Johnson.

"Do not underestimate the value of that woman's soul," said Macy. "But gracious, how Magi can ride. Though not to the pace of your horse, I would guess."

"The Stud," said Johnson. "A Tennessee stud."

"That where you're headed?" asked Macy.

"I must not stray much longer," said Johnson. He pulled himself onto the saddle.

"You've strayed, have you?" asked the preacher. "But of course you have." He mounted Magi. "I'm headed your direction, as you can see," he said.

"Ever since we met," admitted Johnson.

"To lead we must follow," said the preacher.

"I don't see followers," said Johnson, lifting his arm in a circle to include the trees that lined the creek, the grass on the hillock, the sky, just beginning to scud with clouds.

"You've raced that horse, I'll wager. And in a horse race, you want nothing but followers. Same with the good Lord. You might not see them behind you, but that might just be your victory. They go elsewhere, to lead the sanctified life, to bring more followers into the fold, perhaps into glory. All of those behind you might stand for your victory, and yet will not see them as you end the race."

"I've had my sight on one end for some time." Johnson turned his horse toward a shallow in the creek, pushed him up the opposite bank. There, he turned in the saddle.

John Macy was close behind, whipping Magi with a small quirt. "You wouldn't want a race, would you?" called the preacher. "You have any stake but the Tennessee horse you ride?"

Johnson stopped where the stand of trees gave way to grass. At the top of a far hill a lone elm stood. "The Stud is my riches, of course. But my future is my real riches. And that's where I'm headed."

The preacher stuck out his tongue, licked his lips, smiled. "You're right, young man. Our riches are our deeds, in all we give to others. On the other hand, I usually find a bit of gold when I rummage in my bag here." He raised his eyebrows.

"Gold?" asked Johnson. "You've been busy with the collection plate?"

"I give more than I take," said Macy. He brought out two gold coins. "Up to yonder tree, around it, and back," he said. "Leave the money here. First one back collects it."

Johnson took two coins from the small sack he carried. He secured his gear, tossed the coins onto the ground, sat tall in the saddle, patted his horse's neck. "I'm ready when you say *the word*," Johnson said.

"And the word was with gold," said John Macy. "And the word is *go!*" He smacked Magi and the horse bolted up the hill.

Johnson kicked The Stud's flanks and the horse bore down, following Magi. For a brief time he gained on her, then not, and she was four lengths ahead and not slowing her pace. The western landscape, as Johnson had discovered, always lied about distance, and though they threw themselves toward it, the tree seemed to recede from them. When the preacher finally reached it, the wide elm dwarfed horse and rider in their turning. But when he came around to start his descent toward the gold, John Macy was flogging Magi like a sinner in a public square. He raised his fist.

The Stud was tired. His ordeal, like Johnson's, had been long and hard. Neither had eaten nor slept, drunk nor rested well for so many days they'd lost count. This small race seemed nothing to the long race home to Tennessee. He did not want to follow the man back to the money. He rode to the huge elm that had no doubt stood above the green valley with its gradual hills since long before the Testaments had been brought to this God-fearing country by those fleeing its misuse in England. Though The Stud wanted to turn, Johnson urged him down the opposite hill, toward a distant spot where he could choose to move between one of three rises, where, if he hurried, he would be well hidden by the time John Macy pursued him. Let the preacher have the collection.

Down they ran. No rider followed them. In losing, he had won, though he did not let his horse slow down. They finally reached the juncture of hills, and chose a path among trees, where a small creek eventually joined the one they'd just run from. One hill, then another, then they could rest against a bluff.

So they did, as night fell around them. No food, for Johnson could not chance a shot, nor the lighting of a fire. They drank. Johnson leaned against a rock outcrop, rifle loaded and lying in his lap, his ears cocked like the rifle, until he drifted into sleep.

He was awakened by a voice. "Some run from righteousness into sin," John Macy said, his foot on the long barrel of Johnson's rifle.

Johnson removed his hands from the rifle to rub his eyes. "What in hell do you want?" he asked. "More money?"

"I am a man of the Lord," said the preacher. He pulled the rifle from Johnson's lap. "See how you sleep the sleep of the guilty, weapon at the ready? I want to lead you away from your sins." He turned the rifle onto Johnson.

"There's only one sin I want to be led from," said Johnson. "*Your* sin. The sin of righteousness. My father's righteousness is all he has left. He lost his son, then his wife. He's lost me. He hates his neighbors. All because he's more righteous than any of us.

"John Macy, you are no different from me, except your righteousness lets you believe that your mission is sanctified and mine is selfish. But you're wrong." He pulled his pistol from where it lay just behind him. "The pistol is loaded," he said. "The rifle is not."

"Why should I believe you?" asked the preacher.

"Because you are a believer. Or, I could quickly make a believer of you." Johnson leveled the pistol at Macy's chest. He held up his other hand. "When I bring my hand down, let's both pull the trigger. See who lives and who dies."

John Macy threw the rifle down.

Johnson picked up the weapon and fired it into the air. He mounted The Stud, wondering where Macy kept his own firearm. Might the man wait, ride after him, threaten him, maybe even shoot him for his horse and his money?

The man simply smiled. "You should think about becoming a preacher," he said. "Are you off to find your girl, then?"

"I didn't say anything about a girl."

"No need. I have often seen how carnal love clogs a man's heart. You have a good horse, but you might get him in better shape before you reach Tennessee."

"Best advice you've given me since we met," said Johnson.

"Thanks for what you left in the collection plate," said John Macy. He mounted Magi. "I didn't always use my tracking skills for good," said the man.

"Nor I for bad," said Johnson.

"Maybe we'll meet again," said Macy.

Johnson rode away into a morning sun just reddening the horizon. He shook his head. He'd said more before breakfast than he usually said in a week. He longed for the Mississippi River.

A couple of evenings later, seeking shelter against a bluff much like the one where he'd spent the night hiding from John Macy, he saw someone lying down, back against a rock. A woman, he saw as he neared, so still and gray he knew he'd found death. He was surprised no creature had disturbed the body, which rested peacefully, head lifted to the sky. Her thin lips were slightly parted, her eyelids closed, her long brown hair down, framing a round and pleasant face. Her dress was disturbed, wrinkled around her waist, where Johnson saw the dark stain that meant blood. He gagged, nearly retched, and turned for distance. He did not want to have to smell her. Perhaps she'd died of some malady of womanhood, resting in this place, peaceful as it seemed. He turned to her again. The darkness around her throat, just above the plain collar of her dress, made him retch again. And turn The Stud quickly to the woods, toward open country. He'd find another place to shelter.

The next evening he directed his horse toward what he hoped was a cooking fire. As he neared the trace of habitation, he found a path. A log cabin, small like the one he'd built for himself in Tennessee, showed itself. The rock chimney loosed an occasional thread of smoke, but the cooking was probably complete.

He stopped at shouting distance. "Haloo!" he warbled. "Anybody to home?"

A rifle barrel appeared before a man followed it onto a small porch. He was a big man, fully bearded, long hair wild on his head. "Who be you?" he asked. "Any news?"

Johnson almost replied with, *I'm John Macy, a preacher*, but he was tired of being all the things he wasn't—criminal, fugitive, horse thief. "Robert Johnson's my name. On my way to Tennessee, Pleasant View. My girl waits for me there."

"Come closer," said the man.

Johnson dismounted and led The Stud toward the cabin. The sun was nearly set, and the gray trees were turning black against a deep blue sky. The sudden smell of meat came like a fist in his gut. "How far to

Tennessee?" he asked. "I am eager for home." He dropped the reins and held up his hand.

"Good reason to be an Arkansawyer," said the man, leaning forward to appraise the danger that might lurk in this stranger.

Johnson stopped twenty feet from the porch. "I'm hungry. I could trade you work for food, or even pay you in gold."

"I've learned not to trust men who have gold," said the man, though he lowered the rifle. "I'd rather trade the work. I need a horse. You tie yours and come in."

Johnson did as he was told. On the porch he dipped his hands in a bucket and splashed water on his face. "I've been traveling a long time," he confessed, "with a long ways yet to go. If desire could speed me, I'd have been home long ago."

"We've been waiting," said the man. "That slows you down, too. Come in."

Johnson followed and the man motioned to a seat at the table. His rifle leaned against the bricks of the fireplace. A young girl hovered over some dishes next to the hearth. Johnson nodded in her direction, but she would not meet his glance. "I thank you," said Johnson. He'd not had the comfort of a chair in a long time, and he leaned back and stretched his legs.

The man set a plate before him. A slab of venison and some johnny-cakes smothered in molasses. "I can cook you an egg or two, if you'd like," he said. "We were saving them for the morning."

Johnson shook his head. The man took the chair across from him. Johnson's belly had tightened at first, then expanded for more. He knew he should talk, but he was mesmerized by food, plate, table, chair, all luxuries he'd only conjured these past weeks. "I can't thank you enough," he said finally.

"You'll thank me plenty tomorrow. We'll haul rock for half a day before we let you get on your way. Foundation for a barn. New country, and not always easy, but we like it well enough."

"Many people in these parts?" Johnson asked.

"We're filling up. And we're filling up this little cabin, too. My wife, my Katherine, she took a turn, though." He ran his fingers through his wild hair, but he was not a wild man. Tears welled in his eyes.

"Where is she?" asked Johnson.

"That's why we're waiting," said the man. "Daughter?" The girl climbed a ladder into a loft and disappeared behind a curtain. The man lowered his voice. "Woman trouble," he said. "Had a cramping something awful. Worried she'd lose the baby. Thanks to God we got some help." He stood up and paced the side of the table. "Preacher came by. As ugly on the outside as he was kind of heart. Knew the Bible backward and forward. He knew a place where a healing woman lived, someone who'd saved mothers and babies all her life. He took Katherine in his arms a week ago, led Maggie behind so Katherine could ride her home soon as she was well."

Johnson's heart seized his chest. He nearly choked. His food turned to stone in his belly.

"We just have the one horse," the man said. "So we wait. You got our hopes up for a slim bit of time, but she don't have your voice, singing at us like you did."

Johnson nodded. "Did that preacher have a name?" he asked finally.

"John," said the man. "Like the Baptist. Last name of Mackey."

"Ugly, you said?" asked Johnson. "One front tooth dark, like it needs pulling?" He pushed his plate to the middle of the table.

"Something wrong?" asked the man.

Johnson could not bring himself to speak. The little girl's head peeked through the crease of the curtain above the rafters. He stood and walked onto the porch, struggling for air. The man joined him. Together they stared at the sky. A crescent moon tried to enclose a star. "And your Katherine. A slight woman, with brown hair? Round face?" Johnson asked finally.

"You've seen her?" the man asked eagerly.

Johnson could not say *yes*, though the man wanted him to. But the man would not want to know what that yes would mean. "Just heard tell," said Johnson.

"Where?" asked the man.

"Something from a stranger who admired my horse." Johnson took the bucket of water to The Stud. Then he climbed down the porch stairs and took the saddle off his horse, whose head was sunk to nearby grass. "I'm looking forward to a little work in the morning," Johnson said. "I'll lie down on the porch here. I thank you."

The man took a deep breath, sighed. "You didn't see them, then?"

"Not them," said Johnson, as close to the truth as a lie could be.

"Evening, then," said the man.

Johnson waited until silence told him the man and his daughter were settled. He saddled The Stud and rode into a deep night, his heart as shrouded as the moon, which had been overtaken by a gauze of thin cloud. Even The Stud seemed to know they had to retrace their steps, each so hard won. They could find Katherine by midday, return her to her family by the following evening. The man would wonder at Johnson's disappearance, but that mystery, once solved, would be the smallest of the mysteries he'd have to comprehend.

They could not ride fast, because of the night and their exhaustion, but by daybreak their plodding turned to earnest search. Johnson trusted The Stud to know where they'd been, realizing how often his mind had drifted when the horse's senses were alert to their passing. The sinking of his heart told him when they were nearing the outcrop, the bluff where they would find the body. The approach was terrible. Johnson was unsure he could do what he knew he should do—pick up her body, carry her home to the grief that waited there.

The body was gone. They stopped just where they'd stopped on their journey. Johnson dismounted. He neared the spot where she'd been propped against the rock. The earth was still stained with her blood. He rose quickly and ran to The Stud. As he mounted, a rifle shot sounded from above, the whistling bullet close. He weaved his body, trying to elude the preacher's bead. They headed into the woods. Another shot sounded, and Johnson thought to turn, to hunt the hunter, to kill the murderer, to recover the horse, Magi, Maggie. But he could not turn his sadness and disgust into violence. He flew away, stopping only for water from the occasional creeks. The Stud knew the way. Johnson practiced for what was to come.

He arrived at nightfall, hallooing from a distance, just as he had the evening before. Again the rifle, the man. This time, "You stay right where you are. I'll kill you."

Johnson raised his hands into the air. "Kill me and you'll silence the news I have for you. Though it's terrible news."

"Katherine?" asked the man. He nearly crumpled, as though he'd suspected all along what might have happened, kept it locked at the back of his mind. He began to wail. The little girl came out the door to stand over him.

Johnson nudged The Stud forward. As he reached the porch, the man quit wailing and sat up. The girl perched in his lap. Johnson took off his hat.

"Go ahead and tell what you have to tell," the man said. "Kate will learn the cruel way of the world sometime."

Johnson sat on the porch stair, not quite facing them, not able to look into their eyes as he told of the preacher, the horse Magi, the man's unpleasantness, the race, the encounter the next morning, "When I should have shot him," Johnson said. Then Katherine, dead. "I went to bring her to you," Johnson said. "The sad errand nearly cost me my life. May yet cost me." At that, the girl flew inside. "Should you ever see the man again," Johnson said, "John Macy, John Mackey, whatever he calls himself, shoot him dead and I'll be among the thankful." Johnson fingered the coins he'd already removed from his saddlebags. "Do you know people nearby?" he asked.

The man nodded, his eyes streaming with tears.

"I'd get the girl to them before I went looking for the preacher," Johnson said. "You'll need a horse." He stood and held out the gold, pinched between two fingers, ready to drop the coins in the man's hand. But the man stared away. The little girl came back outside, her hand cupped for the money. "I'd best be on my way," Johnson said. "Remember my name. Robert Johnson. If I ever come back, you can consider me a friend. Now, you must forgive me. I must ride. Even if I, too, ride toward sadness." He mounted The Stud and hurried away, bone sick and weary, for who was to say that anything might unfold as wished for in this world.

He'd seen terrible things in Arkansas. But he'd seen horrifying things everywhere. He could settle north, but he'd heard that Missouri was already being called Misery since that territory had become a state. Arkansas, with its grasslands, streams, and woods, game still teeming, seemed only tarnished in its promise. In Arkansas, at least the criminals were vagabonds, whereas in Tennessee they'd all settled down, like the Bensons.

The thought of them made him kick The Stud toward home and away from the man and his daughter, from the horse thief who masqueraded as minister, who mistook murder for righteousness, who would have killed him for The Stud and called it a conversion.

Bonne

from then on, if The Stud had rested well and found rich grass, Robert Johnson raced him once in the morning, once late in the afternoon. The horse had been so mistreated he'd lost muscle. So had Johnson. Occasionally, he studied himself in a still pool at the side of a creek, wondering if anyone would even recognize him when he returned to Tennessee with a curly beard and a ragged ear.

Johnson found himself half scouting for the future, half retracing his journey. He had seen the best and worst of people, including himself. He'd made mistakes, taken advantage of people, but he'd been no worse than the people he'd encountered, and often better. When the trail he followed widened—he'd soon meet the Arkansas River—hoofbeats sounded and a man rode toward him. Johnson hoped he'd pass by with a nod, but the man caught up his reins. Johnson slowed his horse. The man was swarthy, with a fat face, white with Indian features, dressed in the leather and skins of a trapper, but with fancy boots. His horse, a bay mare, broad as a barn, might have been with foal. When he opened his mouth, Johnson could hardly understand his words, even though he knew the man had said, "You have a horse so fine. Of Tennessee," for he spoke with an accent foreign to Johnson's ear. Even though The Stud was rangy from his hard time, his long legs, his color, his distinctive eyes, green now as the woods they rode through, drew attention. Johnson feared another race, but instead, the man said, "So fine you must feed him? Yourself, as well?"

Johnson was always hungry, though he'd become as parsimonious with his appetite as his father was. Even the mention of food released saliva in his mouth, clutched his stomach with anticipation. "You know where we can find food?"

"But of course. I am Joseph Bonne. I have a small inn for travelers such as yourself. Above the river, to keep from the floods."

The inn was anything but small. Johnson had become used to seeing the cramped cabins settlers built in haste while they dreamed of such structures as Bonne had erected. He tied The Stud to the rail of the broad porch that spanned the building's wide front. The sloping roof rose two stories. When they climbed the few stairs, a wide entry gave way to stairs, more rooms, an open kitchen as well as a closed one. "We want for people to stay with us," said Bonne. "This will be a good country for settlers, yes? You are maybe a settler?"

Johnson followed the man into the closed kitchen, where a table and chairs promised a meal. He was tempted to launch into his story, from the injustice of the past right up to his unformed plan to take Jo from her brothers and pa. "I've been traveling," he began.

Bonne interrupted with a sudden call—"Marie!"—and a woman came down the stairs. "A guest," Bonne said. Marie was stout, from her wide shoes to her full face. Her rich hair was braided from each side and coiled at her ears. She nodded to him, went to a shelf, and brought bread and cheese from behind a curtain.

"A settler someday," said Johnson.

Bonne raised his eyebrows. Marie brought a knife to the table, set it at Johnson's hand, then put her hands together, as though prayer might follow. "Eat," she said. "You look very used to being hungry." She spoke to Bonne in a language Johnson thought might be French, but he wasn't certain.

"She saw your horse from upstairs. Wants to take him to our stable," Bonne said. "Give us a chance to get acquainted. My hand will care well for him."

Johnson wondered if the hand was a slave, but he didn't ask his new host. He set to the food at the slow pace of civilization, remembering how he'd eaten before he'd become ravenous, wolfing food like an animal. The cheese was sharp, the bread sour. Bonne gave him time to eat, then described the country surrounding his inn.

Marie returned, humming, and served them coffee.

"Thank you," Johnson said. She nodded, still humming a tuneless air. "Tell me about yourself," he said to Bonne.

Joseph Bonne was half Quapaw and half French, one of the men responsible for the treaties that allowed the settlement of Arkansas, where his family had been trading for years. With Marie, he settled down to build the inn and raise children. A percussion of feet came tumbling down the stairs and three children scurried into the kitchen, begging for coffee. Marie shooed them outside, and they tumbled from the room as though tied together by ropes. On the trail Johnson had seen only sad children. The energy of these young ones was as much jolt as the strong coffee. "A good country, it is," said Bonne, "where we work to have a school to match our church."

"You Catholic?" asked Johnson. When Bonne nodded, Johnson told him of San Antonio, the mission, and its fine dome. Though for all the splendor, it would soon be a ruin.

"I am no priest, as you see," said Bonne. "We French come to live, not to convert. We do not come to conquer. The Spanish, they have a story of blood and gold. We have a story of women and family."

"I'd like that story." Johnson sliced more cheese, tore another hunk of bread, drank coffee even though he was already light-headed. "Only you'd have to add horses."

"Of course," said Bonne. "This will be a story of horses, like your own. Perhaps like mine?"

"You a horseman?"

Bonne promised Johnson a trip to the stable, to see how his own horse was being treated.

Marie brought more bread when Johnson took the last of the loaf to his lips. She'd cut an apple, too.

Johnson took a small bite of apple. He pushed the bread away. "I'd best give my stomach time to catch up to this good food," he said. He'd taken many a bitter apple from trees he passed. This one was almost a peach, juicy and pungently sweet. He washed it down with more coffee. "It's been some time since I ate anything sweet. Anything baked. Mostly I've eaten squirrels shot on the trail."

"And how long have you been on the trail?" asked Marie.

"My story can't all be told in one sitting," said Johnson. "I've been away from Tennessee since spring. But clear down into Texas and Mexico, across the Rio Grande."

"You were looking for a home?" asked Bonne. He held an apple slice above his mouth as though it were a crescent moon.

"I am now," said Johnson. If he were going to find a home in a place like Bonne's, he would tell a story about the future, not the past. Yes, he'd been fugitive. Yes, he'd killed the man who pursued him unjustly. Yes, he was returning to face his accusers. But the important part would be the end, the part yet to be lived. "I believe my sweetheart will take to this part of Arkansas."

"We would welcome her," said Marie.

After they'd eaten, Bonne brought Johnson to the stable, more a barn, but of stone to the height of a man, then beams of pine, cut from the woods around them. Inside, a man pitched hay into an empty stall. Tall and broad, with a brooding profile, the worker was not exactly Negro, but not Indian, French, or Mexican, either. "Francoise," said Bonne, and the man turned in their direction. "This is Johnson. Marie brought his stud to you."

The man set his pitchfork to the floor of the barn and leaned against it, looking toward but not at them, his head cocked slightly.

"I thank you, Francoise," said Johnson.

"It is nothing," said the man. "Your horse has spirit."

"He's worn to the bone," said Johnson.

"His spirit is not worn," said the man. "I can feel it in his flesh."

Johnson looked at Bonne, raised his eyebrow. "Blind," Bonne whispered.

"But not deaf," said Francoise.

"And not a slave," said Bonne, approaching his hand, then clapping him on the back. "You may leave whenever you'd like, you know that, Francoise?"

The big man smiled, as though this was a joke between them. "I'm on my way," Francoise said. "I'll see you again, Mr. Johnson." He leaned the pitchfork by the door and disappeared.

"A good hand," said Bonne. "Knows more about horses than most men with eyes. I thought he'd appreciate your stud."

"Is he French, like you?" asked Johnson.

Bonne looked out the door. "French, but not like me. And Indian. Negro. And English. No doubt he has some German or something else. Of course though we are a country of mongrels, we still turn a man into but one thing. So he is known as *Bonne's nigger*. Though he is not mine, and he has only a little of the African."

"He's blind, so I guess he'll stay with you," said Johnson.

"He stays because I love and trust him like a brother," Bonne said. "See how he's cared for your stud."

Johnson smiled. Not because The Stud was well watered and had been combed, but because he was dreamily chewing clover hay, his bearing as much of comfort as Johnson's had been in the kitchen, leaning back in a chair, Marie singing behind him.

"You'll want a bath," Bonne said.

"I suppose."

"You must if you expect a bed." Bonne started out the door.

Johnson followed. While the men were in the barn, Marie had begun to cook. Onion browned in salt pork. The momentary quell of his appetite forsook him by the time they entered the kitchen. Marie sat before the orange of fat carrots, the lush green of parsley, the dark red of fingerling potatoes, the milky yellow of summer squash. Behind her, dried meat was pounded to a pile of shreds. Bonne stood behind her, rested his hands on her shoulders. When she turned her head to smile at her husband, Johnson's homesickness panged his heart.

"Travelers from the west," Bonne said, "have more need of satisfaction than those from the east. Tonight will not disappoint you. Unless you should disappear in the bath, an apparition of mud." He hung a large iron pot on a hook over the fire. "Come." Bonne led Johnson from the kitchen.

They went through the hall to a back porch, then to a small building that served as springhouse, cool room for milk, butter, and cheese, and where, behind a curtain, a deep tub of rock and mortar, smoothed on the insides and painted with whitewash, was already full of water. "I'll bring a hot bucket or two, but first you must clean yourself from that bucket." Bonne pointed to one of several along the wall.

"One of those will do," said Johnson. "Don't bother with hot."

"The tub will drown the vermin," said Bonne. "But you must make yourself fit for the tub. You are no longer on the trail, Robert Johnson. You must expect some civilization." He left the springhouse.

Johnson slowly peeled away his clothing, dropping everything on the stone floor. He'd not undressed completely for a long time. He'd splashed water on his face, waded into streams where rocks and shallows cleaned with rushing water. But he'd let his clothes dry on him while he hurried The Stud up the trail to Tennessee.

Naked, he was a comical wraith, thin, his bones jutting from wrist, shoulder, and hip. His feet were black, his knees bruised, his pubic hair knotted, his belly like a little pot, waiting to be filled. His hair had curled along with his beard. And he'd thought he might be a sight for Jo Benson's sore eyes. He was a sore sight for any eye. Maybe Hiram and Elizabeth could cut his hair, render him a semblance of the young man he'd been when they first met him.

He cupped water from the bucket. The accumulation of dirt, sweat, smoke, and dried leaves streamed down his trunk, his thighs, his feet, disappearing in the cracks between the rocks. He stepped over the lip of the tub and lay down in the cool water.

Bonne was right. He would have to learn to tolerate some civilization, slow as it could be, for he'd been in a hurry all his life. He'd hurried from bed at night to race horses in the roads and pasture tracks around Pleasant View. He'd hurried from his father's house after his mother died. He'd hurried to build his cabin, stake his claim on contested ground. He'd hurried his courtship with Jo in his desire to make her his wife. That had stirred up the Bensons' plot to ensnare him in crime. And so he'd hurried away on The Stud. Once he'd killed MacDonald he'd hurried home, loping toward Jo Benson, still faithful, still pregnant with their child, scheming for him just as he was for her, both ready to make a home in just such a place as he found himself in the pine bluffs above the Arkansas River.

Though Johnson yearned for Tennessee, the food he'd eaten, the soak in water, the unbinding of muscle and tension, made him drowsy. He had not been so content since those brief days of spring when he'd met Jo in the pool in the creek between their properties. Bonne clomped across the stone floor. Johnson opened his eyes and covered himself. But Bonne pulled the curtain open just enough to pour a bucket of hot water into the tub. He tossed a chunk of yellow soap into the water. "Take your time. I have left a robe. Marie will wash your clothes as soon as the stew begins its simmer. And Francoise, he says your gold is safe with him."

"I'm trusting all of you," said Johnson to the curtain.

"You are wise. We want guests and settlers. We do not set upon wayfarers. We care for their horses, their tack, their pistols and rifle . . ." Bonne waited, hand on the curtain.

"You think I'm a desperado," Johnson said. "I have been, and I may have to be in Tennessee. Circumstances have been hard on me, but I am not a hard man."

"I can show you lowland or bluff. Game—bear, deer, muskrat, duck. Good land for growing crops. A fine valley with rock to quarry, timber to cut." Bonne dropped the curtain.

Outside, Bonne called to his children. "The pigs," he shouted. "They need water. Do not disturb the man at his bath."

Johnson lay quiet. They whispered into the springhouse, filled buckets, tempted each other to laughter, then hurried away. Johnson had been a solitary child, his mother his only companion once his brother died. She could make him laugh. He and Jo had laughed together in the creek, splashing naked after they'd joined their bodies. He'd been both man and child then, she woman and child.

He scrubbed himself, lather and foam, until his skin was raw. He rose from the tub and parted the curtain. He dried himself and put on the robe Bonne had left. He'd been promised a hearty stew. He would know the laughter of children, a bed for sleep. Such simple gifts, yet they had eluded him for many months. He was but several days' hard ride from Hiram and Elizabeth, then on to Tennessee. And yet as he contemplated home, he felt home. He would be an Arkansawyer, drawing his Tennessee line—his own blood and The Stud's—into a new line in a new territory, like so many before him.

in the pines

robert Johnson stayed beyond the stew and bed. He spent the following day riding with Bonne and Francoise through the Arkansas Territory. Johnson imagined three small cabins, one on a bluff above the river, another along the shoulder of a ridge that opened into bottomland, another on a creek. After their exploration, he ate, as famished as though he'd just ridden up to the inn.

That night he lay in bed. *Dear Jo*, he thought. *Here in Arkansas, birds gather everywhere, fish break the water feeding on bugs. So many of them they ripple the streams. Last night, and again tonight, whippoorwills call each other all along the bluffs. I cannot sleep. I have eaten hearty dinners with Bonne and Marie and their three children. Evenings are spent fireside. Marie sings such songs as I've never heard. Breakfast today did not end with a single helping. Plate after plate of ham and biscuits and gravy and eggs from Marie's ducks. This unspoiled country holds sweet abundance. It will be ours when we settle here. I will build a little log cabin and hope we outgrow it soon, as Bonne has shown me the plan for starting with a single room, then adding on. He is a clever man, and friendly. We'd do well to settle near him. I ride tomorrow. I send you my love, soon to be followed by myself, across the hard miles.*

Next morning, his appetite was still keen, as though it grew when he fed it. He took out his pouch of gold and silver. He separated the money into two portions. He clambered down the stairs from the loft and found Bonne in the kitchen. "A favor," he said. He set half of his coins on the table. "Take enough for your hospitality and hold the rest for my return."

"You show me great trust," Bonne said.

"Eggs?" asked Marie from where she tended the hearth.

"Yes, please, ma'am." Johnson sat at the table. "I'm trusting myself," Johnson said to Bonne. "That I can do what I must do and still be alive to return."

Marie cracked eggs. Bonne cracked his knuckles. "I will give this to Francoise for safekeeping," Bonne said. "He is the only man I trust besides myself. And now you, of course. Do you have such a terrible thing to do?"

Marie brought Johnson coffee.

"Thank you," he said. He nearly burned his tongue. "I must face accusers. Though I am falsely accused. I must face those who committed the crime they accuse me of. They are my sweetheart's brothers and pa. If I return . . . *when* I return, she will be with me."

"Let me advise you," said Bonne. "You are wanted, yes? And yet *they* have what you want, your woman. Beyond that, what do they want? Can you not trade for all that is wanted between you?"

"They want my land," said Johnson.

"You will find land here," said Bonne. "Have I not shown you all a man could want?"

"You have," said Johnson. "And it's undisputed land. These Bensons want that small piece of land. That might be enough."

"Dream where you have freedom," said Bonne, "as I have. We leave our homelands. We have found a new world. Join us."

"I ride today," Johnson said.

"Francoise will have your horse ready."

"After he's hidden my silver and gold."

"It will be as blind to every man as it is to him," Bonne said. He picked up the small bag and left the kitchen.

Johnson ate bacon and bread and eggs washed down by the richly roasted coffee. Marie prepared sacks of bread, cheese, and dried meat for the road. The children lined up before him to sing in their high voices a French song that imitated the calls of birds at morning and night.

Johnson stood up, took off his hat, and bowed. "You are more than gracious," he said. "I hope to see you soon."

Bonne helped him gather the few things from his sleeping loft and went with him to the small stable. The Stud whinnied when Johnson entered, eager for the journey. Johnson brought him out of the stall. "I start from here this time," Johnson said to Bonne. "And so I will return."

"Your intention makes me happy," said Bonne. "As does your trust."

"Francoise, thank you for the care of my horse. I'll see you again."

"You will," said Francoise, "if you want your money."

"I'll want it, sure enough," said Johnson. He saddled his horse, tied on the provisions, and led The Stud outside. He mounted and nodded to Bonne. "Soon!" he shouted. He trotted around the inn, found the trail, and set course eagerly toward the Mississippi and Memphis.

Memphis

The rest at Bonne's inn had been good for Robert Johnson, even better for The Stud. Johnson hoped Hiram and Elizabeth could help him puzzle out what awaited him in Pleasant View. They might have a letter responding to the one he'd sent so long ago.

In two days, as his food ran low, he shot a duck, enough good meat to fill his belly for a day. Two more days brought him close to the river. He happened upon a fire in a small clearing, chicken bones blackening on smoldering coals. He pushed his horse past, but after some distance he dismounted and circled back. The colored man who scooped dirt over the bones and coals, a thin man with a face like a blade, was the one who'd called himself Jackson, the one Johnson had given food from the box.

A black man would be fool to live on the edges of the Mississippi, constantly hunted as he had been the night Johnson swam The Flood. An escaped slave would head north, to Canada, if he wanted freedom. Perhaps he stole chickens, foraged the gardens of the cabins that had begun to litter the western bank of the river. Johnson walked into the clearing.

"Thought you'd passed by," said Jackson, not looking up.

"Thought I recognized you," said Johnson. "You know Hiram."

"Don't know nobody," said Jackson.

"You're Jackson, aren't you?" asked Johnson. He stretched out his hands, palms up, to show he was unarmed.

"If that's what you want to call me."

"Is it Hiram sending you food across the water?"

"Don't know no Hiram," said the man. He backed away, glancing over his shoulder, unsure whether Johnson was really alone.

"What do you do in return for the food?" asked Johnson.

Jackson disappeared into the woods.

Johnson smiled. He'd have even more questions for Hiram. And, he'd have the prospect of chicken when he found Hiram William Gillian and Elizabeth once more.

He rode through the bluffs and down to the riverbank. He could have hollered out to the many people traveling along broader paths than he'd seen a few months before, or to those hauling logs on wagons toward where they might be building a cabin, a barn, even a business. One man stood on a half-built dock. "This the best place to cross?" Johnson asked.

The man was laying an inch-thick board of sawn oak over two pilings. Behind him, the broad river moved swiftly. Like a scurf, Memphis crawled up the bank on the other side. Johnson hadn't remembered so many buildings.

"Be a boat here before sunset," the man said. "My partner. With more lumber. You can ride back. Maybe for nothing if you'll help us set some planks. And if you can row." The man stood for another board, and Johnson dismounted and helped him carry it to the farthest edge of the pilings.

"I aim to swim. I'm in a hurry," said Johnson.

"River's rising," said the man. "We've had a might bit of rain for this time of year. That makes us in a hurry, too. River ain't kind when it's up."

"I swam it last spring," said Johnson. "Or my horse did. He ain't afraid of any kind of water." He gathered his saddlebags and supplies. He threw everything he could over his shoulders. He held pistols and rifle.

"I reckon you've picked as good a spot as any. Least it's the one we've chose. But I still wish you luck. The middle is swift today." The man walked across the finished length of his dock.

Johnson did not help him with the next plank. He hadn't hurried from Bonne's only to contemplate the river. "I hope to come this way again," he said, "and with my sweetheart, too." He nudged The Stud forward.

"She waiting for you? That ain't just hope?" The man kicked at the pile of lumber. "I've had my share of disappointment with sweethearts."

"Hope is just a kind of waiting," said Johnson. "I've waited, and I've hoped. I expect she's done the same."

"I guess you'll find out." The man leaned to another board.

Johnson raised his rifle and pistols into the air, as though defying anyone to challenge him. The Stud leapt into the water and walked, then swam toward the swift current. "Wahoo," shouted Johnson. He looked back at the working man, who stood smiling, a board balanced on his shoulder.

They pushed into the river, with its little curls of current, its sticks and leaves bobbing downstream, dunking under then rising again, its brown silt stirred enough to ride all the way to the delta, its occasional whirlpool. The Mississippi was unlike any river Johnson had crossed, more like three rivers—muddy banks and calm water, swiftly flowing sections, then the strong middle, thick as a cable, pulling everything inexorably downstream. The Stud swam strong, head jutting forward, legs sure. Johnson kicked his legs to help, but not at the risk of wetting his powder and the other supplies in his saddlebags, held high over his head.

In the thick flow at the middle of the river, his horse drifted, resting between spurts of the intense swimming. The buildings of Memphis drifted until Johnson lost sight of them altogether. He urged The Stud, but still the horse slacked against the swift current. Johnson swam to take some weight off his horse, but his upstretched arms burned with the weight of guns and saddlebags. Johnson let The Stud drift. They'd make better time on land, no matter how far south they climbed up the eastern bank.

Even rest took effort. He clicked his tongue, and The Stud renewed his effort. "Thataboy," Johnson said again and again, in rhythm with the horse's efforts, in rhythm to the kicking of his own legs. "Thataboy, thataboy," until the repetition seemed a kind of swimming, too, the words encouragement and reward. They pushed forward as they had all these past months, tired, hungry, one step beyond endurance. Yet they had endured, and would endure.

Once they crossed the thick river middle, the current eased. Their efforts purchased more distance. Hope redoubled their effort. The last third of the crossing seemed light, and though The Stud stopped as soon as his legs found the bottom, Johnson didn't mind. Let him stand in the Mississippi as long as he wanted, celebrating muddy earth beneath his feet.

When The Stud finally lifted his hooves and mucked up the bank onto dry land, Johnson dismounted. He reattached his saddlebags and stowed his guns. They'd drifted so far south he recognized nothing. He might be in Mississippi, for all he knew. They walked through brush and into the trees that lined the bank.

Before he found a trail, a commotion stirred around him. Several figures ran through the woods. "Don't shoot, you fool," someone hollered.

"They ain't worth nothin' dead," shouted another.

Three men on horseback, with rifles they wouldn't shoot, rode past where Johnson sheltered in thick honeysuckle. The shadows they chased had disappeared. "Goddamn 'em," said a voice.

"Might need the dogs," said another.

"What did I tell you," said the third.

"Oh, go to hell," said the curser, and pushed his horse into the trees.

"Over here!" a rider shouted. The men trotted toward the voice. Johnson figured fugitive slaves. Men would shoot a criminal, for the value of a criminal was tallied dead or alive. The slave was at least free of the specter of death, even if he might be whipped or sold. Johnson had been enslaved by the accusations against him, and he'd run. Now he was free because he had decided to be. Such was the advantage of white over black.

Johnson started quickly away from these men. Through the trees was a grassy path, perhaps cut for a road, perhaps worn away by years of Indian migrations up and down the Mississippi. Signs of Indians were everywhere along the river, so numerous had they once been in this land. His father had cursed their presence once, saying, "You can't make a single step but what an Indian has already stepped there before you." Johnson was thankful for the swath of grass. He wanted to put distance between himself and the slave hunters.

He rode northwest, along the curve of the river toward Memphis. Before the river straightened north, a wagon rolled toward him, pulled by mules. On the wagon seat was a tall man, lean, with a high hat. Only one man he knew could cut that figure—Hiram William Gillian. Johnson waved, but Hiram jerked back the reins, and, once the mules responded, he stood up in the wagon, musket finding his hands and his aim, all so quickly that Johnson reined The Stud and raised his hands. "What business!" shouted Hiram.

Johnson shook his head. He must be a pitiful version of himself to be unrecognized. He'd expected to be greeted with eagerness for news, with conspiracy for future plans. Instead, another long-barreled musket stared at his heart.

"My horse is to be put to stud," Johnson shouted. "Do you know a Hiram Gillian?"

Hiram lowered the musket. "The Stud to stud, is it?" he said. "He have anything left, Johnson?" He stowed the musket under the wagon seat. "Tie your horse to the wagon. Catch me up on your miserable life."

When Johnson hopped into the seat, he shook Hiram's hand. The Stud found grass. "He won't need tying," said Johnson. "He's been dreaming of your oats too long."

"What have you been dreaming of?" asked Hiram. "Your sweetheart? A new ear to replace that notched one."

"I've had my close calls," said Robert. "Oats for the horse, chicken for me. Then back to Pleasant View."

Hiram turned his wagon in the broad path.

"What are you doing down this way?" asked Johnson. "Where you need such a quick musket to protect you."

"Trading some stock," said Hiram. "Half the men down here are horsemen, the other half are horse thieves." He snapped the reins and the mules lurched ahead.

"I saw men on horses," said Johnson. "They were chasing some men on foot. Slaves, most likely."

"More slaves run away than you might imagine." Hiram whipped the mules.

"They try for the river? Expect to swim across?"

"You swam the river today. Else you wouldn't be this far south."

"Nor be so waterlogged," said Johnson.

Hiram pushed him to the far edge of the seat. "Nor have such a stink on you." He put his fingers to his nose. "You look downright abandoned."

"I've abandoned fear," said Johnson. "I'm not a fugitive. Others will have to see it my way now."

"First a bath," said Hiram. "And a change of clothes. And The Stud will find two of my fillies in heat."

"What about chicken?" asked Johnson. "It's been some time since I ate chicken."

"Chicken?"

"Jackson just finished one. Black bones in a dying fire when I came across him on the other side of the river."

"Jackson?" asked Hiram. He lashed at the mules, who had lost their pace.

"Black man with a hatchet face. Thin as a chicken bone himself."

"Don't know a Jackson," said Hiram.

"When I crossed to Arkansas. I came up the bank pulling the box you'd packed for me. He knew about it. He said someone sent me to him. Someone who knew about horses. A tall man." Johnson pointed at Hiram. "You."

"Have you learned anything since then?" asked Hiram. "Like who to trust? A man can say anything. What have *you* told people these months away?"

"What do *you* tell people?" asked Johnson. "You're down here by the river. You're prickly as a Texas horn toad. Jumpy, too. Trading stock, but no stock with you. Why so far south?"

Hiram said nothing.

"One thing I learned these months. If someone says they don't know something, that's fine. But if two say it, then they both *don't know* the same thing."

"You've become more talkative since I last saw you," said Hiram.

"And you, less," said Johnson.

Whenever the mules lagged, Hiram snapped his whip over their heads. He'd been so easy when Johnson had last passed through. Each time Johnson cleared his throat, readying speech, Hiram called out to the mules.

A rider appeared, hurrying toward them with incautious speed, and Hiram jerked the mules to a stop and bent for his musket. He stood ready.

The rider raised his hand, slowed his horse. "A message," he called out. He trotted up beside the wagon and whispered to Hiram.

Hiram whipped the mules to life once more. The man dug his heels into his horse's flanks and raced on past. Hiram turned to Johnson. "Forget this, if you know what's good for you."

"What *is* good for me?" asked Johnson.

"Your future," said Hiram. "Remember this. There's only one thing harder on folks around here than the river. And that's other folks."

"Give me a river any day," said Johnson. "I reckon that's how fugitive slaves feel."

"I said forget this." Hiram stowed the musket under his seat. He remained silent, ever persistent with the mules, until they reached a wider thoroughfare and Johnson could see in the near distance the buildings of the growing city. They passed other wagons, coaches, and buggies. Hiram tipped his hat, smiled, hallooed greetings. "And how's Elizabeth?" asked Johnson.

"Why, I should have told you. She's in a family way since you were here." His stern countenance melted away in a beaming satisfaction with himself.

"That's mighty nice," said Johnson. "Just like my Jo."

"You left her with child?" Hiram raised his eyebrows. "You took her innocence without marriage?" Hiram frowned.

"I believe she took mine as much as I took hers. I believe everything was freely given." Johnson smiled.

"So she's big with child by now. And she doesn't know where you are, or when you're coming back?"

"No way to get word to her since I left here last," said Johnson.

"Do you know what it's like if you're a woman with child, and you have sickness in the morning and weariness at night? You suppose her brothers and her pa are helping her?"

Johnson hung his head.

"And you out being a fugitive?" Hiram shook his head. "You're a fugitive to your responsibilities with that girl."

Johnson squared his shoulders. "I killed him," he said.

"I was there when you told Elizabeth what to write to that sheriff. You insisted you were innocent." Hiram muttered to the mules, who turned into a narrow lane off the main road.

They passed familiar buildings.

Johnson hoped they'd soon be at the stable. "I *am* innocent. I killed that bounty hunter, MacDonald. Same one we raced on your track. He kept after me. Found me way down in Mexico. He had my horse, even. He called you *nigger lover*. I shot him." Johnson shook his head. "And rode back here."

"MacDonald was a man to hate," said Hiram.

"He hated you," said Johnson.

They were in front of Hiram's home, and Johnson's stomach churned. Hiram must have been hungry, too, for he simply hitched his mules to the post. "My man Jefferson will come for the mules, for your horse," he said. He strode into the house. Johnson took weapons and saddlebag, loosened the saddle cinch, and followed.

"Chicken." Elizabeth stood in the kitchen doorway when they walked into the front room. She was most substantially with child.

"I knew it'd be chicken," said Johnson. He set his belongings in a corner.

"That doesn't mean you know anything much," Hiram said. He stood still, arms folded over his chest. He stared directly into Johnson's eyes, warning him not to speak of their meeting place.

"I know I like chicken," Johnson said. He bowed. "Elizabeth, I have thought of you and your kindness many times these hard months."

"I thank you," she said.

"Hiram told me you are to be a mother. I'm happy for you."

Elizabeth blushed. "And Hiram can be so quiet about so many things." She backed into the kitchen.

"Seems Robert Johnson has a family, too," Hiram called after her. "Told me he's counting on it." He followed his wife. In the kitchen, the air was redolent with roasting chicken. "But he's not even married to the girl." Hiram pointed to a chair at the table.

"I'll bring her back here as soon as I wrench her from her outlaw brothers and pa." Johnson took a seat.

"We'll have the justice of the peace take care of it," said Hiram.

"If he can find time in his busy schedule," said Elizabeth.

"I can make some time," said Hiram. He took plates and cups from the shelves and set the table.

"You're a justice of the peace?" said Johnson. "That why you were away today?"

"Just diddling over a load of hay. They want too much. I often return with an empty wagon." He glared at Johnson.

"You brought Robert Johnson," said Elizabeth. She dipped potatoes from a pot that hung steaming over the fire. "So your wagon was full enough."

"Soon his mouth will be too full to gab. And then his belly. And then we'll hear about his adventures in the Southwest." Hiram tied his napkin around his neck. He put it up over his face, like an outlaw, and raised his eyebrows. He blew the loose end of the napkin into his eyes.

They set to the food, chicken and potatoes and green beans boiled with bacon fat. So hungry for chicken, Johnson had imagined that even plenty could never be enough, but the meat was so rich, with hunks of fatty skin hanging from it, the potatoes so slathered with chicken fat, the beans so laden with bacon grease that he soon pressed himself from the table.

Then they talked, or Johnson did, with stories of his travels and adventures, prompted to detail by Hiram's questions, Elizabeth's concerns, both of them celebrating his small triumphs, wincing at his pain, worrying through his recklessness, understanding his need to dispatch MacDonald and find his way home. "Fatten up a bit," said Hiram. "Then we'll send you on your way. But you shouldn't go from one danger only to plunge yourself into another."

"Bonne said the same thing." Johnson picked up the leg bone of a chicken, bit it in two, and sucked at the marrow.

"Then I'd like to meet him." Hiram stood up. "Men too often counsel toward violence. They do not ask. They take. Soon, they will enslave all of Arkansas, all of the West, to their wills. Be it Indian, African, the land itself, they care for nothing but ownership." He left the kitchen.

Elizabeth stood up and began to clear dishes. Johnson scraped back his chair to help. "He has set his sights on changing the world," Elizabeth said.

Johnson handed Elizabeth the cups and forks.

"I have coffee," she said. "And your cup." She raised her eyes to the shelf where she kept the men's dishes.

"Misspelled still?" Johnson asked. He reached for the cup that read *JONSEN*.

"You tell me," she said.

"Same as it was," he said.

"How do you spell your name?" she asked.

"Teach me," he said. "For I want to sign it properly when Hiram hitches me to Jo."

"Can she write?" Elizabeth asked.

"She knows her letters," Johnson said. "She once sewed my initials into one of my handkerchiefs."

"Then you should know your letters." Elizabeth reached for a large mug at the end of the shelf. She handed it to Robert. "The alphabet," she said.

He recited through *G*, but could go no further. His mother had sat at their table with slate and a hunk of chalk. He heard her voice again, through the letter *G*, and then he heard no more. He swallowed.

"*H, I, J*," said Elizabeth. She put her finger to the mug. "*J* as in Johnson. As in Jo. Right here. A straight line with a backward curl."

He traced it with his finger. Then he put down the cup. He gathered his saddlebag and firearms.

In the barn, The Stud was settled into a stall with water and food. Johnson put his gear with the horse. Hiram was in another stall, grooming one of his mules. Johnson found a currycomb and began on the other mule. "You threatened that MacDonald when he rode against me," he said. "Would you have shot him?"

"I've never shot a man. Shot *at* a few. Wanted to shoot a few. Known lots that deserved to be shot." Hiram patted his mule. "Horses and mules often make better company."

"If I hadn't shot MacDonald, he would have shot me," Johnson insisted.

"I don't judge you," said Hiram. "I know what it's like to be cornered."

"That why you're helping the Negroes?" asked Johnson.

"I don't know what you're talking about," said Hiram. "But such talk gets a man in trouble around here. I'm a generous man, Robert Johnson, but I won't tolerate a generous tongue in you."

Johnson finished combing the mule and went into the stall to brush The Stud.

Hiram watched him. "We've had a letter," he said.

"From who? About me? To me?"

"I wanted you to eat. To settle," said Hiram. He pulled a sheet of paper from his vest.

"Unsettling news?" Johnson asked.

"I took the liberty of reading it, in case I could answer," said Hiram. "I could not, and so I've waited for your return." Hiram held the paper at arm's length. "From your father," Hiram said. And he read.

June 1825
Dear Son:

Your letter has come into my hands by way of Judson. I have studied what I should do. I honored your mother's wish to give you those 40 acres. I might have known it would bring you trouble with the Bensons and now I regret it. We have always seen things differently. You think I expected you to live but by one commandment—honor thy father. I admit I thought you were unruly and disrespectful. Your mother's death made our differences greater. Yet I am proud of the cabin you built and the improvements you made on your land. You have your mother's blessing in Jo Benson. She spoke of that child's rescue many times. I do not and will not believe any accusations against you.

Jo Benson is with child. That may be your responsibility. If so, she is part of you. Your future is more important than ever before. Return. Your land is of little importance when weighed against your responsibilities to Jo Benson and the child she carries.

"So you knew about Jo already?" Johnson interrupted.

"I wanted you to tell me."

"Testing me?"

"You passed the test," Hiram admitted.

Come back for Jo Benson. Abandon the land. Abandon your place. Some of those in my church will be moving soon to Arkansas. They report it as good country. You could start again there. Someday I might go there myself. Pleasant View and Tennessee are ever filled with men like the Bensons. They gain worldly power each day. Sometimes a man must go in search of a new Eden, unspoiled by the sins of such men.

Judson will help you. I will help you. Already I have told Benson that to harm you is to ensure his own harm at my hands. If you receive this letter, make haste.

Your father, Jacob Johnson

"Should I write him?"

"Ride back, don't write back," said Hiram. "Like your father, I will help you."

"You're mighty generous," Johnson said. He reached into his saddlebag for his pouch of money. He brought out two coins, for the one against the other made a pleasing sound. "I want to give you something for your trouble." He reached them over the slats of the stall.

Hiram did not take them. "You've already promised all I asked of you," said Hiram. "I'll put The Stud to mare yet this afternoon. He needs something to do while you bathe and find some new clothes. Save your money for that." He handed Johnson the letter from his father.

"You could use the gold for something besides your own comfort?" he asked.

The two stared, unrevealing, for a full minute. Hiram spat. "There's people I know could put it to use," he said, but he did not reach for the coins.

Hiram poured more water for his mules and for The Stud.

"I'll be wanting to leave most of my gold with you anyway," said Johnson. "All but what I'll need for food, supplies, a fair price for Jo's horse. The one my horse studded before this trouble."

"You're counting on a lot," said Hiram. He shut the stall door behind him and walked away.

Johnson followed Hiram toward the house. "I've imagined a lot," said Johnson.

"You leave some money in Arkansas, too?" Hiram asked. "With Bonne?"

Johnson smiled. "I need something to return to."

"You're right to do it." Hiram turned at the door to his house. "You're leaving your gold here because you might not survive what's in front of you?"

"No sense in those varmints taking it off my dead body."

"You don't return, I'll get the money to Jo Benson," said Hiram.

"You'll give it to *me*, as a wedding gift." Johnson shoved Hiram into his door.

That night, after a bath, Johnson dressed in clothes rustled from the other hands. "I can't look fancy going back to Pleasant View," he told them. They ate a light supper of biscuits with chicken gravy. He slept in the bunkhouse, as he had before, and though the men pestered him with questions about his travels, he wagered that sleep would be better for him than attention.

Robert Johnson had no dreams in which he rode up to the Benson cabin and shot his pistols into the air. Or rode toward the cabin and took a bullet in his chest. Or rode up to a cabin obviously deserted, parchment windows torn and flapping, barn door open. He'd rehearsed scene after scene across Arkansas, but now that he was in Tennessee, his mind allowed him to rest.

"Fat enough?" Hiram asked, watching Johnson next morning at breakfast.

"You'll see me in a week or two." Johnson put a boiled egg in his mouth, chewed extravagantly.

Hiram sliced his egg and loaded it with salt.

Johnson reached for a last piece of bacon. "I can't thank you enough, Elizabeth," he said.

"Thank me by bringing Jo," she said. "We'll help you become a proper young couple." She spooned mush on Johnson's plate.

Johnson swallowed the corn mush in two gulps. He wondered if he'd ever have enough to eat in his life. "I'll return to Pleasant View. Then back to Memphis. Then on to Arkansas. To the piney bluff where Bonne and I scouted land. It's a fine country. And far from trouble."

"A man can carry his troubles right along with him," said Hiram. "You know that."

"I do," said Johnson. "Though I aim to lay them down, more of them each place I return to." He stood up abruptly, as though the prospect of putting trouble behind him had finally dulled his appetite. He reached into his pocket for the leather pouch that held his gold. He tossed the pouch to Hiram.

Hiram weighed it in his hand. He raised his eyebrows. "I'll hold it for you," he promised.

Elizabeth wished Johnson well. Off he went to the barn to saddle The Stud. They had hard riding and high hopes, and no need to tarry.

Onnen

t he ground unrolled beneath Robert Johnson like someone was reeling him home. In two days he hoped to pay Charles Onnen a visit, see how he'd fared in the past months. Surely his young wife had given birth. When the river finally opened up before him, Johnson was but a quarter mile from where the ferryman docked on the west bank. Onnen would be waiting across the Hatchie, where he was more likely to serve travelers; folks headed west in greater numbers than east. Johnson whistled and waved his arms.

The ferryman stood up and waved back. He jumped from the dock into his boat, no longer a group of logs lashed together, but a real flatboat, ruddered and smooth. He began pulling. Halfway to Johnson, he stopped pulling and took a moment to size up his customer.

"I need across," Johnson yelled.

"No," said Charles Onnen. He had a new hat, black with a red band. He took it off to wipe his forehead. He pulled closer for a better look.

Johnson wasn't certain the man recognized him. After all, Johnson had thinned considerably. He had a beard. Everything he'd once owned had been stolen. If Onnen recognized him, it was only because of The Stud. He walked onto the small dock. The ferryman was just twenty yards from Johnson, hand on the rope.

"You got money?" asked Onnen.

"I can pay my way," Johnson yelled from the bank. "Or I can swim across." He turned to his horse. The Stud had thinned, too, though he looked better than Johnson did. They were both tired. But they were in a hurry. Johnson mounted his horse.

"Ain't seen but one man cross this water very easy," said Onnen, "and he had a stronger horse than yours." He steadied himself on the rope he'd strung across the river.

Johnson smiled. "I know that man," he said.

"Spit on him next time you see him," said Charles Onnen. He pulled on the rope and began to back away.

"I believe you relocated your ferry after his crossing!" Johnson shouted.

"Son of a bitch had a smart horse. Knew where to ford. I've followed his lead."

Johnson reached into his saddlebag and the ferryman pulled a rifle from the small cabin of his flatboat. But Johnson was not reaching for his pistol. "Here, Charles Onnen," he said. He took a piece of gold and held it so Onnen could see it. "Let's have no hard feelings."

"I didn't trust you then, and I don't trust you now," said Onnen.

"You don't want my money?" Johnson threw the gold piece. They watched it plunk into the river. The ferryman winced but did not move. Johnson held out another piece, then cocked his arm.

Charles Onnen set down his rifle, grabbed the ferry rope, and pulled hard. "Okay, okay," he huffed. "Stop wasting your money."

When the ferry reached the small dock, Johnson urged The Stud toward it. But they did not climb aboard. Johnson threw his saddlebag over his shoulder and the horse splashed into the river.

"Hold on," said the ferryman.

"Don't really need a ride, Charles Onnen. And you don't seem to need money." Water swirled around his boots.

"You're still mean, ain't you?" the ferryman fumed.

Johnson was ready to wave him away, but turned his horse instead. He *was* being mean, bearing an old grudge when he should be anticipating a future. He swam The Stud back to the bank. "I'd like a ride, if you'll have me," he said.

Onnen secured the ferry to the small dock. Johnson urged his horse onto the craft and then dismounted. He reached into his saddlebag and pulled out another gold piece. "How much?" he asked.

"That'd be fine," said Onnen.

"You were asking four bits last time."

"I've come up in the world," said Onnen, "and so has my price."

His admission was so bold Johnson almost laughed. "If I give you another piece will you be ready for my return in three or four days?" He put another coin in Onnen's hand. "And if I give you two more will you shove away quick no matter what follows me?" He put yet another coin into Onnen's outstretched hand. The ferryman pocketed the money and reached for the rope. "I'll have a woman at my side," said Johnson.

"Who'll be after her once she's with you?" Onnen pulled hard against the Hatchie.

"Will you do as I ask?"

"I've built a small cabin. See it up the hill yonder? My wife and baby snug as can be." Onnen paused and pointed to his crude dwelling. "Right next to it I've rigged a bell. You don't see me, you just ring that bell. I'll come running."

"I appreciate that," said Johnson. "I don't expect to be on the run. But the world doesn't always live up to what I expect."

"You cut my rope," said Onnen.

Johnson wondered why Onnen would bring forth the old grudge. "My name is Robert Johnson. I was on the run then. No money. Afraid. You didn't see my need."

"You showed me a better crossing."

"My horse did," Johnson reminded him.

"Horse sense," said Onnen. "I strung the rope where he crossed. Made things easier, sure enough. Folks been traveling through here real regular these past months." A bell clanged and Onnen waved his free hand.

Johnson reached for the rope and helped pull them to the east bank. Before they eased to the dock, Onnen muttered a thank-you.

"Just remember your promise," said Johnson.

A man in a wagon loaded high with crates waited above the dock. Behind the crates, on the back lip of the wagon, sat two black men.

Johnson and The Stud walked across the dock and onto land.

"See you," said Onnen, and in the same breath, "three dollars. Haven't seen you pass this way before."

"Three dollars?" barked the man from his wagon seat. He spat a glob of tobacco juice that landed between his team of horses. "That's a might steep for crossing a river."

"Six bits for you, six bits for the wagon, six bits each for the niggers."

"You ain't charging me for the horses?" asked the man. He stood up to show his size, a giant of a man, white beard stained brown.

"They're part of the wagon," said Onnen.

"So are the niggers," said the man.

"They ain't hitched to the wagon, are they?" asked the ferryman.

"Not so's you'd see," said the man, "but they sure enough belong to me, as my bonded slaves, and I reckon you'll charge me for them same as the horses."

Onnen pulled the rope and the ferry retreated from the dock. "I reckon I'll charge what *I* say, not what you say."

"I reckon you'll burn in hell someday," said the freighter.

Johnson had more important negotiations to contemplate, so he left Onnen and the freight hauler to haggle. If he had to guess, Onnen could not rely too much longer on his monopoly. Someone else would promote a crossing. He nudged his heels into his horse's flank, but once they crested the rise, Johnson stopped. He wanted to hear what he knew he'd hear. "Okay, how about a dollar then?"

whupped

t he road to Jackson was well traveled, the town bustling—wagon-loads of lumber, kilns for firing bricks, roadways crudely marked, buildings climbing up to second and third stories. Businesses poured into the streets, great bins of apples and turnips, cabbages and carrots, fat barrels in which pickles, eggs, and sausages all floated in the same brine. Boots and tack hung from the porch roofs of stores. The smell of spirits wafted from the many saloons, even before noon.

Robert Johnson passed it all by, slowing The Stud to a walk. He still had three or four long days to Pleasant View. He would sleep few hours, only in the dead of night, owl time, when the big birds might swoop from a nearby tree. He'd wake at the first ratchet of an insect. The Stud persisted as willfully as Johnson, always ready to be pushed, swimming creeks, leaping into forested paths where Johnson thought he might make a shortcut by following the flight of the crow.

He traveled without incident, nodding when he passed horsemen and freighters, wagons of families. He ran by those he overtook, holding up his hand to wave a greeting. And so passed hasty days, short dead nights, and he reached Judson's barn. The old man was throwing hay down to his horses. Robert whistled from the back door.

"Back, huh?" Judson leaned on his pitchfork.

"You doubted me?" asked Robert. "You told me to do some growing up. I've learned some since I've been away." He led his horse forward.

"But not enough to stay away?" asked Judson. He climbed down the ladder from the loft.

"I'm here for Jo Benson," said Robert. "Then I leave. I know who I am. What I want. What's mine. She's carrying my child." He swung the gate of an empty stall. The Stud found his way in. He uncinched the saddle and hung it on the stall slat.

Judson approached him. His beard was white. "Your father said he wrote you a letter." Judson smiled, stroking his long beard. "You sound like him."

"I sound like myself," said Robert. "What have you heard of the Bensons? Of Jo?" He forked some hay into his horse's stall, then dumped half a bucket of water into The Stud's trough.

"The Bensons claim her child is yours. Say you abandoned her after you killed Archibald Krummer at the Lonely Creek Bridge. They're ever set against you." Judson came close then, as though he couldn't stand for even the horses to hear what he had to say. "Everyone else says it's the father's, or one of the brother's. Those folks don't have much reputation left."

"I don't want to clear their bad name, but I'll claim Jo's baby to be mine, sure as we had our relations together in the months before they framed me as murderer." Robert sat on a bench, more tired than he thought he could be. "I did read the letter from my pa. Or listened to it. Is he still well?"

"He got mighty alarmed when the Bensons burned out your little cabin. You'd think he built it himself." Judson took Robert's hand and pulled him up.

Robert took his pistol from his saddlebags. "I was told they'd set flame to my home. I shot the man who said it to me, for he was surely taunting me before killing me."

"He the one took part of your ear?" asked Judson.

"He had bad aim." Robert touched the notched edge of his raggedy ear.

"Your pa write you any other news?" asked his uncle.

"Said he was leaning toward Arkansas," said Robert. "It's a good country. And he's not had an easy life since Ma died. I know that now." They walked out of the barn toward the house.

"I won't like your leaving again," said Judson.

"We'll be in the pine bluffs above the Arkansas River. Beautiful country. Good people. A fresh start." Robert turned at the porch and surveyed his uncle's small place as the evening turned the trees into silhouettes that would soon dissolve into shadow. "I'm counting on you to take word to Jo Benson, so she'll be ready for me."

Judson scraped his boots on the porch stairs, then sat. "Let's eat. Nothing like food to help make a plan. Then we'll have us a drink. Nothing like drink to screw up a man's courage."

They ate cold ham and beans, molasses and cornbread, tomatoes Judson had picked that morning. Robert answered his uncle's questions about the journey, but he didn't regale the man with stories. After all, the important story would come at the ending, next day. "Just a word with her," he told Uncle Judson. "So she'll know to be ready."

"I understand you want her prepared." Judson poured fresh cream over the last slice of his tomato. "But then you'll have them all prepared. Talk is you're dead. Bounty hunter named MacDonald bragged he would hunt you down. Parlayed with the Bensons some."

"He hunted me down, sure enough," said Robert.

"He the one you shot?" asked Judson. "I heard he was more interested in The Stud."

"He wanted both of us," said Robert. "Though he wants for nothing now. Unless it'd be a more decent resting place. I left him under rocks in Mexico."

Judson sighed. He went to a cabinet for his bottle. He poured whiskey into Robert's cup. "Here's what I'd do." Judson sat down, took a substantial pull of whiskey. "Shave that scraggly beard. Curry The Stud. Look presentable. Then present yourself. And nothing but yourself. No guns, no fists, just yourself, a proper bridegroom come back for what you think is yours."

"The beard bears witness to my time away. And this time I have money."

"That's a voice the Bensons listen to," said Judson.

Robert Johnson had planned for confrontation. Bonne, Hiram and Elizabeth, and now Judson all wanted him peaceful. Nobody realized how he'd come to where he was—the murder the Bensons committed to frame him, the months of confrontation, near starvation, suspicion, running for his life again and again. He'd shot a man. Surely the Bensons would not allow peace. Robert had imagined threat, stern will behind a loaded pistol, Jo running into his arms after her brothers and pa backed down.

Robert quaked with doubt, for Jo had become more imaginary than real. She would be big with child, her eyes green and alive, her hair wisping as it did from the prison of a tight bun, her mouth rich with lips that surely waited for his.

Sleepless through the long night, through moon set and star shine and dawn glow, Robert waited. As day broke, he led The Stud from his uncle Judson's barn. He had stowed his pistol. His money was in his pocket. Judson stood on the porch. Robert walked up to the steps. "I thank you," he said.

"You see your father before you leave again." Judson slapped Robert's back.

"I'm away then," Robert said to Uncle Judson. The Stud needed no urging—he ran ahead faster than Robert's thoughts, as though at least *he* knew what he was doing.

Robert Johnson rode straight up the Benson lane and stopped his horse in front of the house. The sun broke through the trees, and each tree suddenly stood by itself—part of the woods, but individual as well. Robert whooped. And whooped again. "I'm out here!" he shouted.

The house was dark, silent. He whooped again, calling them out. "Benson! Manny! Randolph! I am Robert Johnson. I've come for Jo."

Jo appeared first, but Manny followed close behind, a pistol in his hand. Was he protecting Jo, or threatening Robert? Robert was more interested in the swell he saw under Jo's dress. His thrill emboldened him, and when Randolph, then old man Benson, stumbled out the door, he whooped again. "I've come for what is mine," he shouted.

"She ain't yours," said Benson.

"*She* ain't, that's right. But she carries part of me. I can't claim *that* without claiming her, too."

Benson turned to Jo, grabbed her arm, twisted it behind her. "It's true then?" he asked her. "He's the one got you this way?"

"I have said so each day," said Jo. She wrenched her arm from her father's grip and cradled her womb.

Robert wanted to touch her there. When he moved forward, Manny cocked his pistol. "Go ahead and shoot, you thieving murderer," said

Robert. "For you can't kill me now. I am more than just the man standing before you. Part of me is in Jo. And you won't kill that, unless you're even more heartless than I think you to be."

"Many a child has a father he's never known," said Randolph.

"I don't want that fate for my child," said Robert. "Nor would you want that for your sister." He held his hands up in the gesture of surrender. "I love you, Jo," he said.

"Put the gun away, you fool." Benson turned to Manny.

"If we let him go, then who has the trouble of the law?" asked the son, pistol still cocked, aimed at Robert's chest. "If *he* ain't wanted, justice will turn somewhere else."

"When did it ever turn to you?" asked Robert. "I want Jo on horseback. The same mare that The Stud serviced. I'll pay you for the horse. Once we leave, you'll ask McFall if you could have done anything. You'll accuse me of abducting your daughter, stealing your horse. You'll no doubt add that to my crimes, along with the killing of the bounty hunter MacDonald. I believe you might know him."

Benson stood quiet. Manny lowered his pistol. Randolph scratched at his head. "Jo?" asked Benson.

"I'm off for Molly." Jo brushed past her father. Randolph stepped forward to stop her.

"How much for the horse?" Randolph asked Robert.

"I feel generous," said Robert. He flung some gold pieces to the ground. Randolph bent to examine them. Jo broke for the stable.

"Your generosity don't include anything for the girl?" Benson asked.

"You'd sell your own daughter? I'm not asking for any dowry beyond her freedom from you. I've paid you for the horse."

Jo rode up on Molly. Robert smiled and The Stud nickered as horse and rider took their place beside them.

"Not *that* saddle," said Benson.

Jo did not move. Her brother cocked his pistol. "You heard your father," he said to his sister.

"*You* heard *your* father." Her voice was cold and flat. "*My* father will give me this saddle. To remember my mother." Her voice softened, and she reached out her hand as though touching—her father, her dead mother. "I will need the memory of her close to my heart. I have much to do, and soon." She brought her hand to her womb.

"Your horse left something of himself behind, as well," said Benson. "Molly will soon foal."

"I expected as much," said Robert. He reached for his saddlebag.

"Don't you move!" shouted Manny. He leveled the pistol at Robert.

Jo rode between the pistol and Robert.

"I was reaching for more gold," said Robert. "Saddle and foal are worth something." He nudged The Stud to Jo's side. "But I have better payment. My land. Consider it yours. Jo and I will settle in Arkansas. My father will not dispute you." He nudged his horse and slapped Molly's rump, though neither horse needed urging. Neither Robert nor Jo expected gunshot or pursuit, but they rode away so fast anyone might have thought they'd stolen more than their freedom.

They turned into the lane and rode hard toward the Clarksville Road. As they neared the lane that led to his father's house, Robert slowed. "They might be after us already," Jo said. Molly shook her head against the bit.

Robert reined The Stud. "He wrote me a letter."

"Quickly." Jo turned Molly toward the home where Robert had been raised, where his brother and then his mother were buried.

Robert had wondered if he'd ever see the place again, familiar and yet strange now that he'd been gone so long. He rode up hallooing, hoping to raise his father from whatever chore he had put himself to on this crisp fall day. And then his father was in the barn door, waving. Robert had never seen him raise his hand except in anger, nor smile except in the bitter way a man grimaced when he knew the world was full of folly. Robert rode straight to him. "Your letter," he said.

Jacob Johnson nodded. "I see you've taken my counsel. Morning, Miss Benson."

Jo nodded.

"You knew my heart," said Robert. "I've wanted nothing else but to return for Jo."

"The Bensons?" asked his father.

"They took my money. They'll have the land. We're off to Memphis. Where you sent your letter. Then to Arkansas. The piney bluffs along the Arkansas River. Ask for Joseph Bonne. You'll come?"

"I'd need to get things in order. I'd have to decide to leave your mother, you know." Jacob swept his arm toward the graves, surrounded now by a low fence he'd recently whitewashed.

"And James. Sweet baby brother," said Robert. "I leave them, too. Jo leaves her kin. We'd like you to come."

"Haste," Jo hissed.

"We must ride," said Robert.

"Don't fear the Bensons," said Jacob. "They have what they want. Just as you do."

"I have money, too," said Robert, reaching for his saddlebag.

"You made a show of that, did you?" Jacob chastised him. "For riches . . ."

"Father," Robert interrupted. "I care nothing for gold. But others do. You might need some?"

His father stepped into the barn. Robert took it for a rebuke. But Jacob appeared with something in his hand, striding toward Robert and Jo. "For you," he said, and offered Robert a piece of blackened metal.

Robert Johnson took the saddle horn he'd stolen from his father's barn.

"Build another place for it," Jacob said. "I'll expect to see it when I knock on your door."

"I'll expect that, too," said Robert. He put the horn in his pocket and turned The Stud. He nodded to Jo. They trotted toward the Clarksville Road. There, they ran several miles until Robert found a trailhead that he knew led to a spring. Along a tree-shaded path they found their way to the cool moist earth where water sweat, then streamed from a rock outcropping to pool in a natural bowl. The horses drank.

Robert and Jo sat horseback, side by side, and he tasted Jo's lips, leaning to her just as she leaned to him. They lingered against each other, lips brushing, their hands reading each other's faces, and then the heavier text of bodies beneath clothing. Robert drank from the richness of memory, from the anticipation of what they might do next. But when the horses had drunk their fill, and shook their heads, impatient, Jo sat straight in the saddle again. "Not now," she said. "You showed them you have money."

"If they try to rob me," said Robert, "I'll defend myself." He pulled MacDonald's derringer from his saddlebag.

"They're my brothers. My pa." Jo turned Molly so she could face Robert. "Outlaws though they are, as much as I want to leave them, I don't want to see them killed. Especially by you."

Robert leaned forward in the saddle. "They wanted to see me killed," he said.

"I didn't want that, either," said Jo. She stood in the stirrups and pulled her dress up above her waist. At first, Robert thought she'd changed her mind—they might take each other. But she was girdled, wrapped in strips of cloth. He thought she might be bandaged. She unwound one of the strips, threw it to the ground. Then another.

Robert Johnson nearly swooned as Jo, head down, never acknowledging what she was doing, methodically unwrapped herself of her pregnancy. She gasped, finally, as though a weight had been lifted from her. But the weight was upon Robert, sudden and crushing. All that he'd dreamed and conjured those lonely nights in bunkhouses, by campfires, under stars, was unraveled in a moment. He let unashamed tears fall. He shook his head, but not in disbelief, even though belief was the thread that had stitched his life together over all his months away. He shook his head to clear the past and grasp the future.

Jo released the hem of her dress, sat back down in the saddle, and looked at him for the first time. "I lost the baby," she said. "A month ago."

The news doubled him again. The strips of cloth on the ground, like the discarded skins of snakes, told of what had been. He stared down at them as though he could fathom what had been so close to her womb, her heart.

"I wrapped myself. I added strips of cloth each day," Jo said. "I prayed for you to return before my time was due." She reached for him, but he leaned away.

"I prayed for so many things," said Robert. He cleared his head. Ever since he'd run, the world had startled him. He had surprised himself, too. He had survived what he once would have thought impossible. He had forded rivers, starved and thirsted until his throat closed, he had become a thief, a murderer. He'd finally been certain in his return to Tennessee, to Jo, to their child. But the baby had been a mirage. Jo was real. "I prayed for you most of all," he said.

"Would they have let me go if I hadn't wrapped myself in this secret?" she asked.

He smiled. She was smart. She knew her brothers and pa. He'd been able to bluff them because of her bluff. But now, if they came after him for his money, and found her lithe and thin once more, they might well shoot him. "We will have a baby," said Robert. "At least I aim to keep trying."

"And I aim to let you," said Jo. "But not until we're married. I've suffered enough as the Jezebel of that house."

"We're riding to Memphis. To friends. Hiram and Elizabeth. They know of our situation. They've made plans for us that involve a certain justice of the peace."

"That's your marriage proposal, is it?"

"Did you expect me to ask your father for your hand?" He leaned toward her, stretched out his arm, and she took his hand.

"I accept," she said. "I'll whisper it into what's left of your ear." She leaned to him and softly said "yes" into his torn ear.

"It was shot," said Robert, "but I hear out of it just fine. Just what I wanted to hear, in fact."

stirrup to stirrup

obert Johnson's heart was as light as it had been heavy when, months before, he'd ridden away toward he knew not where. This time, each destination was familiar—Jackson, Memphis, Arkansas. Each person, too—Charles Onnen, Hiram and Elizabeth, Bonne on the ridge above the Arkansas River that Robert thought of as Pine Bluff.

Jo took the lead, as though she'd dreamed of flight with the same urgency Robert had dreamed of homecoming. As many times as he slowed his horse and looked behind them, he did not detect pursuit. He began to trust his father's word, just as the old man trusted the word of his Heavenly Father. For once, righteousness might work toward Robert's salvation.

They stopped at dark. In a bower of trees beside a creek, they uncinched the saddles. They drank with their horses, then turned them loose. Robert had jerky and dried cornbread. A small vial of molasses was Judson's treat. "Not as sweet as being with you," Robert said, "but a nod toward it."

They ate, then lay themselves next to each other in the grass, holding hands. "From the beginning," Jo insisted. "You, then me, taking turns until we've caught up. Tell everything."

Robert laughed. She wanted everything in the same way his mother told everything. His father might come in from watering and feeding the pigs and horses, milking and then turning loose the cow, oiling the wagon wheels for the expected trip to town, throwing down hay for when they returned, and when asked what he'd done, he'd say, "Chores." His mother might come in from weeding the garden and all of dinner might be a recollection of the pumpkins her family had watered daily one year when she was eight and how one grew larger than she was, and two men could barely lift it to the wagon to take it to town and show what a pumpkin could be, and they'd made soup from it, pounded it to dry for stews, sold the seeds they didn't eat. And then she'd start in on her potatoes and the one she'd dug up when she was twelve and it looked so much like a human foot she thought someone had been murdered and chopped to pieces and buried part by part and she was the first to learn of the crime.

Robert looked through the trees into the starlight between the branches, and tried to find his way of telling. "I waited in Uncle Judson's barn," he began. "I heard them come after me. I could tell they meant business. So I rode away, and rode, stopping for nothing but water and spring greens."

Jo seemed satisfied as he told of his journey through Tennessee, the swollen Hatchie River, the wayfarers and town builders at Jackson, and then Memphis. He told about meeting Hiram, then stopped. "Your turn," he yawned.

"So you can sleep?" she asked.

"A yawn can be a calming thing," said Robert.

"I knew they were planning something against you, but they kept me locked in the house," Jo began. "And then the worst happened, and I had to listen to their self-praise, their miserable plans for your land once you were brought to justice. All I could do was pray I was with child. I missed you and wanted part of you left behind with me." The intensity of her voice, even in recollection, spoke to the misery of her loss. She'd lost Robert, and then she'd lost their child. She could tell no one once she'd resolved to continue as though she were pregnant, wrapping herself in that lie. They'd treated her as damaged, as whore, but they'd not beaten her as they might have had she not been carrying a baby. The sheet she'd ripped into strips had been one of her mother's, put away in a chest with things meant someday to be dowry. She fell asleep talking.

Robert woke her in soft light. They rode hard, stopping only for water, continuing the stories of their time apart at night. This time, Jo rode behind, because, as she said, "They won't shoot me." Each time Robert turned, he was doubly relieved—her brothers and pa were not in chase, and Jo's expression of determination matched his own.

They approached the Hatchie River on the third day of their escape. The haste Robert had anticipated was unnecessary. Maybe they'd be able to meet Charles Onnen's wife, his child, find a meal. When they saw smoke, he wondered aloud if there might be some cooking ahead.

"Hope and air make a thin diet," Jo teased him.

"Better than my diet of *fear* and air," said Robert. "We'll describe your father and brothers. I'll ask Onnen not to take them across, if they come this way. He'll agree if there's some reward behind the asking."

In anticipation of food he told her about the meals he'd eaten in Elizabeth's kitchen, the chicken stewed in its own juices, the pork, the beans, the potatoes, the gravy. Their appetites keened, and thin trails of smoke ahead drew them forward through the bottomland, the dense trees, the swampy mud from the Hatchie's flood of the previous spring.

Once they smelled the smoke, they knew nothing was cooking, and when they finally came upon what had once been Onnen's small cabin, nothing stood but two half walls and ash. Nearby, the post that held the bell to call the ferry stood intact. The small dock had been burned, the rope cut. Nothing waited on the opposite bank. The smoldering ruins of half a burned cabin turned Robert's stomach, the chimney blackened with soot, the door fallen outward and tattooed where coals had fallen on it. "Like my cabin?" he asked.

"This is not the work of my brothers or pa," Jo said.

"No," Robert agreed.

Jo screamed and pointed. The rope from the ferry had been put to use. Onnen hung from a tree ten yards into the woods, his neck broken, his pants dark where he'd fouled himself. Robert suppressed a cry. Their silence was nicked by a whimpering exhalation, like a lost fledgling. Jo rode to the cabin, threw herself off her horse and into the random smoke curling from the blackened rubble.

She backed away, sobbing. A mewling reached Robert's ears and he jumped off The Stud to join Jo. A charred face. Hair singed to thin threads, black clothing steaming. Yet he saw movement. He jumped over what had been a windowsill and found the baby beneath the dead mother, protected where the tiny creature might well have been smothered. The baby cried when Robert picked it up from beneath her mother's apron. The tears made black tracks down a sooty face. Jo cried, too, and Robert carried the baby to her.

"Who could do such a thing?" Jo cried, holding the baby to her breast. She hurried away into green grass, toward water to try to wash away ash, smoke, whatever haunting memory would plague the suffering child.

Robert gathered the horses and led them after Jo, toward the river, which moved as peacefully as if no violence had ever stained its banks. He held his tongue. Jo wondered who could do such a thing. Robert had met many of that ilk. For him, the question was not *who* could do such a thing, or even *why*, for he'd seen Onnen's gloating negotiations with travelers. Instead, Robert Johnson questioned *when* he would ever escape such foulness. He had committed foul deeds himself. Maybe he was doomed to see himself over and over in what others might do, would do, to each other.

"We'll keep the baby girl," said Jo. They stood together on the bank. Already, to Robert's surprise, Jo had unbuttoned her dress to give the crying baby something to suckle. "She might find something here," said Jo. The tiny girl's gaping mouth found Jo's nipple.

"They might have folks around here. We could ask," said Robert.

"I might have some folks chasing after us," said Jo.

"Best cross the river," said Robert. "Is Molly a swimmer?"

"She has to be," said Jo, "but you should hold the baby."

He mounted The Stud and Jo unlatched the baby from her breast. What had been whimpering cries turned to full-throated objection. Johnson held the baby tight and The Stud moved toward the water. The baby screamed. Johnson smiled. Soon his horse began to swim. The rocking motion soothed both rider and baby. Robert turned to be certain Jo was behind him. Molly balked at the water's edge. Jo kicked her so hard Robert wanted to remind her the horse was with foal, but Jo knew her horse, and the force worked. Timidity was replaced by abandon. Soon they were swimming side by side.

"Easier than spring. There was a flood here," Johnson shouted. "And this time you're with me."

"And you're carrying a baby," said Jo.

This baby, abandoned, had been cruelly disregarded by whoever was bent on destroying Onnen. Could they simply take her away and make her their own? Robert was seized by the question as they swam, the baby peaceful in his arms, exhausted by her ordeal.

By the time they reached the opposite bank, Robert was determined to embrace circumstances. Doubt, Fray Antonio had told him, was the opposite of courage. Courage came from facing death. Robert had cheated death many times since meeting Jo Benson. This baby had cheated death. Should he be less courageous than a tiny girl?

"Yes," Johnson said when they found the road on the other side of the Hatchie River. "I'm carrying this baby."

Jo took the girl in her arms and kept her there through the two long days to Memphis. They stopped on the road as they neared. Robert wanted to find Hiram, make certain Jo's pa and brothers hadn't come to town. Jo stayed in the woods, resting against her saddle, the baby at her breast. She'd suckled the child whenever they'd stopped for water, whenever Robert had disappeared to shoot rabbit, squirrel, bird. Robert wondered at her determination to give comfort, for surely she couldn't give milk. The baby seemed equally determined to be satisfied, for she'd remained quiet through the ride to Memphis.

The city brought no sign of the Bensons. Hiram took him into the house to the kitchen. Elizabeth, bigger with child than Robert thought possible, began to fetch food.

"Jo is in hiding," he said. "I rode ahead, to make certain we're not pursued."

"I've had others looking out," Hiram said. "No news has come to me." He strode out of the kitchen and Robert followed. "I'll go with you, just in case," Hiram said at the door. He went around the house to the stable and soon appeared on horseback, a roan filly.

As they rode to where Jo Benson and the baby girl waited, Robert told Hiram about calling out the Bensons, about their surrender of Jo, about his brief visit with his father, about the sheet Jo had wrapped herself in. Then there was Onnen's ferry, the smoldering cabin, and the baby they'd rescued. He warned Hiram about Jo's determination to suckle the child, milk or not. "Horse or cow, they have to foal or calve to give milk."

"Humans are creatures beyond others," said Hiram. "Sometimes what you can imagine is what you can have. I like your Jo."

They found her asleep in the woods, the baby asleep in her arms, its mouth open as if in midsuck. Jo and the tiny girl both woke when the men approached, and the baby went for Jo's nipple. Jo tried to stand when she saw Hiram behind Robert. The baby released Jo's nipple, her mouth dripping a filmy liquid. Robert was amazed. Jo put the baby on her shoulder and hid her breast beneath her thin dress.

Hiram cleared his throat. Jo motioned him forward. "What's your baby's name?" he asked.

"Nell," said Jo. "That was my mother's name." She handed Nell to Robert and buttoned her dress. She turned to Hiram. "You're Hiram. Robert has spoken much of you."

"And I've heard much of you. And your baby, Nell." He slapped Robert on the back. "Nell has eaten. Now you two must eat."

Jo picked up Molly's blanket, threw it over her back, followed it with her mother's saddle, cinched it tight, mounted, and leaned over for Nell.

"Nell suits her just fine," Robert said.

They rode into Memphis as quickly as the baby could tolerate.

Elizabeth had filled a tub in the small room off the kitchen. "I always eat better when I'm well scrubbed," she said. She drew Jo into the room with her and shut the door.

Hiram lifted a brown jug from the same shelf where Elizabeth kept the cups with the men's names on them. Robert reached for the one marked *JONSEN*. In it was his pouch of gold. "I thank you," Robert said.

"You can take the cup with you," said Hiram. As he poured whiskey into the cup he spelled Johnson's name correctly. "Someday, you'll know all the letters. Be sure Nell goes to school. Then she'll teach you what she learns."

"Jo can teach me, too," Robert said, taking a sip of the strong drink. After the first mouthful, the others came smoother and richer, as did a second pour. "Don't get me stinking drunk," Robert told Hiram. "I haven't had drink in a long time."

"A bath will sober you up. And cure the stink, too. For you're already *stinking*, if not stinking drunk." Between small sips he rose from the table to stir the stew that keened their hunger.

By the time Elizabeth and Jo and Nell came from the tub room, Robert was afraid he might not be able to stand up. He wobbled. But they looked so fresh—the baby now in a blanket, cheeks red, hair so light it lifted off her head, and nearly as blond as Jo's. Robert stood straight, staring at them. "Go make yourself decent," said Jo. "I'm hungry."

In the tub room, sitting content in the same water that had cleaned his soon-to-be wife and recently found child, he wondered where in

Memphis a man could buy clothing. His pants nearly stood on their own where he'd stepped out of them. He scrubbed until his skin was raw, then shook out his clothes and put them on. He wasn't the new man he wanted to be, but he was fresh.

Jo had put Nell in the small crib Hiram had made for his and Elizabeth's baby. They made a long meal of the stew, cornbread, greens, and fried apples. At the end, more whiskey for the men. Robert pointed to the first two letters on his mug. "*J, O*," he noted. "That's your name, too," he said to Jo.

"I never learned my letters," she said.

"But you sewed my initials, *R* and *J*, into that handkerchief," said Robert.

"I had your handkerchief, I thought I did. But I lost it." She wrung her hands as though knotting the missing handkerchief in her fingers.

· "Your brothers? Your pa? Someone sewed my initials in that handkerchief. Someone took it to the Lonely Creek Bridge, as sure as someone rode The Stud there."

"I don't know," she said.

Robert pushed his whiskey away and stood up. He paced the floor, feeling as trapped as he'd been all these months, but this time in the tight trap of his mind. He put his palm against a wall. "If you had known, you would have spoken for me?" he asked. "You couldn't get me word? You couldn't tell *anyone* that your brothers and pa plotted against me?"

"I was prisoner in that cabin until you came back." Jo stood up and walked to the other side of the kitchen.

Neither Jo nor Robert spoke. Each breathed deeply. Elizabeth interrupted the silence with the clattering of dishes.

"You couldn't have come back sooner?" Jo said. "*They* were your accusers, not me. Don't you try to change that now!"

They stared at each other across the room. "I reckon we were both trapped," said Robert. "You couldn't speak. I couldn't return. We can't either of us change that now."

Nell woke up and screamed as though another cabin was on fire and she was caught in the hot flames.

"And now we're together," Robert said. He went for Nell, just as she did. They met at the corner, and Jo reached for Nell, and Robert reached for Jo.

"I have a fine trap for you both," Hiram said. He drained his whiskey and stood up to help Elizabeth at the table. "Tomorrow, if you still want hitching."

"I do," said Robert.

"I do," said Jo.

"Save it for tomorrow," said Hiram.

They had saved so much for each other that neither had known how hard it would be to realize what they'd saved. One had been rescuer and another rescued; one had been hunted and the other kept; one had become criminal—murderer, horse thief, liar—and the other implicated in the criminal machinations of murderers, horse thieves, and liars. Both had lived on longing and hope. Both had thought their reunion would bring them nothing but happiness. But both were leaving home and family no matter how they'd been treated there. Robert Johnson knew almost nothing about Jo Benson; she did not know him. They had sought each other as escape. Everything they did now would be inescapable. They would marry. They would raise a child. They would become Arkansawyers. They would build a cabin, expand it when more babies came. They would raise horses, become citizens of a new place, become people who could be trusted to do honest business in the world, who would have open hearts and an open hearth. But first, Robert realized, he had to undo his words. And after that, unravel the knot of all his experiences in his travels, just as she had her own knots to loosen.

They lay down in the tub room, on thick blankets, Nell beside them. "Like Hiram said, it's a fine trap," Robert said when Jo sighed.

"I don't like that word," said Jo. She propped her head on an elbow.

"What word do you like?" Robert faced her.

"*Together*," she said. "And *now*." She touched his cheek. "And *someday*."

"Then how about I use better words myself," he said, reaching for her hand.

"That'd be fine," she said.

"*Marriage*," he said. "*Mississippi River. Arkansas. Bonne's. Pine Bluffs.*"

"*Nell*," she said. "*Cabin. Foal. Baby.*"

They named things as though they were the first to invent the words. *Mother. Home. Sweetheart. Sweet dreams. Love. Care. Dare.*

side by side

after they'd cleared the breakfast table, Hiram suggested that Robert Johnson give Jo Benson some gold pieces. "She needs proper attire. Elizabeth will help her, of course, if she'll agree to be seen in public in her condition."

"You're the one embarrassed by my condition," said Elizabeth, and before Robert could fish in his pouch for gold she had put a bonnet on her head and a shawl around her shoulders.

Jo took up Nell in one hand, clutched gold in the other, and set out.

"And you," Hiram said to Robert. "Never did a man need new clothes more."

They went to the dry goods, a much less refined mercantile establishment than where Jo and Elizabeth stopped, for, as Hiram said, "Let new be the same as fine, for once you head to the territory, muslin will be an improvement on linen." Hiram pointed to a sign of a beer mug with *GOODS* painted below the rim. "Sells beer he makes himself, Steinbock does," said Hiram, "but he gives sixteen ounces to a pint, sixteen ounces to a pound and thirty-six inches to the yard. Along with a hearty laugh."

Steinbock did more than laugh when he saw that Robert Johnson had gold, but Robert insisted on nothing more than new boots, pants, and shirt. "I'm traveling light. To the territory," he said. "Just as soon as I get married."

"Once you're married, you'll not travel light again," said the shopkeeper, running his hand through long brown hair. He led Robert to his best line of pants.

"You don't know my Jo," said Robert.

"That's a fine attitude," said Steinbock. He stroked his goatee, staring at his merchandise. Then he brought forth wool pants, and a drop-sleeve linen shirt. "These should fit you, if you like them."

"I do," said Robert, "but I'd like them better if they were muslin."

"I like a simple man," said Steinbock, "though I don't usually find much in his pockets for myself." The shopkeeper put his hands in his vest pockets and pulled a gold coin from each one. "You might consider a vest," he said. "Dress you up just a little. And keep your money handy."

Robert nodded. He'd worn his father's vests until he moved onto his own land. Then he'd bought one for himself, of leather. He thought of it, black and brittle, in the ashes of his cabin, set afire by the Bensons. "Leather," he said, and enjoyed Steinbock's raised eyebrows.

The shopkeeper pointed to a chair. "I have to order the boots," he said. He measured Robert's foot. "But I have two pairs made for a man who never came back for them. I think they'll do for you once you break them to your feet."

"I'm lucky, then," said Robert, thinking of the fat man in Laredo so far away.

"You seem so," said Steinbock. "If you can break yourself to a woman, then what's a pair of boots to that?" He took two pairs from the shelves. "And I'll give you a good price if you buy both pairs."

"One pair," said Robert.

"I'll buy the other," said Hiram, "if it'll bring the cost of each lower."

Steinbock looked at Hiram, puzzled. "I have to have yours special made, a foot and a half from heel to toe, it seems."

Hiram looked at his long foot. "The men I hire, fresh in from wherever, they can use them. I keep a few extra."

"You're a thoughtful man," said Steinbock.

"I hope to think about others more than they think about me," said Hiram.

Steinbock looked around the store. The several customers who had come in while he was waiting on Robert were toward the back. "You know my sympathies," Steinbock whispered.

"I know you're sympathetic to Robert here," Hiram said loudly, "getting hitched today as he is."

Steinbock's eyes widened at the booming voice.

"Yes, my sympathies, boy. My heartfelt sympathies." He led them to the counter where he kept his ledger book and receipts.

They paid for the clothing and started toward Hiram's.

"You can be mysterious," Robert said.

Hiram strode ahead.

Elizabeth and Jo and Nell were still away. "Go dress in those clothes." Hiram pointed to the tub room. "Best break them in."

Robert emerged from the tub room stiff and awkward, but he soon forgot himself. Elizabeth sat in a rocking chair, nursing Nell, a shawl covering her breast. A second woman giving milk, neither suckling her own child. Hiram was right about mystery. "Where's Jo?" he asked.

"Changing into a fine dress," said Elizabeth. "We'll wash your other clothes before you leave. Though I can't say they're worth keeping."

"Make good rags, as my mother used to say," said Robert.

Hiram came into the kitchen with a wooden box. The same box Robert had floated across the Mississippi. "We'll make sure they have plenty," Hiram said to Elizabeth. "Enough to take them to those Arkansas pine woods Robert keeps talking about."

"Did you go to Steinbock's?" asked Elizabeth. And when Hiram nodded, she said, "I suppose you purchased beer?"

"No. Nor whiskey. You fixing to put on a party?"

"I'm fixing to keep Jo's milk coming," said Elizabeth. Under cover of her shawl she took Nell from one nipple, readjusted her dress, and set her to the other. "My mother always said, 'Nothing brings milk like beer.'"

Jo walked in wearing a blue gingham dress and new shoes. Her hair was pinned into a bun. She stood for one moment to present herself to all of them, to allow Robert to present himself to her. Hiram left the room. Jo went to Elizabeth and Nell. "She's nursing?" Jo whispered.

Elizabeth smiled, content. She lifted her shawl. "She'll sleep right through your vows."

Hiram returned with two witnesses. He moved everyone into the small parlor and performed what passed for a wedding ceremony in the Memphis, Tennessee, of 1825. No rings, no preacher, no family. As predicted, Nell slept through the short passages that Hiram read in his deepest voice.

Afterward, Robert Johnson signed the marriage certificate as best Elizabeth could show him how. He wrote "22." Elizabeth worked with

Jo, too, who wrote her name twice, once with *Benson*, "For the very last time," she said, and once with *Johnson*, "my forever name," then wrote her age, "16."

The witnesses marked their lines with Xs and grumbled out the door to return to their work in Hiram's stable, two men who had as much chance of marrying soon as they did of winning a horse race against The Stud, who was too busy with first one mare and then another to run the track that day.

After the ceremony, Hiram disappeared. Elizabeth put Nell in the small crib. She and Jo began packing the wooden box Hiram had left in the kitchen. "We'll make sure you have plenty," she said.

Hiram lugged in a second box, which he labored to place next to the one Elizabeth packed. He motioned Robert into the parlor. There, he pointed to a chair. Robert sat. Hiram did, too, stretching his long legs so that the heels of his boots each rested in the middle of the two flowers woven into the carpet. "I'll take you to the river tomorrow," he said. "Elizabeth is packing a box of provisions, but once you take the box across you'll want to put everything in the bags and tie them to your saddles. You'll leave the box along the bank."

"Like last time," Robert said.

"Like last time," Hiram repeated. "But I'm going to ask you to take the other box, too. Leave it where you leave the smaller one. Someone will take care of it."

"You do business both sides, then?" asked Robert.

"I promised myself not to talk to you about this." He drew his legs up and put his hands on the armrests of his chair.

"This is more than horseflesh, is it?" he asked before Hiram could stand up.

"Flesh," said Hiram. He stretched his legs again. "Elizabeth says I have to stop once the baby comes. I could end up dead."

"You running slaves?" asked Robert.

"The slaves are running," said Hiram. "I help them."

"Jackson one of your men?" Robert wasn't certain how much he should know. "That's risky business." He told Hiram about Bonne and Francoise, how much Bonne's attitude about ownership seemed like Hiram's.

"My family has been in this country since Pilgrim days," said Hiram. "They escaped the tyranny of England. They wanted religious freedom.

For generations, we've sought freedom. We've found it by moving west. Me, I want freedom from those who worship ownership in a place where none of us has much to own. Senator Jackson knows the common man. But he still owns slaves. Too many men care more for their ownership of slaves than their Bibles, more for their property than their principles."

"And so you break the law? Risk your life?" asked Robert.

"To give others the chance for life. You'll be carrying my last donation to the cause. Elizabeth is right. I have to be responsible to the baby. You have a new life, too, suckling at the breast of your wife."

Robert grinned. "When she can get Nell away from Elizabeth."

"Jo will make you a good partner."

"I'll be glad to float the box. No doubt the boots you bought are in there?"

"As are the clothes you left in the tub room when you changed into your new duds. And a dozen percussion rifles." Hiram stood up, tall as an exclamation point. "That's another reason I tell you this. Those who have been working with me will need rifles to protect themselves."

"I've come a long way," said Robert, standing next to Hiram. "I left Tennessee a fugitive for a crime I did not commit. Since then, I've become the outlaw I was accused of being. And now you ask me to continue in my lawlessness."

"You don't have to do this," said Hiram.

"You didn't have to help me," said Robert. "But you did."

Elizabeth was so taken with Nell that she and Hiram banned Robert and Jo to the parlor, encouraging them to "get acquainted."

Theirs was no longer a hurried rush from possible pursuit, nor shadowy doubt about what they might do next, nor even a time to parse out what had been. They talked about their future in Arkansas, with the prospect of a cabin in the piney woods, with horses and children growing up in sunshine. In their slower reacquaintance they put aside whatever doubts they'd had about each other in the space of their separation.

"I want you to be more than the mother of Nell," Robert said once they'd retired after supper. "I want you to be the mother of *our* children."

"Nell *is* our child now," said Jo. "But we can have *our* babies, too. And soon."

"How soon?" asked Robert.

"Come here," she said. She spread out the blankets Hiram and Elizabeth had set on a chair for them. She pulled up her dress and lay down. "Would right now be soon enough?" Jo pulled her dress up over her head, and then off. Her underclothing came off next.

Robert followed her example, stripping off his new clothes. He studied Jo Johnson, the woman he'd only conjured over the months of their absence. Her breasts were fuller, her hips broader, her navel deeper, her knees knobbier. But her skin was softer, her hair more pliant, her eyes greener, her arms more eager for him than ever before. And then he put imagination aside, for the sensation of pleasure was richer than what the imagination could render.

Both were rendered by their passion, their happiness in being together at last, their commitment to a future. This was a marriage celebration. Their love would make the future.

When they awoke next morning, they made a little more of their future, and dressed and breakfasted, and packed their few belongings, and readied The Stud and Molly. Elizabeth left the kitchen when Hiram did, she to her room, he to the stable for the mules.

the flood

hiram slapped the reins until the mules took to his pace. Robert Johnson, for the first time in months, did not care who might see him. He was unafraid with Jo at his side, little Nell in her arms. "Elizabeth," Hiram said as they left, "was nearly swooning. Worried about the two of you, I believe. But we'll find some help for the crossing." He fell into silence.

The buckboard was loaded with the two boxes, and The Stud and Molly were tied behind. The travelers shared the wide seat. Hiram's silence might be sadness at their parting. Or the quietness that sets in when someone is doing something for the last time and will miss it, though the danger of his missions would surely make their end a relief. Or perhaps with Jo and Nell beside him, he contemplated his upcoming fatherhood. Nell broke the silence, suddenly screaming, her mouth round, her face red, her eyes squinched and flowing with tears.

Before Jo could quiet her, a horse galloped down the street after them. Hiram jerked on the reins and the mules dug their hooves into the dusty street. He pulled his musket from under the seat, but the rider was one of the hired men who had served as witness to the marriage ceremony the day before. He was hatless, riding without a saddle in his obvious hurry. "Your missus," he called to Hiram. "She needs you home. And Missus Jenkins says she'll need help with the baby."

"Baby?" Hiram's disbelief left his face vacant.

"Take the horse," said the hand, dismounting and handing the reins to Hiram. "I'll get these folks to the river."

Hiram put his musket under the wagon seat, jumped down, and threw himself on the horse.

"You want us to come back with you?" asked Jo. "We could help."

"No," said Hiram. "You'll be helping me by getting yourselves across the river. Robert, take care." He lifted his hand.

Robert could not tell if the gesture was a salute or a caution. The hired man climbed into the wagon, but Robert had already picked up the reins. "I know my way to the river," he said. The man shrugged his shoulders.

Nell quieted in Jo's arms. They drove in wary silence. As they neared the river, the wide water laid out before them, the man finally spoke. "Those your boxes?" he asked.

"I aim to take them across," said Robert. He slowed the mules and stopped the wagon near a small dock Hiram had shown him on his last trip through.

"Then what?" asked the man. "You can't carry them horseback."

"I can carry what's in them," said Robert.

"I'm not certain you will," said the man. His shrieking whistle pierced Robert's ears, brought Nell from her sleep, brought Jo to her feet. Robert reached under the seat at the same time as the hired hand. They struggled over the musket. Robert managed to grasp the gun. He used the barrel end as a staff, pushing the man from the wagon. Then he aimed directly at the man's face. "Raise your hands," Robert commanded. The man did as he was told. Robert jumped off the wagon. The man's whistle hadn't brought anyone yet, but Robert kept the musket truly aimed. "You will carry the boxes to the edge of the dock. Now!" Robert Johnson shouted.

The man did not move. Johnson backed to the horses. "Jo," he said. "Get on Molly. Take The Stud to the dock." He did not want to shoot the man.

Jo, Nell in arms, mounted Molly. She reached for The Stud's reins, then into the saddlebag. She pulled out the pistol. "I'll cover him, Robert, if you want to get the boxes."

Robert strode to his horse to stow Hiram's musket, then hurried to the back of the buckboard. The hired hand lunged toward him. Robert readied himself for a fistfight. Jo shot the pistol. Nell cried out. The hired hand did not move. He looked to the sky, gave one more whistle, then fainted.

Blood oozed from his rump, and down his leg. "Hurry, Robert," Jo said. She'd found the powder bag and the shot, and was preparing the gun.

Robert heaved up the heavier trunk, already attached to a rope, and staggered to the dock. The Stud followed. Robert tied the rope to the saddle horn. He hurried back up for the trunk of their provisions. Three men rode toward them. "Jo!" Robert shouted.

She turned and waved the pistol, then readied herself to shoot. Robert grabbed the smaller trunk and ran to the small dock. He tied that rope to The Stud's saddle horn, too, then threw the box into the river. "Steady," he said to his horse. He picked up the heavier box and threw it in after the first. Both soon pulled with the current against The Stud as his hooves clattered against the wood of the dock. "Jo!" Robert shouted.

The riders had pulled pistols from their vests. "Into the water!" Robert shouted. But Jo, cradling Nell in one arm, the pistol outstretched in the other, took steady aim. She shot at one of the men. His hat flew into the air. She kicked Molly and flew down the planks, across the dock, and into the Mississippi. Robert pulled his rifle from The Stud's saddle. He took his own shot, and one of the men clutched his leg. The other two held their ground and Robert mounted The Stud just as the horse dove off the dock, the trunk taut and pulling them downriver.

"Stay ahead!" Robert yelled at Jo. She swam Molly out of rifle range. Robert would not be so lucky, with The Stud weighted with the boxes. The two pursuers clattered onto the dock and took futile shots with their pistols.

"Come on, boy. Now or never," Johnson said to The Stud. The men lifted their rifles. He thought of cutting loose the ropes, saving himself even if he was left with the little that was in his saddlebags. But he could not disappoint Hiram's final plan. Once again, he was ambushed by cowards. Jo swam ahead. "Now or never," he repeated.

Two shots whistled past, but Robert felt nothing, saw nothing. The Stud redoubled his efforts at the sounds, as though he knew the men on shore had to reload their rifles. Boats plied the river, and Robert urged his horse toward the nearest one, for surely the men who wanted to stop him would not shoot at passing strangers in a longboat. Jo, Nell, and Molly, unencumbered by boxes, stayed upstream.

A second volley found truer aim and the water pocked in front of him. The Stud shuddered. He bled from one ear, and Robert leaned close.

A flap of the horse's ear was torn away, nothing more, though blood trickled into the water to snake its way downstream. Robert slipped off The Stud. No use losing a horse when he was the one the men wanted to stop. And he could take his turn tugging the boxes.

The men in the longboat heard the round of shots and picked up rifles. They steered the boat to where Robert struggled with the ropes, trying to bring the boxes closer together. With the third round from the shore, the men in the boat answered with warning shots. The boat finally came within shouting distance. "My wife!" Robert hollered. He pointed upstream. "I'm not sure they'll make it." He couldn't see Jo, Nell, or Molly, and fear gripped his heart, greater fear than he had of the rifle shots that came one more time.

"Stop your fire!" yelled a man from the longboat. Another man discharged his rifle toward shore, this time with more aim.

"They're my wife's kin!" Robert shouted. "We've just married! Help *her* across!"

The longboat continued toward him. Two of the crew trained rifles on the eastern bank of the river. "You first!" shouted a burly man who held the rudder. He carried a large pipe, which he promptly stuck in his mouth. Smoke issued forth as though from a chimney.

"My wife!" yelled Robert, bobbing in the water. "They're after *her!*" Panic pulled Robert down. He held the ropes as though drowning. He pointed upriver, where two pursuers now swam their horses.

"Your wife is halfway across!" shouted the burly man. "She's swimming stronger than they are, she is." They were nearly alongside Robert. The man gave the rudder to one of his companions and strode to the side of the boat. He leaned toward Robert, his pipe still sending up clouds of smoke. "Course she doesn't have the boxes, does she?" He was next to the ropes. He jerked them up, looping them to a gunwale bracket.

"Her dowry," said Robert. "Our new start in Arkansas. Her brothers are mighty jealous." Robert used the ropes to pull himself toward the boat.

"Must have been a wedding at gunpoint?" asked the man. His short beard was gray as the smoke that issued from his mouth.

"Seems to be now," said Robert. He was next to the boat. The man reached down for his hand. Robert kicked and the man pulled him onto the deck.

"Not much flesh on those bones," the man said, wiping his hands on his leggings. "If you was a fish, I'd throw you back in."

"Done some hard traveling," said Robert.

"Your missus, too?" he asked. He shouted at his crew to turn the boat and grab their oars for a push upstream. Two of the men pulled the boxes to the boat.

The Stud swam close. Robert leaned over to check his ear, still seeping blood. "We're on our way," he told the horse. He straightened and stared into the distance, straining for a glimpse of Jo. "She has the baby with her," said Robert.

"Baby?" The man turned to his crew. "Dig in, my lads!" he shouted. The longboat turned and the four men plied the water with deep strokes. "We'll be to her soon," said the captain, smoke streaming out with his words. "Sooner than they will," he said. He pointed upstream where two men on horseback bobbed in the water. The captain made a sour face, tapped his pipe against the gunwale, and pocketed it in his red vest. "Two fools who don't know better than to test *the flood*. There's whirlpools, eddies, driftwood that can jimmy up from the deep and knock over a boat."

"I've swum it twice before," Robert said. "Over and back. First time it was all swollen up with rain."

"Fool's luck," said the captain.

"Good horse," said Robert.

"Looks to match you, with that ear chewed away."

Robert touched his ear.

"Your wife have a good horse?" The man dipped the rudder deeper into the water.

"A fine horse, yes. A horse that will soon foal," Robert bragged.

The man smiled. "You seem a right fruitful family," he said.

"I hope so," said Robert. Jo came into sight, holding onto Molly, baby Nell's head next to hers. The men on horseback swam slowly, rifles in the air to keep flint and powder dry. They'd have to be closer to train an accurate shot.

The crew put their shoulders to their oars, skimming the boat steadily against the current, making faster time than Robert had imagined they could. Still, patience disappears during pursuit, and when he lost sight of Jo momentarily he was sure she'd been sucked under the water. Molly might finally weaken under her burden. Jo might weaken under hers.

All he'd hoped for, past and future, might sink into the river. Her head bobbed to the surface again, her arms outstretched, holding Nell aloft. The captain moved the rudder back and forth like a paddle.

"You have guns," Robert said to the captain.

"We're merchants," the man said. "Speed is the best speech now. We've twice what they have."

"They have rifles," said Robert.

"You'll have your wife and baby. Distance is freedom," said the captain, "and that's what we'll give you. More than you'll need." He pointed. The riders floundered in the water, their horses drifting downstream. Occasionally they shouted. One of them fired a shot into the air, perhaps to threaten Jo, or Robert, or the longboat. Jo held Nell and Molly held her own. They had out swum the swiftest part of the current. The captain directed his crew upstream, where they might turn and intercept Molly and Jo and Nell as the boat swept back down. "Where were you wanting to land?" he asked Robert.

"We'll be fine anywhere," Robert said with a smile.

"There's more mischief in the woods on that side of the river than you'd imagine," the captain warned him.

"I reckon mischief knows mischief," said Robert. The captain frowned. "Not you," Robert added. "I speak of myself. When I speak of you it is only with thanks."

"So be it," said the man. He pulled his pipe from his vest and stuck it in his mouth. He pushed hard against the rudder and brought the boat around so that the snout of the bow pointed directly toward shore.

"Jo!" shouted Robert, testing the shortening distance between them.

She raised a hand into the air. She spoke encouragement to Molly. Robert took relief in the sound of Nell, squalling in her new mother's arms, as eager for the crossing to end as any of them.

The captain smiled. "Don't know if my men will want a crying baby on board," he joked. "They most of them took to the river to get away from such creatures." The men put oars ever more deeply into the gentler current, and dug their way toward the mother and the baby as though Jo and Nell were each man's sweetheart and future.

The captain shoved the rudder again and they were alongside Molly. Robert reached for Nell, still shrieking her distaste for swimming on a horse. The captain took Nell from Robert and paced quickly, bouncing the baby. Robert pulled Jo off Molly and onto the longboat. She fell to the deck, and he bent down beside her, rescue replaced by fear. Her left shoulder was matted with blood, a stain through her dress. She winced when he moved his hand toward her.

"Where's Nell?" she asked.

"She's fine, ma'am," said the captain, bringing the child to her sight. His finger was stuck in her mouth and she sucked on it contentedly. "I've six of my own on the other side of the river."

"Thank you," she said. "Molly?"

The men had not been able to bring Molly any closer to the side of the boat. She swam next to The Stud, the two of them lighter now that their burdens had been removed. The riverbank neared.

"Robert," said Jo. She tried to sit up. He sat and laid her head on his thighs, stroked her hair. "They shot me," she said. "Are they still following?"

"Can't anybody follow what you've done, ma'am," said the captain. Indeed, the two men had disappeared, whether returned to shore, or far down river in the fast current, or drowned, they would never know. "You crossed *the flood* horseback. You brought your baby safe to us. And you're scraped up, to boot. I don't understand how any brother could take a shot at a sister, and her baby, too."

"Brother?" asked Jo. She frowned at the captain, then looked up at Robert, eyebrow raised.

"I told him about the dowry in the boxes, how your kin was dead against our marriage. I told you we'd likely be pursued." He hoped they might avoid questions about the boxes, about his errand for Hiram. He should have told her of the danger.

"Half brothers don't know any kin," Jo spat. She tried to rise. "'Half sister,' they said, 'so half dowry.'"

"Cussedness is everywhere," said the captain. He was smiling, Nell sucking at his finger, the other men watching him curiously, as though he held something explosive in his arms.

Robert smiled in spite of himself. Jo's dowry was Molly, and the saddle soaking up Mississippi River water as the two horses swam behind the longboat. And Jo's wit, too, quick as it was.

They soon ran to bank in a small eddy. A sycamore, fallen into the river, was white as a skeleton. They tied to it. Jo sat up. "I can take her." She reached for Nell in spite of her bloody shoulder.

"She'll squall when I give her up," said the captain. "They always do."

"You miss them when you're out on the river?" asked Jo.

"Babies are ever a blessing, though my wife curses as she brings them into the world." He removed his finger from Nell's mouth and she screamed.

"There, there," said Jo. She stood and rocked the baby as she walked.

Robert jumped from the boat into waist-deep water and coaxed the horses to him. He blessed the horses and his luck, blessed Jo for her strength, blessed the longboat captain and his crew. He wasn't certain about Hiram. Having a cause meant having enemies. Perhaps having anything—a good horse, a good woman, a good cabin, a good little piece of ground—would bring you enemies. He hoped not.

The Stud climbed onto the bank, sinking into mud. His hooves sucked into and out of the holes they made. Molly found surer ground. When they were among the brush on the bank they lowered their heads to leaves and bunchgrass. The Stud closed his eyes. Molly nickered. Robert went for the boxes, pulling them to shore.

"How far you aim to get with those?" shouted the captain. "Without a cart."

"Travois, like the Indians do," Robert shouted back, heaving the ropes over his back and leaning forward. He tugged at the heavier box. Robert whistled and The Stud perked one ear. The bloody one drooped. The horse grudgingly stepped back to the bank and waited for Robert to climb up to him. "Need some help," Robert apologized. He tied the rope to the saddle horn. "Together now," he said, and pushed his horse up the bank. They brought the box to the edge of land and Robert secured the rope to a willow. He pulled the smaller box easily to him and lifted it onto the bank.

He waded out again to where Jo stood with a bawling Nell on the edge of the boat. "Can you sit on the gunwale?" he asked her. She did, her legs dangling into the water. He reached for her, to carry her the ten yards to the bank, to Arkansas.

Before she slid into Robert's arms, she reached back for the captain's hand. She squeezed it. "I will remember your kindness all my life."

"Since it's kindness you'll remember, I hope you have a good long life for the memory."

She dropped her hand and scooted to the edge of the boat and into her new husband's arms.

"If you're ever this way again, you come see me," said the captain.

"Where will we find you?" asked Robert.

"Hiram knows me." The captain winked. "We were aiming toward that little dock when your hell broke loose. You had a rougher go of it than Hiram wanted." He nearly hopped with his news, now that he could let it out. "Dowry, indeed! Half brothers! Travois!" He laughed with each pronouncement and his crew joined in. "Jackson should help you haul that big box to land, soon as he gets here." He saluted. "Heave to," he barked at his men, and they set to their oars.

Robert and Jo and Nell stood in the water, soaked, tired, and relieved. Help would soon find them. They would dry themselves. They would tend Jo's wound. She would nurse Nell. They would eat and drink. They would unpack their saddlebags and set everything to dry while they rested. They would wait for Jackson and then pack everything back up. Everything, that is, but a tarnished totem of bad luck, stolen from a barn. Robert's granddaddy was wanderer, adventurer, hard drinker, the man who wished the ocean was whiskey and he the duck, the man who had never come up.

Robert found the saddle horn and threw it to the bottom of the Mississippi. Later, they rode toward their new life in a new place, near the piney bluffs above the Arkansas River, near Bonne and his wife and children, near Francoise, who would lead them to their stake in this new world.

baby, colt

When mail arrived in Arkansas Territory, sent to the area Bonne was calling Pine Bluff, the letter found its way to Bonne's inn. There, Marie Bonne served generous food and drink. And her son, Paul, having taken to school, could decipher any hand. Just six years old, he would sit on a little stool by the hearth reading mail aloud to grown men and women who stooped close to better hear him.

Listening, on the day before Christmas of 1825, were Robert Johnson and Jo, baby Nell in her arms. When Bonne summoned them with news of the letter come to them from Memphis, Tennessee, they had ridden eagerly from their cabin through crisp December air.

Robert knew Elizabeth's hand. He conjured her at her table, writing. He was proud to be able to read his name, and Jo's, on the envelope. Someday, he reckoned, little Nell would go to school with the priest, same as Bonne's Paul, and when she did, Robert and Jo planned to learn everything they could right along with her.

"We'll be leaving," said Bonne. He motioned to Marie.

"No need," said Robert. "We want no secrets from you."

"*Dear Robert and Jo Johnson,*" little Paul read to them all, "*I heard an account of your narrow escape. I apologize sincerely. Those of my men who plotted against me are well disposed of, and with harder justice than a shot to the rear as dispensed by Jo. I applaud your courage, both of you. My communication with a man across the river has assured me that you did all I asked, and with good results.*

"May this letter find you well, and Jo recovered from her wound. Such men, to shoot a woman to try to trap a man. Such men deserve their fates. And you, friends Robert and Jo and Nell, deserve all the promise of your plans. Have you realized your destination, built your cabin? Has Molly foaled? Does Nell thrive? Does The Stud maintain his dignity even with a ragged ear like his master's? Elizabeth and I hope so.

"Nothing seems more like boasting than writing good news to those who might not have experienced similar luck. Please don't think us too full of pride. When my hired man called me back it was ruse, but Elizabeth turned it to truth. She gave birth to a baby girl. We have named her Josephine and hope she will grow to have your pluck, Jo. We are building an addition to our house, adding to the clamor of construction Memphis is known for. To walk the streets is to soon feel the pounding in your head. Our stable will soon need additions, as well, for as Memphis grows so does the number of men who will race their horses. We will add two more colts within the year, as The Stud was successful in his services while he was with us. When you venture to Memphis for the visit we expect you to make, you may have your choice of one. I am sincere in that offer, for I know you plan to raise horses. From what I know of horseflesh, I would say there never was a horse like your stud.

"We have immediate news. Your father has been with us, Robert. We gave him shelter and as much information of you as we could. He starts for you at the same time as this letter, so perhaps he has overtaken this news already. If so, you have learned what has transpired in Pleasant View between him and Jo's brothers and pa. If not, please be assured that nothing he says will cause either of you grief. He looks forward to a land of promise. The Lord, he says, has spoken to him. But I must tell you that the Lord doesn't look as though he has shined upon him. He does not look well. His travels might be difficult and Elizabeth and I predict he will need care once he finds you.

"Please let us have news of you. I live more safely now. I must. But I am happy to, now that Josephine has joined us. A man needs settling. After all of your unsettling, Elizabeth and I hope you are finding peace. The challenges and hard work and rewards of building will be well beyond the excitement of adventuring. Such is the beginning of contentment. Our regards to you and Jo, and Nell, and to the man Bonne who has shown you a way. He sounds like a good man and I wish I knew him. I am, sincerely, Hiram William Gillian."

"I wish I knew *him*," said Bonne.

Little Paul folded the letter along its creases and handed it to Robert.

"Thank you," Robert said to the boy. And to Bonne, "Perhaps you *will* meet Hiram some day," said Robert. He looked at Jo. "Your name is Josephine?" he asked.

"You knew that," she said.

"I never," he said.

"So your father will soon be here," she said.

Marie brought them coffee. "If he needs caring for, we have the inn," she said.

"We'll see," said Robert, not resigned, but eager. They *would* see—how his father fared, what his father would need, how he and his father would finally come together so long after the death of son and brother, of wife and mother. "We'll see," he repeated.

They drank coffee, then left Bonne's inn, riding through the woods to their cabin above the river. Robert had felled thin pines for stable enough to keep The Stud and Molly and her coming foal from the winter wind, the chilling rain when it came. He had much to do, but he could see it all. The cabin, expanded as their family grew. The substantial stable. The pretty little babies on the floor. The colts frisking around the stable door. He saw his father on the cabin porch, in a rocking chair, basking in spring sun, a slight smile on his face, saying, "I never," and shaking his head. After all, he would have found his Eden.

I ever, Robert thought to himself, with the same smile. *I ever*.

Acknowledgments

s I researched the past and the geography of *rode*, I found help everywhere I went. Jimmy Bryant, director of archives at the University of Central Arkansas, hosted my visit to the Jimmy Driftwood Collection. Ricardo "Rick" Villarreal, director of the Republic of the Rio Grande Museum in Laredo, helped me with background on Laredo and Nuevo Laredo, those two sides of the Rio Grande. Keith Asmussen, of El Primero Training Center in Laredo, let me watch the 5:00 a.m. training of horses and patiently answered my questions about horses and racing. This travel was made possible through the generous support of research grants from Washburn University of Topeka, where I've taught for the past thirty years.

Early consultation with Jim Hoy, of Emporia State University, about cowboys, horses, and vocabulary, helped me write. Thanks, too, to Steven Hind, for his consultations about animals and firearms, and his expert reading of drafts.

As I wrote, I shared. Special thanks to the Topeka Men's Group, for listening and encouragement on those Saturday nights during our weekends together. Thanks, also, to the editors of literary magazines who took early interest in pieces of *rode*: Steve Sherwood and David Kuhne at *descant* (Texas Christian University); Grant Tracey at *North American Review* (University of Northern Iowa); Bob Stewart at *New Letters* (University of Missouri–Kansas City) and Ande Davis at *Blue Earth Review* (Mankato, Minnesota State University).

Ric Averill, my brother and fellow writer, read the manuscript with particular interest in plot; Libby Rosen, my sister, read with her usual interest in lactation consultation. Thanks to both for being such great siblings and such experts in their fields.

Howard Faulkner and Sarah Smarsh, my Washburn colleagues, read and commented with great insight. Greg Barron, who knows horses and Westerns, gave helpful suggestions. And Miguel Gonzalez-Abellas, friend and professor of modern foreign languages, read for the Spanish.

As always, and in all ways, I give special thanks to Jeffrey Ann Goudie, tireless reader, proofreader, best critic, friend, and wife.

Final thanks to Clark Whitehorn, my editor at University of New Mexico Press, for his belief in the manuscript and his enthusiasm for the project.

In spite of all this support, I'm sure I've made mistakes. I claim them all for myself.